SACRED TEARS

The Dance of Iris

TIFFANY GRANT

Cover designed by: Emilie Haney, eahcreative.com

Edited by Lisa Thompson at www.writebylisa.com You can email Lisa at writebylisa@gmail.com

Paperback: 979-8-9877973-0-3

Hardback: 979-8-9877973-1-0

Ebook: 979-8-9877973-2-7

For my friends and family who refused to let me quit when self-doubt and depression were at their worst. Your ferocious love and support fueled me through some of my darkest days.

Just because something starts in darkness, doesn't mean it has to end in darkness.

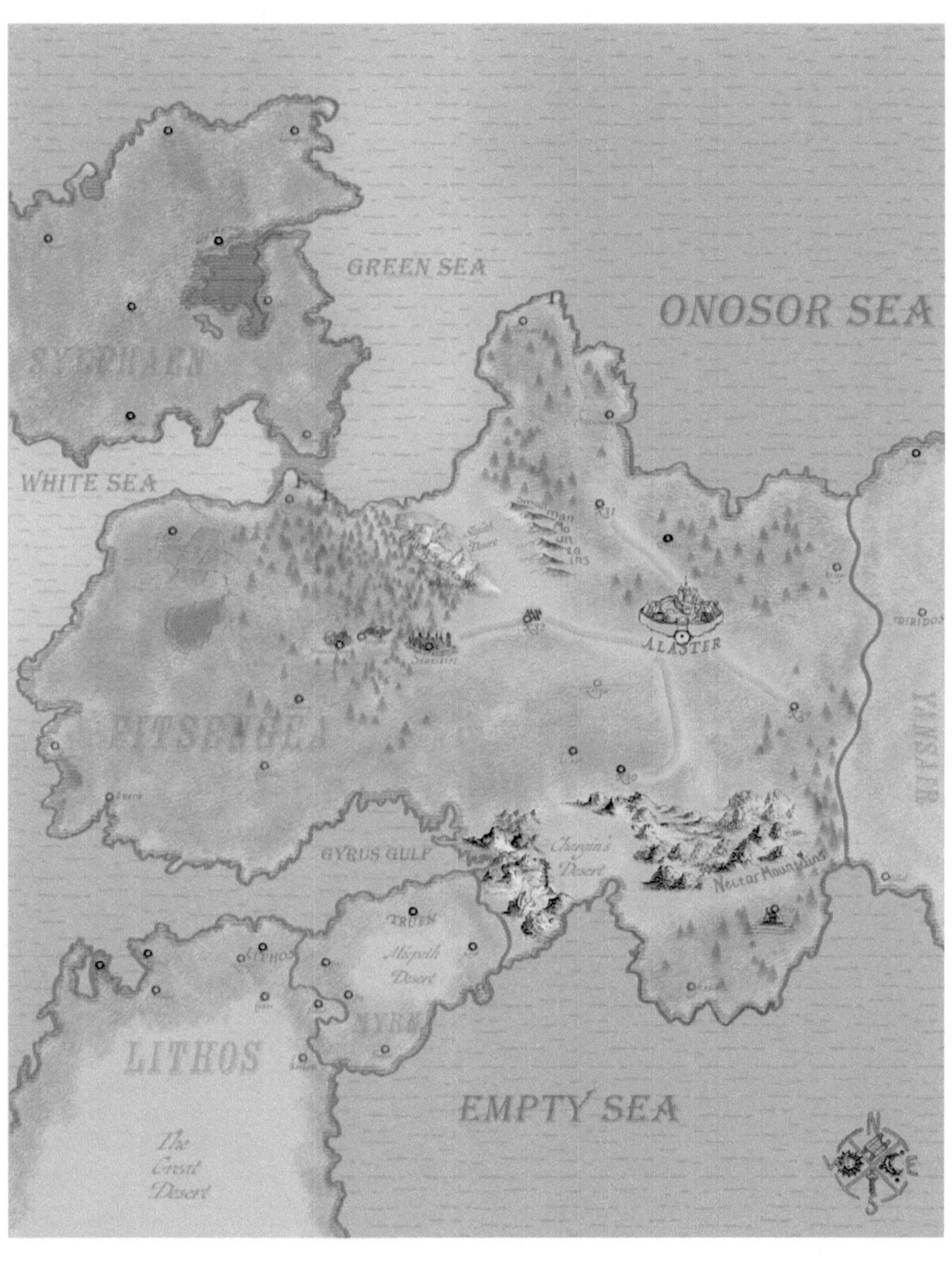
GREEN SEA
ONOSOR SEA
SYDRAEN
WHITE SEA
Sand Desert
Snowman Mountains
ALASTER
TRIRIDOS
PITSENGEA
YANSTIN
GYRUS GULF
Chopin's Desert
Nectar Mountains
TRUEN
Mizrah Desert
LITHOS
MYRM
The Great Desert
EMPTY SEA
N S E W

Chapter One

Please! Holy Father, save us! Please, stop this! Iris Straton inwardly screamed to her Creator as she tore through her town of Throansburrough. A cacophony of terrorized cries, stray gunshots, and raging fires assaulted her ears. Iris dashed a hand over her eyes to clear her vision of tears. She chanced a look back at the soldier pursuing her. She didn't recognize his foreign uniform or the simple eye-shaped design carved on his leather chest plate. He was gaining ground, firelight glinting off the metal tips of his shoes and the sword held in his hand. *Get to the Holy House! I must get to the Holy House!* Iris didn't know why, but she just knew her only safety was in that blessed place of worship at the town center. The closer she wove toward it, the more buildings were engulfed in flames.

"Holy Father, where are you!" Iris screeched in terrified anger, passing by numerous fallen victims who had once been dear friends.

Rounding a turn, the Holy House came into view. The large simplistic wooden structure had yet to be touched by the fire, but the surrounding blaze of the burning buildings would quickly change that. Iris slid to a stop, realizing the absurdity of her plan. She'd be trapped if she went in! She whipped her head back at the angry, frustrated yell of her assailant as he closed in on her. *Go! Inside!* The thoughts pushed her feet into action. Iris thrust herself through the front door. *Hide. You need to hide!*

The Holy House consisted of one large meeting space with wooden benches placed in an amphitheater structure curved along the walls. The center of the room was left bare to make room for the worship dancers and each night's speaker. Iris ran to the far end of the building. Spying a small gap between the benches and the wall, she worked her way in between and underneath them. Smoke had already begun to pour in as the roof crackled with newly caught flames. The front door to the Holy House flung open once more as her terrorizer angrily stomped through. Smoke created a thick wall of haze, forcing him to walk slowly as he searched for Iris. Iris peeked through the small slats between the benches as the man inched forward toward her with his sword drawn. Squeezing her eyes shut and curling up on the floor under the tight gap, Iris prayed desperately. *I don't want to die. Please, Holy Father, do something!*

The wooden structure groaned loudly and cracked as the flame-eaten ceiling began to collapse. A scream rang out but was swiftly silenced as more burning timber came crashing down. Iris shuddered as dust and smoke swirled around her. Peeking out once more, the soldier lay prone, a timber pierced through his chest. *At least he went quickly.* If only she could be gifted with such a fate.

The door was blocked. Iris didn't think she could even escape from her wedged hiding place. Struggling to breathe, she coughed violently as her lungs fought for clean air. *At least . . .* Iris thought with morbid consolation. *At least, I'll be joining my family soon . . . Holy Father please, please just don't let it hurt.* Darkness edged in around Iris's vision as the Holy House collapsed around her.

———> ⬥ <———

"Iris, I need you to watch Lori and Jacob today. Dan and I have to go to the market," Julie called out from the back bedroom.

Iris sat on the wooden floorboards of the main room. She looked up from the game she had been playing with Lori and Jacob and laughed. "Sure, no problem. I promise not to beat them too hard when they misbehave." Iris teased, ruffling her niece and nephew's blond hair in turn.

Her sister returned to the main room, smiled, and knelt down to give her kids a hug. "Now, you two listen to your auntie. She's in charge while we're gone. So whatever she says goes."

The six- and four-year-old nodded happily and hugged their mom back, then hugged their dad who stood next to his wife.

"Love you, kiddos." He smiled, breathing in their essence.

Each parent then took a turn hugging Iris before they left. They turned away and then . . . vanished.

"Julie?" Iris called. Her stomach sank in dread. "Julie? . . . *Julie!*"

"Julie . . ." The whispered name escaped as consciousness tugged her awake. Memories flooded in with the horrific imagery from the night before. A tear slipped through her eyelashes. *My family . . . my home. Is everything really gone? How am I alive? Where am I?* Prying open her violet-blue eyes, light floated in small streams around her. Debris from the fire covered her, and the smell of charred timber permeated her skin. A ragged cough irritated her already raw throat. Could she move? Shifting positions, she slowly tested the weight of the rubble on top of her. It gave way easily. Fear flitted through her heart. *Is it even safe to leave?* Pushing her long reddish-brown hair out of her face as best as she could, Iris peered out, making sure she was alone. As far as she could see, she was. *If they're there, don't let me be seen,* Iris prayed and pushed her way out. Climbing over debris and kicking charred remains out of her way, she worked her way free from the wreckage. Standing erect, she took in the broken shell of what was once the Holy House, the destruction of her home all around. Shock stilled the pain that battled to overtake her.

Stepping away from the building's remnants, Iris walked in a daze. Nothing of her home of twenty-four years was recognizable. Absent-mindedly dusting the dirt off her pants and tunic, she took in the full extent of the damage. Fires still smoldered on the collapsed beams of buildings. Clouds of ash danced around her with each disturbing step. *All you've ever known is gone.* The thought twisted through her heart. Silence enveloped her. Panic bubbled up within. Why was it *so* quiet? She quickened her pace as she worked her way through the ruins of Throansburrough. No soldiers marched around; no enemy encampments remained. Their slaughterers had vanished as quickly as they came. Was there no one left? *I'm alone . . . I can't be alone! It can't be just me! It can't!* A terror and anguish unlike she had ever known seeped into Iris's heart and mind. The fear that had initially closed off her voice shifted to a need for sound.

"Hello?" Iris called out to the ruins. "Hello? Anyone? Hello!"

Staggering around debris, she cried, "Please, can anyone hear me!"

All caution about the possible danger of remaining enemies evaporated as her desperation to see one more living soul possessed her. The weight of the answering silence pressed in, deadening her legs and numbing her thoughts. A dark hole opened up inside her. Iris stopped her search and fell to her knees on the ground. Everyone was gone. Only the smallest flicker of hope kept her heart beating. Maybe some of her townspeople had escaped. Perhaps they fled into the surrounding woods.

Iris remained on her knees until her legs began to ache. She had to leave this place as quickly as possible; if she didn't leave now, she might never be able to. She had to move on. Already, Iris felt as if it were closing in on her. Still, she had one thing left to do. She needed to find her family and bury them. The thought of seeing their lifeless forms terrified her, but they deserved a proper burial.

Wandering around the town, clambering over broken items, she searched. Her confusion mounted; she couldn't find any bodies. What had they done? Did they even go as far as robbing her of a resting place to give her family, her townspeople? Maybe they had already buried them. The idea of a mass grave somewhere curled her stomach. What a hideous and disgraceful thought. One of these days, she'd somehow make this right. Her gentle town—her family—deserved that.

Finally surrendering to this defeat, Iris stopped and looked down the main street of her village. Nothing left to do here. Ripping her heart from the ties of her home, she stumbled to the entrance of the town where she finally reached the road. It split off in two directions. To the right, tracks and ruts laced the road, the trail left behind by this phantom army. To the left, the path was smooth and peaceful, beckoning as a way to safety. The towns and villages along the path to the right were in danger, and she alone could surely move faster than an army, giving her time to warn them. And yet if some of her people had survived, they had possibly fled to the towns on the left. She had witnessed the death of her parents and brother-in-law, but she wasn't certain of the fate of the others: her sister or niece and nephew. She might yet be able to reunite with them! Taking a deep breath, she stared at the decision before her. Iris turned right.

Swaying back and forth in their cramped wagon prison, the tangible hopelessness hung in the air. Children sat in a large wooden cart with metal bars around the sides and ceiling. The old tarp tied around it all kept them from looking out and prevented any prying eyes from looking in. Jodie's eyes roved over each silent, terrified face around him. Roughly forty of them were crammed together, sitting on one another's laps, scrunched up as small as they could get. Ranging in age from two to no more than thirteen, anyone outside that age group had been slaughtered back in the village. The weight of being the eldest in the group carried such responsibility. He needed to protect these kids, but how could he do that when he was only a child himself? Tears of frustration stung at the corners of his eyes. If only his big brother Sigmund were here. He'd know what to do, how to help, how to get out. They needed help! They needed the heroes from the ancient Sacred Texts. He thought of how Sigmund had told him the stories about those champions each night before bed. Those men and women, some of them even Jodie's own age, had faced horrors such as Throansburrough experienced last night. Yet in the end, through the Holy Father, they always defeated their enemy! *No matter how horrible the situation becomes, you must always hold on to hope!* Sigmund's words bounced around in Jodie's mind. But how could anyone find hope in the midst of so much despair and fear?

Jodie looked around once more, his eyes settling on the Mainfield's little boy. An idea struck him. "Jacob, sing with me?"

Four-year-old Jacob hid behind the dirty blond hair that hung down in his eyes. He sniffled and looked at his feet, his head lolling lazily side to side, rocking with the movement of the cart. He wiped his nose on his sleeve but remained silent. Lori, Jacob's six-year-old sister, scooched closer to him and wrapped her arms around him; he leaned into her.

Jodie shifted his attention to her. "Lori? Will you sing with me?"

Frightened deep blue eyes looked up through wisps of pale blonde hair at the older boy sitting in the opposite corner of their crowded little prison. She held onto her brother more tightly but nodded her head. Softly they began a verse from an old hymn often sung at the town's nightly worship meetings.

The path may be long and hard
But I will carry on
My goal may seem so far away
But I will carry on
I do not walk this road alone
He walks beside me as I go
His grace and aid make me strong
I will carry on.

Slowly the rest of the children's fragile voices joined in. Soon the kids in the second cart riding beside them began to sing along. The atmosphere around them began to change as courage rose up within them once more.

Thwack! An iron rod came down violently on the side of their wagon from a soldier walking next to them. The younger ones screamed at the sudden sound and huddled closer to the floor.

"Shut up in there! Next sound I hear from any of you will be your last!"

They all looked nervously at each other, some trying to keep the others from crying. Once again, quiet settled over the little group, interrupted by sniffles and an occasional hushed sob. A small voice fearfully reached out in the silence.

"Jodie?" she whispered, "Are we going to die?"

"Hush Lori, keep quiet. Everything will be okay." Jodie prayed to Holy Father that he was telling Lori the truth.

Chapter Two

Sweat trickled along Iris's brow and neck, causing her long hair to cling uncomfortably to her. The dry red dirt of the road dusted a new shade over her clothing and skin, mixing with the gray ash layer. As she navigated around the ruts in the road, she fought the chaos of thoughts that threatened to consume her. Tears escaped now and again. Shaking her head and breathing deeply, Iris shoved the emotions back down, refusing to let herself crumble in the wake of all the devastation.

"Don't you dare break down girl. You won't make it if you do," Iris chided herself. "The task ahead, that's what I must focus on . . . Please be safe, Jaralynx."

A shudder of fear rippled through her at the thought of Throansburrough's sister village, Jaralynx. The two places had supported each other for many seasons, sharing in celebrations and carrying each other through trials and tragedies. Faces of friends, of her cousins, her aunts and uncles, floated past Iris's mind's eye.

"Please, *please* be safe!"

The desire to pray tugged at her heart but anger quickly strangled it. The Holy Father hadn't done anything for Throansburrough; why would she think He would step in for Jaralynx instead? War raged inside between a longing to cry out to the Holy Father and hurting far too deep to even try. Iris's steps slowed to a stop as tears welled up in her eyes.

"You left me . . . we were a good and faithful people, and You left us . . ."

Shaking her head in an attempt to empty her mind, she squared her shoulders, lifted her chin, and continued walking. Her thoughts soon focused on the steady pace of her feet, a sluggish rhythm that stuck in her head like a song. The beat of her footfalls reminded her of old songs from her home. Before she realized it, she was humming a tune in time with their patient drumming.

When Iris no longer remembered the words to the songs, she made up her own, finding the most ridiculous ways to keep up with the rhyme schemes. Her eyes fixated on her feet, unable to look anywhere else. The mind-numbing rhythm put her in a semi-trance, one which she was too lazy to break out of. She was almost thankful for the temporary escape.

Flitting her eyes to the sky, she followed the path of the sun, which had dipped down since she began. She knew she would reach Jaralynx in only a few more miles. Exhaustion threatened to take over. She had been walking all day and would likely not reach her destination until right around sundown. Would she come upon the enemy sometime soon? Would it be wise for her to stay along the road for much longer?

A breeze swirled around and past her. The temperature began to drop as the night drew near. Her sweat from earlier now captured every gentle wind and chilled her skin. She rubbed her arms, then crossed them over her chest in an attempt to hold in her warmth.

"And me without my coat," Iris mumbled.

"If it's warmth you need, I think I can be of assistance."

The deep, masculine voice stopped her in her tracks. She whipped her head around in its direction. The outline of a towering male figure was barely visible against the tree line. Now she cursed her haste in leaving the village. She hadn't even brought a weapon for protection. How could she have been so stupid?

"You look tired. I have a place you can rest if you'd like."

The sneer in his voice sent chills down Iris's back. She slowly backed away from him, her heart thrumming in her ears. She did her best to calm herself before she replied, she didn't want him to sense her growing fear.

"I'll be just fine, sir. I do not have time to stop right now. I thank you for the offer, nonetheless. Good evening to you."

"Oh, but I must insist," he cooed as he advanced toward her. "It is still quite far from the next village."

"Please, sir, mind your own business. I must be on my way, so goodbye!" she stated firmly as she continued to back away.

"Now, now, no need to get an attitude, my dear. I have *made* you my business." The glint of a large knife, now unsheathed, flashed in the dusk.

She couldn't deter him; talking would accomplish nothing now. The energy of anticipation coursed through her veins. She spun on her heels and ran down the path as his heavy footsteps thundered behind her. Panic seized her heart, driving her to pump her arms and legs as fast and as hard as she could. The growing volume of each footfall warned her that he was gaining on her. She didn't want to look back, but she had to see, had to prepare for her next move.

Iris glanced over her shoulder as she ran. He was almost on her! Desperate to put more distance between them, she cut to her right to dodge through the trees. The path gave him the advantage of a straight shot, but between the trees, her small frame could more readily squeeze through the tight spaces.

He crashed through the undergrowth. His dogged determination terrified her. Would he chase her until she collapsed from exhaustion? She needed help, someone to rescue her. Out here, she was alone with no one to protect her. All she could do was run. The branches clawed at her arms and face; roots and vines threatened to trip her feet. Small depressions in the earth lay set to trap her. So many obstacles were before her, but they were still worse for him. Every once in a while, he growled in frustration when he met a perplexing barrier. The distance between them grew, but her pace was slowing.

She did not have the energy to keep this up much longer. No sleep, no food, walking all day, and the trauma she had endured were taking their toll. Her initial surge of adrenaline was fading. Still, she refused to surrender. He would not have her without a fight! Casting a pleading glance to the sky, she begged for a savior.

That one glance was all it took to miscalculate her next step and go crashing down the steep hillside. She tumbled head over feet, then banged on her side, tossed around between saplings and glancing over rocks. She lost count of the number of times she rolled. *Will I ever stop?* Down, down she went, narrowly missing the larger trees. Suddenly, she flew through the air, flung off the edge of something and now plummeted downward. Disoriented, she tried to brace herself for impact. With a heavy thud, she bashed into the ground. Her body screamed in pain as she landed on the rocks.

She had no idea where she was. Before she could investigate, her mind shut down, and everything went black.

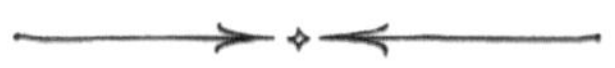

"Auntie Iris? Why is the sky sad?" Lori asked as she looked out the window of her grandparent's home.

"What?" Iris laughed at her niece's question as she played with the small girl's soft hair.

"The sky, it's sad. Jodie says that when water comes down, that—that it's crying. Why is it sad?"

"Haha, Lori, the sky isn't sad! It's just rain. Rain is a happy thing that makes plants grow and everything pretty."

"Oh," she responded as she looked out the window once more and thought for a minute. "So rain is—is a gift that the Holy Father gives us?"

"Exactly! How did you get so smart?" Iris smiled.

"Well, I *am* four!" she stated proudly, lifting her chin.

"Well, I had no idea I was in the presence of such a brilliant person," Iris stated in mock awe.

"Mmhmm!" Lori replied, even though she didn't really understand some of the words Iris used.

"Oh, come here you!" Iris laughed and scooped Lori into her arms, tickling her. Lori squealed with delight as they both giggled gleefully.

The laughter rang in her ears as Iris slowly opened her eyes. In the brief moment before her vision adjusted to the new light, she expected to see her little niece leaning over her. Her mind slowly returned to the present, and she focused on the sound. She had mistaken the trilling song of a small bird perched nearby for a child's laugh.

Slowly tilting her head to the side, she got a better view of the creature, a tiny brown thing. As her eyes focused, Iris put together the pieces of the last few moments. What exactly had she fallen into? Still sore from her fall, she remained lying down, as she moved only her eyes and sometimes her head to take in her surroundings.

She was in some kind of deep rocky pit or hole, medium-sized in both width and length. She could make out plant life circling the upper rim with a few vines creeping down the sides. None of them near long enough to reach down to her level on the floor. She had really taken quite the fall.

"I wonder if anything is broken," she mumbled aloud.

Flexing her fingers and toes, she knew she was at least not paralyzed. She gingerly sat up. Pain radiated throughout her body from the abrupt landing, but that was to be expected. As far as she could tell, all she had managed were some nasty bruises and to tear her clothing. There was also the matter of the splitting headache that pounded with a vengeance once she stood.

Placing a hand on the back of her head, she checked for any signs of bleeding. She alternated her hand between her head and her eyes, checking her sight. She was finally satisfied that she had not split open her head.

"How I managed that, I'll never know," she muttered in amazement.

Taking a step toward the rock wall, a sudden pain surged up her left leg. Hopping on her right leg for a few steps, she leaned against the side. Inspecting her leg further, she looked at her ankle, now swollen and throbbing. But she was pretty sure that it was only sprained.

She sighed and hung her head for a second as she contemplated the seriousness of this new obstacle. Her injury would make climbing out of this hole even more difficult. Recalling the brute that had gotten her into this mess, Iris paused for a good while to listen to the sounds around her. Satisfied by the prolonged lack of human noises, she refocused on her escape from the pit. Studying each side, she examined the area for the place that allowed the easiest ascent. Not too far from her was a section where the roots of the trees grew farther down the sides. But they still did not quite reach her level. Even so, those roots were probably her best bet. Using the wall as a crutch, she limped over to the spot.

She searched for footholds and mentally planned out her moves. She hadn't done any climbing in a long time, but maybe all those years playing in the trees would help her now.

Shaking her head and smirking sarcastically, she stated aloud, "This will be fun."

She took a deep breath, shifted her weight to her right leg, and stretched out her arms. Grasping firmly onto the indentions in the rocks, she pulled herself up. Reaching a spot with a toehold for her right foot, she once again shifted her weight, using her right leg to push her higher. She continued this difficult routine slowly as her left leg dangled uselessly to the side, occasionally bracing herself against the wall with her left knee.

Her headache increased along with her fatigue. Sweat ran down her back as her hair stuck to her face, making her long for a pair of scissors to chop it all off. She swore that she would never grow it so long again.

Left hand, right hand, pull up. Right foot, push against the knee, push higher. Pushing and pulling, her breath caught during a few heart-stopping moments when she slipped on a loose rock. Her hands were sore, and her legs were badly scraped. Only a few more inches before she could grab onto a thick, strong root and pull herself up to the top. All she had to do was stretch her left hand out a little farther.

Almost there! Just push off on the tiptoes of her right foot, straining against her grip with her right hand. *Reach! Just a little more!* Grip slipping, her foot slid out of the slot! *Grab onto the root now!*

With a gasp and one final thrust, Iris clutched at air, but her hand connected just in time. She breathed deeply, calming herself down as she clung to the root and swayed slightly side to side. Carefully, she continued her ascent, pulling herself up and over the edge.

Leaves crunched and rustled on the ground as she crawled through the dirt away from the edge. When she was satisfied that she wouldn't accidentally fall back in, Iris rolled onto her back and just lay there for a minute. Her arms and legs felt like jelly; she couldn't have moved even if she wanted to. Her heart pounded, veins pulsating.

Lying still on the soft bed of leaves and staring at the top of the trees, Iris entertained the idea of sleeping right there. The smaller branches danced in the slight breeze. Since it wouldn't be wise to spend too much time in the woods, she rolled back over onto all fours and stood up. Investigating her surroundings, she let out a pleased "Ah-ha!" when she came across the perfect walking stick. Grabbing it, she smiled and thanked the Holy Father, for this would support her as she walked with a sprained ankle. Using her right hand to shield her eyes, Iris checked the position of the sun. It was slightly higher in the sky than it had been when she had first encountered the man from last night. So that meant she must have lost an entire day by now. *Well, at least* he *won't be anywhere around here then.* She sighed with relief. Plus she must have put quite a bit of distance between them when she had careened down the hillside. Iris had fallen for what seemed like an eternity. Looking around, she tried to figure out which direction she fell from.

Finding what she hoped was the right place, she trudged back up the hill. When she finally reached the top, she looked for signs of broken branches, anything to show that someone had recently passed through. Between the trees, a few last tendrils of smoke spiraled up lazily. Curiosity sparked; she cautiously made her way in that direction.

Drawing closer, her suspicions were verified. The smoke came from a low-burning fire in the center of a small camp. Maybe whoever set up this camp could help her find the road. Hopeful that she might finally be headed in the right direction, she increased her pace. "Hello? Is anyone here?" she called out, trying to avoid barging into someone's home.

When she received no response, she moved in closer for a better look. One small well-used tent was set up. Perhaps it belonged to a wanderer or some sort of hermit. Whoever they were, they were apparently male. Undergarments hung from the lower tree branches, obviously placed there to dry. By the foot of the tree lay extra hunting arrows and a skinning knife. At the sight of the weapons, warning bells sounded in her mind. She had no idea what had happened to the man who had chased her. For all she knew, this could be his camp, and she had walked right into it!

The hairs on the back of her neck stood on end, and she became deathly still. She held her breath and strained her hearing, making sure he wasn't nearby. Crunching footsteps of a person lazily making their way through the leaves and underbrush crept up from a short distance. Her heart beat faster. *It's time to leave.* Turning as quickly as possible, she backed out of the campsite. But she wasn't fast enough. A deep masculine voice shot ice into her veins, and she halted in her tracks.

"Why, hello there."

Chapter Three

Run, you fool, run! Her mind screamed at her, but her legs wouldn't cooperate. He was coming closer. Well, if her body refused to flee, then she would just have to fight. She adjusted her hands around her walking stick to grip it more securely. She waited for him to move a little closer.

"I said, 'hello, there.' Can I help you?"

His voice told her his position. Close enough! Pivoting on her good right foot, she swung her stick with all her might. She let out a scream and involuntarily closed her eyes. *Grunt!* Her weapon connected with something solid. *Thud!* Something fell to the ground. She peeked out of one eye to look tentatively at her assailant, now face down in the dirt. She took a hop-step back from him, still standing at the ready if she needed to take another swing. The man moaned and moved slightly. This was her moment to flee, a perfect chance to escape. So what in all the lands was she doing just standing there? Was she waiting for him to get back up just to knock him down again? Was he to be her outlet so that she could finally release her pent-up rage? She clutched her weapon, aching to hit him again.

"What the *hell* was that for!" the man shouted irritably as he crawled up to his hands and feet.

Iris half-hopped back in surprise, faltering a bit. His voice sounded nothing like the stranger's from last night. Still, she maintained her hold on the stick. She hadn't just accidentally accosted some innocent hunter, had she?

"Are you—were you—what were you doing last night?" she stammered, searching for an appropriate question.

"What?" he asked as he closely looked at her for the first time, swaying slightly as he fought to recover. "Who are you? And *why* did you attack me!"

"Just answer the question! Please."

"I was here, cleaning the meat I just hunted." He glared at her.

"Stand up."

He glared again and rubbed the side of his head. Slowly he stood, dusting off the dirt from his forest green tunic and brown trousers while picking a few leaves from the top of his knee-high worn, leather hunting boots. The entire time, he eyed the stick in her hands. Iris studied him more closely, her stomach twisting in knots. He looked about her age, mid-twenties, and was taller than she was but still shorter than her attacker. He had a leaner but solid build with short shaggy hair and no beard. She had made a huge mistake, all because of her paranoia.

"Oh no," she whispered under her breath.

Her face flushed in embarrassment, and her mind raced, trying to figure out what to do next. She opted for a guilty grin as she slowly lowered her walking stick.

"What is wrong with you?" He glowered at her in confusion.

"I . . . uhhhh . . . seem to have mistaken you for someone else." She blushed more deeply and wished she could just disappear as she nervously pushed hair behind her left ear.

She swallowed past the lump forming in her throat and continued. "I am so very sorry for . . . um . . . attacking you like that. Are—are you alright?"

He stared at her a moment longer as his brain struggled to figure out what had just happened.

"You . . . you came into my camp, attacked me without looking at me, and now are taking the time to apologize?"

"Umm . . . yes . . . I really am sorry!" Panic and shame swirled within. "I suppose I should leave you to your business. G–goodbye." She quickly nodded and turned to leave.

As she did, she forgot about her sprain and stepped on her left foot. Pain shot up her leg signaling her mistake. Quickly she tried to switch to her right foot but her feet tangled with the walking sticking, ungracefully tripping her and toppling her to the ground.

Spitting out the dirt in her mouth, she let out an annoyed "*Ow.*" She was tired of constantly falling.

"Are you . . . okay?" the man asked from behind her. His voice proved how insane he thought her.

She sighed, shook her head, and moved to get back to her feet. "Yeah. I mean no . . . I mean . . ." She sighed again. "I don't know." Her voice echoed the defeat of her slumping shoulders.

Grabbing her walking stick once more, Iris used it as leverage to help her stand erect. Looking ahead, she took a deep breath before mumbling over her shoulder. "I am very sorry for bothering you, sir."

She decided to find the road on her own; she had already caused this poor man enough problems.

"Wait!" he called out in concern.

Iris paused, curious as to what he could want now. He took a few cautious steps toward her.

"Look, you came into my campsite for a reason, and based on your appearance and . . . um . . . attitude, I suppose that you need some kind of help."

Hmm, nice guy, Iris thought as she turned to face him again. This time, she made sure to focus on her feet so that she wouldn't end up on the ground again!

"Really, that is very kind of you, but—"

"Please, at least have something to eat or maybe a drink. Just come and sit down. You're barely standing as it is." His eyes matched the genuine concern in his words.

She couldn't argue with that. Her stomach growled at the mere mention of food. He didn't seem dangerous, and after all, she had already attacked him. Would she dare insult his hospitality as well? Releasing a sigh, she gave him a slight smile and nodded her head.

The hunter grinned in response. "Good. Now here, let me help you." He moved to her side and put his arm around her. She allowed herself to relax against him as he helped her over to a fallen tree next to the fire pit. The last man to be this close to her was her own father. It felt strange yet wonderful to have his presence so near. She knew it was ridiculous, but that didn't stop the quickening in her heart. She wondered briefly if she'd ever find love. Shame quickly swept over her at the thought. *Your home lies in ruins, and an evil army may well be on the rampage, and yet you're thinking about marriage! How stupid, how selfish can you be?* Stinging with a renewed sense of self-loathing, Iris forced her thoughts onto making her way to the felled log without tripping and bringing down the man with her. *You already knocked him down once. I'm sure he's reached his quota for the day.*

As she sat down, he eyed her left foot with concern. "Did you sprain it?"

"Yes, I believe so." She smiled weakly and touched it tentatively.

He frowned in concentration for a second and then stood. "Hold on, I think I might have something for that."

He rummaged through his travel pack for a minute and then, apparently finding what he was searching for, turned back to Iris. He held a small cloth bag about the same size as a coin sack. Opening it up, he revealed a collection of strange green leaves. He carefully grabbed one and held it up for her inspection.

"It's a Mantriok leaf. If treated chemically and kept in the proper conditions, they have a healing quality."

"What kind of quality, exactly?" Iris eyed them suspiciously.

"Well, they help enhance your body's natural healing abilities so that you heal faster. Yet they really only work for minor injuries. They aren't very useful for anything serious."

"Alright . . . so do I take them in a tea or just place them on my ankle?"

"Actually, you have to chew them plain. If you add anything else to them, the effects are neutralized."

"Oh. I see."

He handed the one he was holding over to her; she held it gently and nervously studied the plant.

"Look, I'm not trying to drug you or anything."

She shot him a wary look.

"Here, I'll take a bite of it first to prove myself to you." He sighed, grabbed another identical leaf, and ate it whole. He made a couple of faces as he chewed; the taste was clearly unappetizing. He swallowed with no apparent ill effects.

Iris slowly turned the leaf between her fingers. "It must be good for you if it tastes so awful," she mused sarcastically.

Taking a deep breath, she made up her mind and stuck it into her mouth. The leaf was much tougher and chewier than she had expected. And so vile! As she continued to chew, the taste worsened. It was all she could do to keep from spitting it out. She thought she might choke for a moment or worse yet, lose the breakfast she did not have. With her eyes watering and nose burning, she finally swallowed it all. Next time, she determined to just suffer through the sprained ankle.

"Here, drink this," the man directed, handing her a beat-up old tin cup.

Iris greedily gulped down the water, desperate to wash the taste from her mouth.

"Why must what's good for you taste so horrible?" She coughed after finishing her drink.

The man smiled and shrugged as he took the cup from her. "Who knows? Always seems to be the case, though, doesn't it?"

She smiled at him and watched as he put the items back in his pack. He really was rather handsome with dark black hair, stubble on his face from not shaving that morning, and strong broad shoulders. She studied his features more closely. His irises were such an interesting coloring. The outer rims were a solid green with a mixture of light blue-green and golden flecks in the center. Even though he wasn't the biggest man she had ever seen, he was still very fit with solid arm muscles. Just then, he looked back in her direction and caught her staring.

Mortified, Iris quickly focused on her hands. She suddenly realized how awful she must look and prayed that she didn't smell. Keeping her eyes on her hands, she gathered her courage to speak as he went about his activities around the campsite.

"I–I . . . umm . . . want to say thank you for your kindness and generosity Mr. . . . ummm . . ." She faltered as it dawned on her that she never asked for his name. Not only that, but she hadn't introduced herself, either. Did her rudeness know no bounds? Yet he didn't seem too taken aback at her obvious lack of propriety.

"It's Darren," he smiled.

"Just Darren? No last name?" Iris teased gently.

"Just Darren. No need for titles."

"Alright. Well, *just* Darren," she said with a laugh, "I am Iris Straton. It is a pleasure to meet you. You may also call me *just* Iris if you'd like."

"Ha ha, very well then, just Iris." He responded with a wink and shook her hand. "It is a pleasure to meet you also, and you're welcome."

Lori lay by her brother in their little prison, the warmth stifling her. She didn't like the heat. It came from those bad men, bad men that burned down people's homes wherever they went. She wanted her mommy to come and sing their goodnight song to her. Then her mommy and daddy would say their prayers, all of them together. She wanted her daddy. If only he were here. He was big and strong; he could protect everyone from the bad men. Nothing could hurt him. She wanted her mommy and daddy to hold her and take her and Jacob back home where she would be safe. Nanny and Pop Pop would bake cookies and tell stories. Auntie Iris would play with them. Home. She wanted to go home. Lori curled closer to the sleeping form of her little brother. Slowly, she, too, fell asleep.

Across their prison, two voices whispered nervously in the darkness.

"They're going to separate us?" twelve-year-old Sara asked with rising fear.

"Especially those related to each other," Jodie answered.

"Are you sure?"

"Yes. I heard the guards talking to each other the other night. They thought we were all asleep."

Sara was quiet for a minute, taking it all in. Finally, she spoke, "When?"

"Right before they reach Alaster. They still want to stop at a few villages along the way."

"Why?"

"More children to collect."

"What do they want with us?"

"I don't know. But I'm going to try and find out."

That answer scared her. If these men found out that he was listening in on them, he could get into a lot of trouble.

"Jodie, please . . . can't we just escape? Run for help or something?"

"And how do we do that, Sara? How would we get everyone out without getting caught? Kids like Jacob or Donovan would never make it! We don't even know where we are!"

"I–I know, but I just–I just can't be separated from you!" Sara choked back tears and grasped onto his arm.

Jodie was silent for a second and then wrapped his arms around her, hugging her tightly. "I know Sara, I know. I'll–I'll try to think of something."

Chapter Four

This is awkward, Iris thought as she sat in silence by the fire pit. She had gratefully eaten Darren's food, and now the plate, scraped clean, sat at her feet. He had been studying her while she ate. She could only imagine how she must have looked as she shoveled it all down. When she realized he was watching her, she made a conscious effort to slow down. Food had been her excuse for not talking earlier, but now she had no reason to stay quiet.

As darkness settled in around them, Darren collected more wood for the fire, setting it up to chase away the encroaching coldness of night. Iris hated this silence, but she didn't know what to say. Her mind was almost numb with all that had transpired so quickly. Even thinking was exhausting. Instead, she quietly continued to watch her host as he moved about. Occasionally, he paused to think and rub the side of his neck where she had hit him. Shame grew in her stomach, finally forcing her to speak first.

"Darren, I–I am so sorry for hitting you earlier. I really am."

Darren turned his attention back to her, breaking free from a troubling thought. "Hmmm? Oh, that! Are you still worried about that? No, it's quite alright. No harm done, well, nothing permanent, I promise.

But really, the Mantriok leaf I ate took care of the worst of it. Your ankle should be walkable by now as well." He smiled reassuringly.

Iris gingerly put pressure on her left foot from where she sat. "Well, would you look at that!" She gaped in amazement at its barely present tenderness.

Darren chuckled softly. Watching Iris for a second he hesitated before asking, "Exactly why did you hit me, though?"

Iris began to play with her own fingers. "I–I was scared. I thought you were . . . someone else."

Darren eyed her thoughtfully and then moved a little closer to her. "Iris, I don't mean to pry, but . . . are you in trouble?"

She thought for a moment, assessing her situation. Was she actually safe right now? She didn't think she would ever feel safe or at least feel like she wasn't in danger for a long time. Taking a deep breath, she finally answered him.

"No, no, I'm fine now. I think. But—" she gasped as she suddenly realized how much time had been wasted here. How could she have let herself become so caught up, so lost in this reprieve of slight normalcy?

"But what? What's wrong?"

"But many other people may not be!" A sense of urgency made her stand abruptly. "Darren, do you know how to get to the central road?"

"Yes, why? Iris, what's wrong?"

"I have to make it to the next town immediately. Could you take me to the road?"

"Right now? But it's already getting dark! That road can be dangerous at night."

"Don't I know it," Iris scoffed under her breath. "Please, Darren, this is urgent! People's lives are depending on it!"

"What do you mean? We're not doing anything until you tell me *why* people's lives are in danger. Tell me what's going on!" Darren looked at her with stubborn determination.

Iris didn't want to waste any more time talking, but she realized that unless she explained herself, she would be stuck trying to find the way on her own. She would have to talk quickly.

"My home, my village, was attacked by some strange army a few nights back. I don't know why. They killed everyone and everything, burning our town to the ground. The next morning, they were gone. They are moving east along the central road, and all I know is that I have to beat them to the next town. I have to warn those people! I can't let them be taken; I can't let that happen again!" Shaking, Iris took a deep breath. She quickly clenched her fists and tried to steady herself.

Darren's stubbornness quickly melted away. "W–where did you say you were from?"

"Throansburrough," Iris's voice quivered.

Darren's eyes widened at some sudden realization. "Throansburrough . . . destroyed by a mysterious contingent . . . professor." He ran a hand through his hair, his mind racing. "My family. They're in danger! Uncle, what have you done?"

Iris breathed in sharply as she worried for his family as well. "Darren," she said, trying to keep her voice calm. "What town do they live in?"

He shook his head, returning from some far-off place. "Al–Alaster. They live in Alaster."

Iris blinked with confusion. That was the capital city of Fitsengea. Wasn't it supposed to be impenetrable? It housed the royal family, after all. What did he have to fear? Iris could tell from the distant panicked look in his eyes that explaining this now wouldn't gain his cooperation. Instead, she walked over to him and placed a hand gently on his arm. "That's still about three weeks or more away from here. They still have time, but we need to go now. We can move faster than that army since there are only two of us, but they already have over a day's head start. Darren, *please*, help me." She looked into his eyes, holding his gaze.

He nodded firmly and pulled away from her. "Right. First help me pack up camp. Then we'll go." His jaw set into a grim line as he quickly began his task.

Iris followed his lead, picking up the stray utensils and bringing them to his pack. Not really sure where anything went, she instead turned to help take down his tent and resign herself to folding the cloth and any other clothing she came across. They soon packed everything and were ready to go. Iris shifted one of the packs to a more comfortable position on her shoulders. They didn't have much to carry overall, which would allow them to move even faster. Darren used the fire to make himself a torch and then kicked the surrounding dirt onto the little pit to put it out.

The darkness deepened without that main source of light, and it took a moment for her eyes to adjust to the flicker of Darren's torch. The moon was covered by the clouds, obscuring the path. Darren didn't wait for her eyes to fully adjust to this new lack of light but instead barked out a gruff, "Come on," before disappearing into the woods. Iris jogged up behind him. He wasn't easy to follow. He darted through the trees and underbrush with more ease than she could. She battled to focus, constantly juggling her attention between watching her footing and watching Darren's figure slip through the trees.

How far was it from the road? If only they could reach it, then she would be able to keep up with him. Iris worried she might lose him on the way. Still, she didn't dare ask him to slow down. She wanted to get there just as badly as he did, but his desire to protect his family drove him onward with hasty determination. *At least he has the chance to save them*, she thought with a growing bitterness.

At that moment, a small branch smacked her in the face, reminding her to do less thinking and more jogging. Just as she wondered if they would ever reach the road, they emerged through the trees with it before them. Iris briefly entertained the notion of kissing the ground but had to keep step with Darren's increasing pace. She understood his desire to reach the next town as quickly as possible, but she knew if they expended too much energy now, they wouldn't be able to make it very far. Taking a deep breath, she forced herself to surge forward and jog next to him.

"Darren . . . please . . . slow . . . down." Iris gasped with each labored breath.

Darren shook his head stiffly. "No, we have to move fast. You said so yourself; there's not much time." With that, he picked up the pace even more.

Panic for his family was overtaking him. She wouldn't be surprised if he soon broke into a dead run. She would have to reason with him or else he would leave her behind. Wiping sweat from her brow, she forced herself to keep up with him.

"Darren! If you keep up this pace, you'll be spent before you're even a quarter of the way to Alaster. How can you protect anyone if you pass out from exhaustion?"

He didn't seem to be listening. He was lost within his own thoughts and fears as his pace continued to increase. She had to make him understand. Unable to think of any other options, she stuck out her foot in front of him, hooking him around his right ankle. Darren flew to the ground.

Angrily he sat back up and yelled at her, "What's wrong with you! Do you think this is some kind of game?"

Iris picked up the torch to make sure it wouldn't go out on the ground and took a minute to catch her breath before answering. "No, I don't, and that's why we have to be smart about this. Too much is at stake just to go barreling along without any sort of a plan. So get a hold of yourself!" As she snapped at him, she surprised herself with her fierceness.

By the look on his face, she could tell that he was surprised too. She did her best to temper her tone. "Now get up and let's go, but at a more reasonable pace." She offered him her hand. He ignored it and rose on his own.

Why was she so angry at him? She needed to calm down as well. She forced herself to relax her tense muscles and picked up the few items that had fallen from Darren's pack. He took them back with a glare and carefully secured them.

"Look, I'm sorry for tripping you," Iris spoke, attempting to appease his bruised ego.

He sighed, and his shoulders slumped a little. "And I . . . I'm sorry for ignoring you. I–I should have been more considerate . . ." His words trailed off as he looked Iris up and down. She felt uncomfortable with his sudden look of pity. Did she really look that awful?

"No really, I understand. I would be the same way if it were my family." Iris broke in, hoping to distract him from her pathetic appearance. *But it's too late for your family*, her thoughts taunted her. *You couldn't save your family! You failed your family!*

The silence grew between the pair as they resumed walking, this time at a steady, brisk pace. Iris kept step with Darren mechanically, but her thoughts swirled in doubt, disappointment, and shame. Doubt in the future, disappointment at the past, and shame for not protecting the ones she loved, not a single one of them. No, she had hidden like the coward she was. Oh, a wretched, worthless coward. But she wasn't hiding now! Maybe she could atone for what she had done. Atonement didn't bring people back from the dead, though.

How would her new ally react if he knew that truth? She stole a glance at him. Mentally, he was miles away. If he knew, he probably would leave her behind. Who would ever bring a coward into a battle? Maybe he *should* just leave her behind. He would be able to travel much faster. No, he needed her; she had to give an account of what she saw. Iris shuddered. It would have to be a detailed account at that so that the leaders of the town could identify the threat through their actions. Certain groups were known by specific actions when they waged war. Iris didn't know these signs, for she had never previously been exposed to them. She would have to force herself to relive every gruesome detail to make sure nothing was left out, that no clues were lost. Once again, she shuddered as the horrible images flashed through her mind. She needed a distraction.

Iris cleared her throat gently and swallowed, working up the nerve to strike up a conversation. "Um, so . . . can you tell me about your family?"

The sudden break in silence caught Darren off guard. "What would you like to know?"

Chapter Five

The torchlight danced across her face, casting a glow over her features. Her long reddish-brown hair, although messy, reached midway down her back and framed her petite face and neckline. Dirt and grime smudges were everywhere. The corners of her mouth lifted in a faint smile, an attempt to be lighthearted, as he talked. An overwhelming shadow of sadness flashed across her violet-blue eyes more than once. And yet she was truly listening to him. He wasn't used to that. This Iris girl wasn't tuning him out and just nodding numbly when appropriate. It helped talking to her like this. Describing his family distracted him from imagining thousands of horrible situations that could happen to them.

"So you have an older brother and sister, one sister the same age as you, and two younger brothers?" Iris reiterated, making sure she had her facts straight.

"Yes, the two youngest are twins, Mikkel and Trevor."

"And your older brother is Devon; your oldest sister is Marguerite, and your other sister is . . .?"

"Liesel," Darren grinned slightly, impressed by her effort and her memory.

"Liesel! That's right! Goodness, there sure are a lot of you! Your poor parents must have been exhausted." She smiled, and Darren laughed in agreement.

"I suppose so. Four boys in any household are never easy. Boys do tend to get into all sorts of trouble; I know we did."

She laughed as he winked at her. "Well, I don't know about boys being the main issue. I mean, my sister and I . . . we . . . um—so did any of your sisters get married? Did your brother Devon settle down?"

Darren caught the glint of a tear as she hastily wiped it away. "Actually, yes. They all did. Well, Liesel is still engaged, but the wedding is taking place next season."

He studied Iris out of the corner of his eye. She was exhausted, perhaps even still in shock from whatever horrors she had witnessed. She looked so fragile and scared, but she was trying to be brave. She wouldn't allow herself to slow down.

"That's wonderful! A wedding in fall—that will be beautiful." Iris smiled at him.

"Yes. They're excited about it." Would she make it to the next town? She didn't seem like the type to give up. Well, at least when they reached the safety of Jaralynx, she could rest there. He, on the other hand, would find a quicker means of transportation. He had to beat this mystery army to Alaster. *Please, professor . . . be wrong for once in your life!*

"So, who's the lucky guy?" Iris gently pressed through the silence once more.

"Hmmm?" Darren refocused his thoughts to the present.

"Your sister's fiancé? What's his name?"

"Oh, him. Well it's–um–it's–uh . . ."

"You don't remember?" Iris tilted her head slightly in surprised disbelief.

Darren raked his hand through his hair with a sheepish look. "Actually, no, I don't!"

"Haha! That's awful!" Iris laughed playfully.

He shrugged. "It's been a while since I've been back home." Darren sensed where this line of questioning might lead and wasn't too eager to go there.

"How long is a while?"

Darren forced a light tone but kept his eyes forward. "Five years."

"Five years! Goodness! Did you get lost or something?" Iris asked, half in shock and half in jest.

He shrugged again, hoping to play off the subject as a non-issue. The last thing they needed was for him to pour more turmoil and strain on their desperate situation with his answers. Not that this conversation could ever come at a good time. Still, he felt an odd connection with this Iris woman. For some reason, she might actually understand him. *You're a fool who's been alone for too long.* Darren let the silence settle around them.

They walked on steadily for a while without speaking. Tactics for future possibilities spun through his thoughts. Darren's desire to know exactly what they were up against, if it was as bad as he feared, ate away at him. Still, he knew that Iris was likely traumatized, no matter how calm she might act, and he couldn't ask direct questions.

"Even though I was gone for so long, I had yet to travel as far west as Throansburrough. That was actually going to be the next town I'd pass through. Iris, do you mind . . . could you tell me what it was like living there?"

Iris slowed her pace and subconsciously played with her fingers. Her voice lowered, but she pressed on. "Throansburrough, my home . . . it–it wasn't much really to look at, I suppose. Not that it was unattended; it had its charms for sure."

"Was it as pious a place as I've heard?"

Iris chuckled sadly. "Pious? Well, I suppose the majority of us did believe and follow the Father. No one is perfect, to be sure, but they were kind-hearted people."

"Was it a small town?" Darren pushed for more specifics.

Iris pressed her lips together and took a breath. "I'm not sure. Perhaps a thousand people or so? I really haven't been able to do much traveling myself, so I don't know exactly what you might call large."

Darren watched as her face twisted into hurt confusion. She bit her bottom lip and took a moment before she continued speaking, "I just don't get it. Why us, Darren?" Her eyes pled for an answer that made his heart shudder. "We were no threat to anyone! Throansburrough had no significant role for Fitsengea; we had no quarrel with any other villages or any other people groups, really. What did they have to gain? Why us? Why—" Her voice hitched with emotion as she cut herself short. Iris quickly jerked her head to the side, doing her best to compose herself once more.

"Iris, I—" Darren stopped himself. He wanted to say he didn't know why, confirm that it made no sense, console her, and somehow help her believe this would get better, but for some reason, walking next to her like this, he just couldn't bring himself to lie. "I'm sorry. I shouldn't have brought it up. We don't have to talk about your home anymore if you prefer not to."

Her shoulders lifted as she took a deep breath and then slowly exhaled. Turning her eyes back to him, she smiled weakly at Darren. "It's alright, but thank you for your concern." She turned her eyes forward once more and focused on walking.

Darren's thoughts flitted in a dozen different directions as he searched for topics to discuss. Maybe it would be best if he just didn't talk anymore. He glanced back over at Iris. She was shivering something fierce, and no wonder, she only had her day clothes on. She must be freezing. At least he had on a night coat; otherwise he'd feel that night breeze piercing through his skin. He had made sure to leave it out while packing up the camp.

"Hold this," Darren ordered as he passed his torch to Iris.

Though cocking an eyebrow suspiciously, she obeyed. Quietly shifting his pack off his shoulder, Darren took off his night coat and held it out to Iris.

"Here. I'm warm enough already."

She looked at it and then back at him to protest.

"No, please, I insist. I'll be fine." Darren persisted with a half-smile.

She smiled through quivering lips and took it gently. Iris passed the torch to Darren so that she could use both her arms to take off her own pack, put on the coat, and then put the pack back on. Once she was situated again, she looked at him and smiled. "Thank you."

"You're welcome." He smiled back gently.

He wondered what she was thinking, her face so pensive and sad. But when she talked to him, she would force herself to smile. What had her eyes seen? What were they up against? He wanted to ask for more details, but she was clearly too hurt to discuss any of it. It really was a wonder that she could function at all. Darren thought again that Iris was still likely in shock. That was the only answer that made sense; how else could she keep herself so calm and composed? Even with all who had wronged him back in Alaster, Darren knew he'd be a completely useless wreck if his home had fallen. *And it still might.* He shuddered at the thought. If Alaster fell, then all Fitsengea would follow. But perhaps this wasn't what he thought it was. Maybe this was simply just a chance attack. Just because Throansburrough was hit didn't mean that one prophecy was beginning its fulfillment. It could just as easily be a cruel coincidence. Surely this was not the beginning of the end. He was just over-reacting; once they came to this next town, they would likely find them safe and untouched.

Even so, Darren knew that Iris would still need to report this attack on Throansburrough, at least to the lord in the nearest town. He would accompany her that far. It wasn't safe for a woman to travel long distances alone. He was thankful that they weren't much farther away from Jaralynx. If he recalled correctly, this town wasn't that large, even smaller than Throansburrough. *It'd probably be more proper to call it a simple village than a town, really,* Darren mused as he remembered that he had never visited this place, either. Not much that such a small place could offer in trade or supplies. A new face stood out like a glaring beacon in small villages, and the last thing he wanted or needed was to be noticed or recognized.

A wooden marker sign came into view in the moonlight now shining brightly in the clear sky.

"Jaralynx," Iris read as she inspected the sign under the torchlight.

A hopeful smile rested on her face. "This village is like a second home to my people. We should be able to see it around the next bend."

A breeze wafted towards them, hitting them both with a heavy scent of smoke. The hairs on the back of Darren's neck stood on end at the implications of that thick smell. Iris looked at Darren with wide, nervous eyes. They simultaneously quickened their pace. Soon they shifted from a jog to a worried run, the smell of burning wood intensifying with every step. They raced in silence, fear supplying new energy.

When they reached the hill at the top of the bend that led out of the woods and into a clearing, the village of Jaralynx came into view below. Or rather, what was left of it. The blood drained from Darren's face in a mix of shock and horror. The moon cast its eerie glow over the heap of smoldering buildings, some still kindling small flames, testifying to the force of the raging fire that had destroyed the town. Darren and Iris stood transfixed at the rubble. They were too late. A lump grew in his stomach. Was everyone dead? How long since the army had left? His heart beat quickened; what if they left behind a scout? What if they were camped on the other side of the town? This was dangerous, and they needed to proceed with caution.

"No . . ." Iris whispered under her breath, finally breaking the silence.

Darren tore his eyes from the ruins to look at Iris, her whole frame rattled in anguish. She shook her head as her face shifted between pain and anger, unwilling to accept the destruction before them. *She just lost her second home,* Darren realized in sympathetic horror. Taking a step toward her in an attempt to comfort her, Iris suddenly raced off and down into the village.

What is she doing! Darren froze in disbelief. Coming to his senses again, he quickly chased after her. He had to stop her; it wasn't safe. Sprinting down into the valley, he quickly caught up with her just as she entered the debris. They bounded over crumbled wood and broken glass, ash kicking up with their steps. He followed her into one of the few buildings left partially standing. He had to get through to her! She was panicked, and this building wouldn't stand much longer. Darren used his torch to help him pick his way around the larger obstacles.

"Iris?" he called to her but kept his voice as low as possible. "Iris, stop! Come back!" His frustration mounted.

He waited for her response but heard only light footsteps racing from one room to the next. Rather than try and search for her, he waited by the doorway to catch her as she ran past. She appeared again after just a minute. Her bright eyes were opened wide in shock, all the more mysterious against her pale face. She was scared and unaware of his presence. He grabbed her arm as she tried to run by, not even noticing him.

"Iris! Stop! Get a hold of yourself."

Her eyes finally focused on him. "Where are they?"

"They're dead. Everyone's gone. We were too late." As he talked to her, he gently led her from the creaking building.

She shook her head numbly. "No, no. Where are they? The bodies, they're gone; they're all gone! What did they do with them?" She looked up at him, tears in her eyes. "They couldn't possibly have had time to destroy them, much less bury them. Where are the bodies?"

They both became quiet. He looked around them. She was right; there were no bodies. With the devastation that surrounded them, how could there be no visual proof of death? He didn't want to see those lifeless forms, and part of him was glad that he couldn't. Still, it was beyond odd that no people—living, dead, or even wounded—had been left behind. What kind of an army was this?

"They have to be here somewhere," Iris breathed out quietly. Slowly stepping a few feet away from Darren, she peered through the moonlight and turned in a circle. "They just have to be." She spun back around and faced Darren. "Come on, we have to keep looking."

"Iris, wait—"

She didn't listen, forcing Darren to run after her yet again. Racing over debris and around crumbling buildings, Darren did his best to keep her in sight. He now understood her frustration as he had run along the central road. Having someone completely ignore you was more than enough to cause him to bristle in annoyance. If Iris were a man, he could think of a few choice words he would like to shout out. Yet crass behavior was never acceptable in the presence of a lady, even if the *lady* was the recklessly barreling through dangerous territory, bashing innocent strangers on the head, and tripping men so that they fell flat on their faces type. And to think, he had even begun to pity her. Apparently she wasn't as exhausted as he had first thought. She had no qualms about sprinting through the village or rather what was left of it. Why couldn't she at least be quieter? Didn't she comprehend the danger of their situation? It would be just his luck to be saddled with the village idiot as the only surviving witness to a great threat.

He stumbled over some debris, barely catching himself before falling, giving Iris time to widen the gap between them. He let a curse slip out as he picked up the pace. *Why couldn't she just slow down?* he thought angrily as she turned another corner.

"Ah!" He let out a surprised gasp as his feet screeched to a halt before barreling into the back of Iris's sudden stone-like stance.

That could have been messy, he thought, glancing at his torch. She probably wouldn't have appreciated being set on fire accidentally. He collected himself and turned his attention back to Iris. Moving around to her side, Darren watched as this woman came to grips with her world collapsing around her. He could almost see the chasm opening up inside her. Shame swept over Darren for any anger he had been directing toward Iris. She swayed and then slowly sat on the ground. Not knowing what else to do, Darren knelt down beside her. They sat quietly together for a while with only the slight sputtering of the torch in Darren's hand breaking the silence. As he held the torch, his arm began to ache. Darren looked for a spot among the debris to safely wedge it upright so that it didn't burn out. Once successful, he sat back next to Iris.

"Is it hopeless?" Iris asked softly without turning to look at him. "Can we really do anything to stop this?"

Darren stayed quiet. There were no right answers to give this fragile heart before him.

"I'm such a fool," Iris chuckled ruefully.

Her silhouette trembled in the moonlight. He hurt for her, for the souls lost in these disgraceful massacres. Anger roiled within him at the injustice and worse, at his helplessness in it all.

"Why have you abandoned us, Holy Father?" The hoarse whisper just escaped Iris's lips.

Her trembling intensified as cries rose in her throat. The slight reflective sparkle of tears streamed down her face. She looked so alone weeping there. He couldn't stand it! Shifting in closer, he gently put his arm around her and drew her in to a protective hold. The kind gesture broke through the last of Iris's walls as she burst into guttural wails of sorrow. Iris reciprocated by burying her face into Darren's chest as her screams of brokenness overtook her.

—→ ✧ ←—

Iris and Darren left Jaralynx in silence. Iris kept her eyes down, watching her feet washed in a mixture of moonlight and the second torchlight she now carried. Her emotions both drained and sustained her, fueling her desperation to not fail anyone else. Every friend she had ever made in Jaralynx, every family member, was now dead, and once again, it was all her fault. She had taken too long getting there. She was too late. How many more would die because of her? She prayed that she wouldn't have to go through yet another destroyed town.

Though, Saunskirt, which was next along the central road, was more of the fighting kind. Maybe they could withstand a sudden onslaught. That is, if their soldiers weren't too drunk from one of those festivals. Which one was it this time of year? Mid-summer festival? End-of-the-summer festival? Pre-fall festival? The Festival of Festivals? Oh, she hoped it wasn't that one. That was the worst of them all, which was saying a lot, for Saunskirt was notorious for throwing an over-abundance of festivals. Their defense was often in a drunken stupor or just reviving themselves from a hangover. But in between their festivals,

Saunskirt was a wonderful ally. They loved battle and had mastered many areas of weaponry. It was no wonder they had grown so expediently. They had a high-demand trade system, making them quite prosperous. Yet their entire existence sadly depended on tools made for death.

War dehumanized people, taking away the soul of the man behind the armor and turning him into a mere object, as if he were a game piece for that board game, Rule or Ruin. War created black-and-white thinking where the enemy is a monster with no conscience. Where you know you're right, and that's all that matters. You don't consider the fact that your enemy is the mirror of you. They were raised to believe that they were right and that you were the wrong monster. They didn't consider the fact that the man felled by their blade had created a widow, abandoned children, and broken a parent's heart. They have family just as you have family. They fight to protect their loved ones just as you do. The only thing that had made them your enemy was that you had been told that they were. Who knows, as children, you might have even played together. War was a cruel monster with a terrifying power to change people forever.

Iris's conscience was pricked by her self-righteous diatribe. Could she extend the same thought process over the army that had stolen her home from her? She didn't want to think of them as having their own families. She wanted them to stay soulless monsters, justifying the feelings in her heart. Truly, how could anyone claim mass murder as right in any shape or form? It wasn't, and that was the end of that!

"I need a horse!" Darren fretted to himself.

Iris jumped at the sudden sound of his voice. She had forgotten that he was even there! What had he said? "Sorry, what?"

"I need a horse or a transport vessel. Anything to help go faster!"

"Transports don't come out here yet. They can't run along the dirt road, and they haven't finished building the new path out this way. You won't find one of those until we're closer to Alaster."

"I know that. It's just that we'll never make it on foot!"

She knew he was angry because he was so worried. Could she

blame him? She felt the same way. Still, she couldn't help but notice how he had only cried out for one horse. He must not be used to company, accustomed to only looking after himself. She wondered how many of those five years away from home were spent in the woods. Would that classify him as a hermit? If so, he was surprisingly personable for a hermit. He was right, though, they did need to find some mode of transportation, or it would all be pointless.

The sudden sound of movement in the trees up ahead stilled Iris's thoughts. She glanced at Darren. He stopped walking and listened. So he had heard it too? Shoot! She had hoped it was just in her head.

"Put out your torch," Darren whispered to her.

She cocked an eyebrow at him for a second and then followed his example, stooping down and kicking dirt onto her light.

"Be quiet. We don't want to give ourselves away until we know what's ahead," he explained.

She nodded and hoped that whatever was in front of them hadn't heard them coming. *No rest for the weary, eh?* she whined. Darren slowly started forward, his steps light and practically soundless. *No fair. Mr. Woodsman here is practiced at stealthy maneuvers. I, on the other hand, will be lucky not to run face first into whoever is up there. I'd much rather prefer it if I stayed behind while he checked to see if it was safe. I mean, really, what could I do to help in a fight if it came to that? I've never been in a fight my whole life! Well, at least not a physical one. Maybe a scrap here or there with my sister but never a full-blown brawl. Whatever happened to the gentleman protecting the lady? The kind-hearted man who kept a woman far from even the semblance of danger?* Iris's thoughts continued to swarm through her head as they neared the sound. A part of her realized her rambling thoughts were ridiculous and just a ploy to distract herself from her rising fear. She knew that she needed to pay better attention to what was going on around her instead of allowing herself to become so distracted. And yet what if the sound was just some animal running through the brush? Their caution could be misplaced. Wouldn't that be wonderful? It would be a nice change of pace.

Iris prayed that it was nothing more than a little creature, a cute furry bunny would nice. They were sweet and soft; no harm would come from them. Or perhaps a squirrel. They were cute too. She looked at Darren a few feet ahead of her. He was crouching lower, peering through the leaves, and had unsheathed a dagger. Her heart sank. No, not a bunny. By now, she could hear the muttered cursing of an irritated man. Well, maybe she would be able to get in a few solid punches before it all went wrong. Then again, maybe she should just let Darren do all the dirty work. He sure looked like he could handle it. It was probably best if she just followed his lead. Who knows what sort of calamity she would cause otherwise? Her most recent actions had certainly not proven fruitful.

Suddenly Darren cut to the right. He made a wide circle and then burst through the bushes. He had moved with such agility that she hadn't had time to follow him. *I thought the point was to* not *be noticed,* she thought angrily. Instead of following, she stayed out of sight and moved in slowly. Why had he acted like that without the slightest bit of warning? She strained her ear as she heard more sounds, and then a harsh whisper came from someone she assumed was Darren.

"Move an inch, and I'll slit your throat."

It *was* Darren speaking, and his tone chilled her heart. Was he about to kill someone? She moved forward and tentatively pulled back a branch. Darren stood behind a man with his dagger pressed firmly to the stranger's throat. A thin line of blood trickled down his neck. If the man even sneezed, Darren could accidentally kill him!

"Please . . . no more death," she breathed out the prayer.

Chapter Six

"Please, no! No! Don't kill him! Leave him be! Stop it, stop!" Sara sobbed, unable to watch any longer as her friend was tortured.

Her cries racked her frail frame. The heavy hands on her shoulders kept her from running to his side. Tears blurred her vision as she continued to plead. The huge demon-like man held Jodie's limp frame up by his hair and smirked at the girl.

"Had enough of this, have you? Can't stand it anymore?"

Sara wept. The man nodded proudly and tossed the boy aside. He walked swiftly over to her and grabbed her chin harshly, bringing her face within inches of his.

He glared into her panicked eyes. "Now let that be a lesson to you. You'll behave from now on, won't you?"

Despite his tight grasp, she managed a slight twitch of a nod as more tears ran down her cheeks.

"There's a good girl. Now get some sleep. After all, we've given you children such a cozy place of your own. Would be a shame not to make good use of it."

The man holding her shoulders let out a cruel chuckle. The other released her face and walked back over to the semi-conscious boy. He grabbed Jodie carelessly and tossed him over his shoulder as if he were nothing but an empty sack. He then handed Jodie off to another man within the tent.

"Take these two back to the cages, and when you're done with that, take care of the body."

The men nodded attentively and began to leave.

"Oh, and girl," he called out. "Make sure to spread the word so that others will know what happens when you try to escape." He chuckled smugly as they left.

Sara forced herself to stare at her feet. She couldn't bear to see Marcus's body nor look at the bloody form of her friend. She allowed herself to be led back to their prison, remaining silent but for a few bitter sobs. Sara climbed the steps without resistance into the crowded wagon cell. Jodie was tossed in haphazardly after her. She rushed to catch him before he hit his head. A murmur arose after the door locked into place. The group gathered around the pair.

"Sara, what happened?"

"Are you okay?"

"Sara, what did they do?"

"Sara, will Jodie be okay?"

Sara sat numbly, cradling Jodie in her arms. She blinked her eyes back into focus as a little hand pulled on her sleeve. It was little Lori Mainfield, her eyes wide with worry and fear.

"S–Sara, where's Marcus? What happened to Marcus? Do the bad men still have him?"

Eyes turned from Lori back to Sara. Sara buried her head into Jodie's chest and cried. Several gasps sounded around her. Lori tugged on Sara again.

"Where's Marcus! Where is he?" she demanded

A voice spoke gently beside Lori. "Lori, sweetie . . . Marcus isn't . . . he isn't coming back."

"Why not?" Lori moaned, perhaps already knowing, perhaps hearing the pain in the other girl's voice.

"Lori—uh—why don't you go see your brother?"

"Why? Why isn't he coming back? Why?"

Her questions were rubbing Sara raw. She lifted her head just enough to whisper, "He's dead, Lori. Marcus is dead. Now go to Jacob." She laid her head back on Jodie and huddled closer to him.

Lori whispered an okay in agreement as the others settled back in their own spots. A few stayed beside her. Someone took off their ragged coat and laid it across her back. Everyone became silent.

Lori reached Jacob and squeezed him tightly; he latched onto her in response. She decided to never let him go. The bad men wouldn't get her brother. She whimpered again, memories of her mommy crowding into her thoughts. Lori ached for mommy to be there. She scooted closer to Jacob in an effort to calm them both.

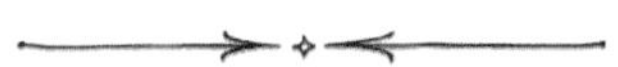

"Are you alone?" Darren questioned as he kept his skinning knife pressed against Malachi's throat.

The man stiffened but answered quietly, "Yes."

"Don't lie to me." Darren tightened his grip and moved the blade up Malachi's neck a tad, a small reminder that he would not be toyed with. "I can tell when you're lying, Malachi. So let's try this again. *Where* are your comrades?"

The man's pulse quickened at the mention of his name. "How–how do you know me?"

"I ask the questions, not you! How far away are they, and how many are traveling with you tonight?"

"A mile into the woods, and there are four of us total."

"How long ago did they leave? When are they due back?"

"An hour ago. They'll be back when the sun rises."

"Alright. I believe you, but that doesn't give me much time. Now time to say good night, Malachi."

Panic flew through the man's body. "Wait—"

Darren raised his hand and struck him heavily across the back of his head, and Malachi collapsed to the ground. A scream rose through the bushes as the man fell. Hysterical, Iris rushed forward and dropped to her knees by the man's limp frame.

"What was that for! Why did you kill him? What is *wrong* with you?"

If he didn't shut her up soon, she would give them away! She hadn't seen what had actually happened. "Iris, stop it! Calm down!" He grabbed her arm.

She tried to shake him off. "Get away from me!"

"Iris, please." Darren attempted to pull her up to him.

"Let go!" She fought back.

"Iris, be quiet!"

She spun out her left arm and punched him square in the jaw. He staggered back a step in shock and released her. She jumped to her feet and backed away.

She glared at him, her voice like stone. "Don't you *dare* touch me."

He rubbed his jaw and looked at her. Maybe he hadn't thought this through. He sighed and tried to keep his voice calm. "Iris, it's okay. He's not dead."

She faltered for a second but looked at him in disbelief.

"I only knocked him out, I promise! You can check him over if you'd like."

She looked at the prone figure on the ground and then back at the knife in Darren's hand. He followed her eyes, his shoulders sagging. He slowly bent to the ground, set down the knife, and then kicked it in her direction.

"There, are you happy now?"

"Your pack too."

His temper rose, but he complied and tossed it at her feet. He held out his hands in front of him and took a few more steps backward to give her more space. Refusing to take her eyes off him, she knelt down slowly and picked up the knife, keeping it defensively stretched toward Darren. Then she walked over to the man. Juggling her attention between the two of them, she took her time looking him over. Finally satisfied that he was, in fact, not dead, she rose and looked at Darren.

She still held onto the dagger, and her steely glare had not softened in the least.

"Why?" The one word covered a multitude of questions, which he knew was her intention.

"Because I know these men. Malachi, here, is too dangerous to keep conscious. We may need him as leverage if his compatriots are who I think they are. They're quite dangerous, but we may be able to bargain a second horse from them." He pointed to a group of trees a few feet away. "See, Malachi's horse is tied up over there. The other men must have ridden theirs down to the river. I'd say we should take the one and be on our way, but one horse with two riders would only last so long."

She was relaxing a little, but she still didn't trust him. Could he blame her? He did come up with this on the spur of the moment. She eyed him more closely, studying his expression.

"How do you know his name? How do you know so much about them without him recognizing you?"

A good question, one that he didn't particularly feel like answering. She was already on edge, and the details would probably shove her over, but staring at her blankly wouldn't calm her down.

"Malachi and the group he runs with are somewhat infamous back in Alaster." That was true. "I've heard tales and seen pictures. They're criminals, which is why I know them, but he didn't recognize me." That was also partly true. Partly.

"Rather strange for a man who hasn't been home in five years to recognize a man he's never met. And in the dark, no less."

Shoot! She was right. He fumbled for a response. "Well, just because I haven't been home doesn't mean I don't like to stay updated on Alaster's news. These men are always near the top."

"Alright then. You've followed the news of Alaster for the past five years. I'll buy that, *maybe*. Then again, you follow stories of this man so closely that you recognize him, but you can't remember the name of your sister's fiancé?"

He shrugged and tried to seem nonchalant. "Guess I just found the stories more interesting. I remember what interests me."

"Even so, how did you receive news of Alaster when you were so far away?"

"People talk in towns. I knew where to look. It's really not that big of a deal, but we don't have time to sit here and chit chat like this. Those other men might be here any minute, and that scream you let loose probably drove them faster." *Oh, please, just let it go and listen to me,* he begged inwardly.

She remained silent for a minute. He could tell that she didn't trust his story nor did she like the way he side-stepped her questions. Whatever safety and comfort he had brought her while in Jaralynx had clearly evaporated. Still, she recognized the danger of the other men's soon arrival and knew that standing around bickering over the full truth could land them in some serious trouble. She sighed, pressed her lips together, and then nodded.

"Alright, then, you win. For now. But what do you propose we do? Tie up this Malachi and just wait for his companions?"

"Well, in a sense, yes. Though I think we could benefit if we looked through some of their things here."

"Hmm, okay, so you want to steal their supplies, steal their horses, and threaten the life of their friend. Sounds like a fine plan to me. That is, except for the part where they become so angry that they hunt us down in revenge. After all, isn't that what these types of men would do?" Iris snapped in angry sarcasm.

Did she have to analyze everything? "Look! Do you want to make it to Alaster or not?"

"Fine, I get it. I was just hoping that along the way, I wouldn't turn into the very people we're trying to stop."

What? Why should she worry about that? It was all his idea anyway, that and his rash actions. And where did she come off comparing a murderous rampage to a little light, and necessary mind you, thieving? Darren chose to completely ignore the rest of Iris's comments while he looked for a rope to tie up Malachi. Once found, he tossed it to Iris and ordered her to tie it tightly.

"We don't want him waking up and breaking free on us."

That taken care of, he made sure they had thoroughly rummaged through all the items that the others had left in Malachi's care. He also made it a point to remove all their weapons from the vicinity. Of course, they would have some on their persons, but at least, he wouldn't have to worry about them rearming themselves. He could handle sword play, possibly even arrows, but anything with black powder would be one messy mistake.

Satisfied with his preparations, he walked over to Iris who was kneeling beside an unconscious Malachi. She had done a wonderful job on the knots. The only way he'd get out of that was if someone cut him free. Eyeing the surroundings, he made sure that their position would be well hidden. He knelt down beside Iris to whisper a few last words of caution.

"When those men get here, I want you to stay here with Malachi. Don't come out for any reason unless I call for you, understand?" He sternly stared to drive his point home as he repeated himself. "No matter what, don't come out unless I say so."

She nodded, intently watching him. "Ummm, Darren . . ." she bit her lip hesitantly then proceeded. "What are you going to do?"

"Well, I . . ."

"You do have a plan, don't you?"

Darren fumbled. He didn't want to admit he was still working on that. "Of course, I do."

She looked at him, her gaze digging deep. He felt uncomfortable to be scrutinized so, especially when he was actually lying. Her eyes widened at this realization, and she gasped slightly.

"You have no idea what you're doing!"

"You don't know that—"

"Oh yes I do. You're just making this up as you go! Don't be a fool, Darren! Let's just get out of here before it's too late!"

Not only did she not trust him personally, she apparently didn't even trust his abilities. Well, she just didn't realize what he was capable of. Nor what these men were capable of either, but that was beside the point. He squared his shoulders, trying to make himself look more impressive.

"Well, that's how most plans are made anyway. Spur-of-the-moment genius."

"That's just reckless stupidity!"

The neighing of horses in the distance cut off his reply. They were back early. Now it really was too late. He shot a warning look at Iris, telling her to be quiet. Then he waited for the other men to draw closer. Now what would he do? Jump them? No, there were far too many of them for him to take. They would obliterate him and the girl in a second. He could just walk out in the open and hope to gain the upper hand through surprise at seeing him. Yet that left him wide open if they had any weapons on them. *Come on, think of something! You need those horses!*

"Hey, Malachi!" a drunken voice called out. "Give us a hand with these horses. Seems Bryant's gave him the slip. We got the horse but lost Bryant!" He laughed loudly.

Sounds like Aaron . . . so that means the other one might be . . .

"Probably passed out somewhere in the woods," mumbled a second voice, not quite clear enough for Darren to make out.

So now he was down to two of them, and one of them was drunk. His odds were starting to improve, but they were still getting closer. He would have to come up with something fast.

"Malachi! Get up here!" The voice shouted more clearly, giving away the identity of Malachi's older half-brother.

Kyle. The name dripped with venom through his thoughts.

Darren decided to act. He took off his pack so that he could move more freely and made an arch through the brush toward Kyle and Aaron. He held his bow and a couple of arrows. *These should at least make them keep their distance.*

"Malachi! Where are you?"

Now was as good a time as any. Darren emerged from his hiding place. "Malachi is a little preoccupied right now."

Chapter Seven

"What the—who are you? Show yourself!" The sober rider scoffed.

Iris fidgeted slightly, trying to see and hear better. The one coherent man looked to be of similar build and age to Darren with short chestnut-brown hair and a fairly prominent scar on the left side of his square jaw. The second man, who struggled to stay atop his horse, looked a good bit younger and had a mess of curly auburn locks. Well, the men were definitely from Alaster. She could tell by the stone lights attached to the front of their horses. Only the people of Alaster had mastered that technology; they acted as a controlled torch, shining light in only specific areas. Hopefully they wouldn't spot Darren or her with them.

"I'd rather not," Darren spoke, mockingly calm.

"I don't take kindly to threats," the man with the scar warned.

Iris didn't like this. So many things could go wrong here. Why couldn't they just ask them for their horses? Surely they would want to help them; after all their own family might be in danger because of this army. They had a common enemy. If only Darren hadn't attacked that

Malachi guy! Then maybe they could have actually talked to them. *Darren, you fool! What will we do now?*

"Throw down your weapons!" Darren called out.

"What weapons? You've already taken what we had as well as our provisions by the looks of it. Why don't you come out of hiding, you coward, and tell us what it is that you want?"

Darren softly chuckled before responding. "Do you think I'm a fool? No man would enter the woods without some sort of protection!" A twinge of guilt settled over Iris as she remembered her own foolishness. "Not even the Brethren of Five!"

So that's what they called themselves! Iris wondered who the fifth man was. Two men were standing in front of her here; another lay tied up and unconscious beside her, and apparently the fourth was off somewhere in a drunken comma. The one sober man, who she assumed was the leader, suddenly sat up a bit straighter as if something vital had just occurred to him. Though he was a little distance away, she was still able to see a wicked smirk creep across his face.

"The Brethren of Five, eh? So you know us then? Still, you're mistaken, for we haven't been the brethren for a while now. No, not since our fifth member betrayed us and then fled into the barren woods. But I needn't repeat the tale now, do I? For you know it well . . . Darren."

What? Darren was one of them! She was traveling with a thieving murderer! Okay, so she didn't know if he was a murderer or not, but still! She was surrounded by dangerous people, and she had no idea what to do! She obviously couldn't trust Darren at all. After all, he had even betrayed these men, men who didn't look or sound like the gentle type! How did he betray them? Did he steal something from them? Maybe he actually did something good, something legal that made them think he was wrong. Oh, she hoped that was it! If only she could get away. Maybe she could sneak over to Malachi's horse. Maybe she could escape them all . . . maybe, just maybe.

"Alright then Kyle, you know it's me. Perhaps we can be civil about this."

"Civil? For what you did, you should be thankful that I haven't killed you already!"

"For what *I* did! Apparently time has clouded your memory, for the events that occurred were through no fault of mine!"

"Or so you say to soothe your conscience."

"Bah! Enough reminiscing and pointing fingers you two!" called out Kyle's drunk companion. "For the love of it all, just spit out what you want, Darren, and what you've done with Malachi, and we'll decide if we're gonna kill you or not!"

"Always a good head on your shoulders Aaron, even when you were sloshed! I need two of your horses and your word that you won't be following me."

"And why should we give you either?" Kyle shouted angrily.

"Because I have your brother—"

"*Half*-brother!"

"As I was saying, I have your . . . *half*-brother, and as long as you cooperate, I won't kill him."

Again with the death threats! Were these men unable to come up with any other solutions to a problem? It was downright ridiculous!

"Why two? Why do you need two horses?"

"For my own purposes, which have nothing to do with you."

They were wasting time. And she had enough of this ridiculous bantering back and forth! These men were crazy and bloodthirsty. She was probably going to die here anyway, so she might as well put her two cents in before it was all over. And it was really starting to hurt crouching down like this. The sun would be rising soon and give away their positions if something else didn't first. Iris tilted her chin up, pushed her shoulders back, and took a deep breath. *Holy Father, help me!*

Standing up abruptly, she stepped out of her hiding spot. "Hey! Over here!"

"What the—who are *you*?" Kyle called out, startled.

"What do you think you're doing!" Darren hissed furiously.

What am *I doing?* "Listen, Kyle and Aaron, right? My name is Iris."

She spoke as she walked toward them. "I don't know what Darren did to you, but that doesn't matter now. Bigger things are happening, bigger than anything you guys could bicker about!"

"So you're a friend of Darren's?" Kyle asked unhappily as he shifted in his saddle. "The reason for two horses."

"Yeah, we need two horses. But the friend part, well, let's just say that's still up in the air," she stated crossly and then waved her hand as if dismissing the thought. "But as I said, that doesn't matter now."

"And why not?" Kyle leaned forward on his steed, his expression as if he were a cat toying with its prey.

That look frightened her as well as angered her, fueling her drive to get her point across. "Because everything you have ever cared about is in danger! Every person you have ever loved, everything you consider normal or good, is about to be destroyed!" Her cool gaze held his.

"What are you? Some kind of misled prophet?"

"No, a witness. A witness to the destruction of the world around her. Villages along the east of the central road are being destroyed, slaughtered by a deranged army. And if you don't help us, who knows how many will die! The speed at which they're traveling, it won't be long before they reach Alaster." *Here's hoping that his family actually resides in Alaster!*

"Alaster would never fall!"

Oh, thank you, Holy Father! At least that part of Darren's story wasn't a lie.

"You haven't seen what they can do. I've seen the aftermath, Kyle. Even Alaster wouldn't stand a chance if caught off guard." Darren appealed to Kyle's heart as well. Maybe the emotion in Darren's voice struck some sort of chord in Kyle, because for a second, his expression had softened. But that warmth disappeared just as quickly as it came. She needed him to recapture that feeling.

"Kyle, please. I'm not asking you to forgive Darren. I'm not asking you to even pretend to like him. All I'm asking is that you lend me some horses so that we can at least give others, give Alaster, a chance."

"Why should we let you go? Why can't we just deliver the message ourselves?" Aaron cried.

Iris massaged her forehead in frustration. It was like talking to her niece or nephew, but worse!

"I already told you why! I was *there*. I saw what happened. I know how they work! It's imperative that *I* go!"

"Fine, then. *We'll* take you and leave Darren here instead." Kyle stated as he jumped down from his horse and walked over to Iris.

"Hold it! Not going to happen!" Darren called out as he stood up, holding his bow with an arrow notched and ready. "She doesn't go anywhere without me."

Kyle stopped, glared at Darren, and mumbled, "So that's where you were hiding . . ."

"What the hell is going on here!" a familiar voice cried in the distance. But Iris couldn't recall why she recognized it.

"Oh, there ya' are, Bryant!" Aaron laughed "Have a good rest?"

"Rest! I was knocked out because of that dumb horse! Thanks for checking on me, by the way. Could someone tell me why our stuff is all gone, and why a man has an arrow trained at Kyle? And why there's this nice little tart standing in the middle of it all? Hello there, sweetness, and what might your name be?"

Iris's skin crawled; she wanted to punch him. Turning her head to reply, her heart stopped. It was him! The creep from the other night! The monster that had tried to—tried to . . . A lump formed in her throat as her hands shook. *Please don't recognize me!* Her mind screamed as she quickly turned her head away, focusing instead on Kyle.

"How about this? We don't trust each other. You're worried we're going to steal from you. How about you come with us, Kyle, to make sure it isn't a lie? That way, you can get your horses back." Iris inwardly pleaded he would listen to reason.

"So there would be two against one? I don't think so."

"Is anyone even listening to me?" Bryant cried angrily, approaching Iris.

"Hey, stay put, Bryant!" Darren shouted as he, too, walked closer, stepping out from the bushes.

"Darren! Is that you? What are you—"

"Keep your hands away from your knives Bryant."

"Darren, you can't take us all on!" Aaron growled.

Kyle kept his eyes on Iris as he spoke. "Aaron's right, Darren, but so is the girl in a way. I have a better idea, miss Iris, was it? Let's make it two on two. The both of you and the two of us. Then I'll know we won't get cheated."

Iris nodded. "Fine, agreed. In a good faith measure, I'll let your brother go." Iris turned back to her hiding place and proceeded to cut Malachi loose. Darren positioned himself between Iris and the others, refusing to lower his guard or his weapon just yet.

"Right. Aaron, off your horse. You're not sober enough to come. Bryant and I will escort them."

Iris shot back up from her position, "What? No!"

Kyle looked at her strangely, "Why not?"

"Because he–he–I don't–I don't trust him!"

"And we don't trust you! Besides, no one else can go. My half-brother is apparently unconscious or else he would have freed himself by now. I don't know how much longer Aaron can stay on his horse, which leaves only me and Bryant. And as you keep stressing, there isn't time for this bickering, so either take it or leave it."

A sob welled up from within. "Fine. We'll take it, but I want your word that no harm will come to us."

"Only if you give us yours as well."

"You have my word."

"Then you have ours, right, Bryant?" Bryant nodded, still utterly confused as to what was going on. "Darren?" Kyle's mouth twitched upward.

Darren stood silent, still holding his arrow. Iris glared at him and gestured with her head. He sighed finally and lowered his weapon. "Fine. You have my word as well. But if either of you try anything, I don't have to keep mine!"

"Fine."

Yes, they were definitely worse than her niece and nephew. Children in grown men's bodies! But why did Bryant have to go? At least he hadn't recognized her yet. Maybe it would be safer for her if he didn't. Whatever the case, she stayed close to Darren. She might not be able to trust him completely, but he was still better than these new men were. At least she hoped he was and that it wasn't all just an act. *Can't catch a break, can I?* She sighed bitterly.

It took them only a few minutes to ready themselves. Aaron was left to tend to Malachi as he woke up slowly and not too happily. Darren dispersed the supplies that he had hidden earlier between each rider but made sure to keep the extra weapons with himself. Yet when Darren wasn't looking, Iris also made sure to grab a short sword for herself. With this group of men, she would not be caught off guard.

They kept their horses at a steady canter. The cold and biting wind from their speed stung her face and occasionally blew her hair into her eyes. Still, she was happy for it, well, as happy as she could be. A little wind and other annoyances were a small trade-off for reaching Saunskirt in time. She was afraid to allow herself to hope that the things would be okay. At least she wasn't dead yet.

The silence of their ride allowed her mind to wander over painful thoughts. She fought bitterness over the fact that these horrible people were given the chance to save the ones they loved when she, a faithful follower of the Father, was given none. She was angry and confused by the abandonment of her Lord.

Why didn't He save her family? Why didn't He send a messenger to save *her* home? Better yet, why did He allow those murderous people to even exist? Was she perfect? No. Was her family holy? No. But they had been faithful. They had prayed and obeyed, read His word and done His will. Where was the protection He promised His children? If He loved them, why didn't He help her? Kyle had moaned about betrayal earlier. Had the Holy Father betrayed her? If so, why? What had she done wrong? Why did this happen? And why was it still happening? He had the power to stop it, but He didn't. *Holy Father, where are You? Why are You doing this to me? Have You stopped loving me?* It wasn't fair or right! She didn't even want to talk to Him anymore, but she still had so many questions. Her head was swimming; nothing made sense. She was tired, and her body ached. She longed to rest, to sleep, and then wake up from this strange nightmare. Her eyes grew heavy, and her body could not even hold her up anymore. Only the jarring motions of her horse kept her awake though not exactly alert.

The sun was rising in the sky so that she could at least see where they were going; otherwise she was sure that she would have veered off the path. She leaned forward in the saddle to stretch her back a little. Surprisingly, the position was rather comfortable. Staying there, her head drooped. Would this horse just follow the others even if she slept for a while? Her head fell down farther but was suddenly smacked by the horse's jarring head. Pain surged through her face, waking her so that she abruptly sat up. Her hand flew to her nose, checking to see if it was bleeding. *That really hurt! Did anybody else see?*

"And *that* would be the reason why most people sit up while riding." Kyle laughed smugly beside her.

Blast! They did see. How embarrassing!

"Leave her alone Kyle." Darren growled his warning. "Are you okay, Iris?" Darren questioned in a softer tone.

"I'm fine," she responded shortly. "Let's just focus on riding."

At that, everyone grew quiet again. It wouldn't be much longer until they reached Saunskirt. Good thing, too, for with the sun out, the day would soon grow warm, making it harder for the horses to maintain their arduous pace. Iris wondered once more about the state of Saunskirt. Maybe this city would be the savior she needed. She could tell them what she knew and then go on her way and let them take care of this mess. And yet where would she go? She had no home to return to, no other family with which to seek refuge. She had the clothes on her back, excluding Darren's night coat. She had a short sword for protection but even that wasn't hers. She had nothing. She still clung to the hope that survivors had escaped to the villages elsewhere. Maybe, just maybe, she could find her people, her family, again.

"Welcome to Saunskirt! City in five miles!" Bryant shouted out the words from the sign at the front of the group.

The sound of his voice still made Iris's skin crawl. Keeping her eyes forward, she watched for the large city to come into view. *Please . . . please . . . please!* Their horses pressed ahead as the road exited out of the woods once more. A large expanse of buildings came into view before them.

"Looks like all is well!" Kyle shouted out over his shoulder.

Relief exploded through Iris's heart. They had done it! They had actually made it in time!

Chapter Eight

Oh no! Don't tell me it's . . . Iris frowned with disappointment as they entered the city. Saunskirt was packed so tightly with people that it was nearly impossible for them to ride their horses to a stable. People were everywhere, pushing and shoving, laughing and screaming. Colorful banners danced in the air; odd assortments of musical instruments battled with each other for the crowd's attention. All of Saunskirt's population seemed to be within the city center as well as a number of foreign visitors. Iris sighed, hanging her head momentarily. *It's the Festival of Festivals! How will we ever gain an audience with the lord of the town now?*

"Hey, you lowlife! Keep your grubby hands to yourself!" Darren shouted, kicking away a stranger that was picking through Iris's saddle. "Pay attention Iris, or these people will rob you of the very horse you're sitting on." He scolded her loudly in order to be heard above the crowd.

"I'm not a child! I know that!" She glared at him, then quickly checked to ensure that she still had the short sword at her side. Finding it securely in place, she sighed with relief, then forced herself to be on higher alert.

Iris and her three-man escort continued to weave their way farther into town, looking for a place to keep their horses as well as board up for the night just in case they'd need to stay more than a day. It took them nearly an hour to find accommodations. Once they had taken care of their horses, they all gathered inside an inn to discuss their next course of action. Iris was surprised at Kyle's decision for he and Bryant to see this whole event through. By all rights, they had held up their end of the bargain and could now return with their four horses to Malachi and Aaron in the woods, especially if they were as nefarious a group as Darren had hinted at earlier. Kyle and Bryant walked about in public, apparently comfortable. Saunskirt was possibly the sort of place where certain company was more common. Ratting out one side only gave space for the favor to be returned.

Iris eyed Kyle who sat across from her at their little round table. Did these men really believe her? Was their concern genuine? Or were they just bored and looking for a little adventure to pass the time?

"So how does one actually go about requesting an audience with Saunskirt's lord?" Bryant questioned after swigging more than half his mug of ale in one gulp.

Iris cringed as he belched and then used his forearm to wipe the liquid off his beard. At his every movement, she involuntarily inched a little closer to Darren.

"I suppose we could try contacting his second-in-command," Darren suggested.

"Or perhaps going to the courthouse and see where we get from there," Iris offered.

"No, that's how you'd do something if you had time to waste! If you go through the proper channels, you'd have to wait for every person in each station to jump through a million little hoops before the request itself ever reached the lord. Even then, you don't know if he'd be willing to hear you out." Kyle spoke grimly, staring at his mug.

"Then what do *you* suggest we do, *Kyle*?" Darren questioned, his distaste for their company obvious.

"I *suggest*"—Kyle looked up, matching Darren's tone—"that we take a more *direct* approach."

"A direct approach?" Iris looked at Kyle nervously. She didn't like how that sounded.

"Yes, we go to his home and *make* him listen to us."

And the violence ensues! These men really don't know any other way to handle things, do they? "I don't like the sound of that. Things could go very wrong very fast." Iris frowned

Kyle smiled at her slyly. "Can you think of any better ideas, princess?"

Iris burned with anger and was about to respond in kind when Darren interjected.

"Leave her alone, Kyle." Darren glared at Kyle, then looked at Iris and sighed. "I hate to admit it, but he's right. This appears to be the best course of action to take. It will just take too long otherwise."

Iris looked down at her hands. She didn't like this. People would get hurt. What if someone were even killed? The whole reason for coming here was to help protect people.

Darren looked at her gently and placed his hand on top of hers. "Hey, you don't have to go, you know? We have rented a room already. You could stay here and rest up for a bit if you wanted."

That look of pity filled his eyes again, as if he thought her too frail to handle a situation like this. She had to bite back a bitter laugh. She had already dealt with far worse than a little scuffle with nobility.

She looked up at him defiantly and shook off his hand. "No, I'm going."

"But Iris—"

"I said I'm going! If I'm not there to tell them what happened, then they won't believe any of you. They'll just think you were some crazy festival people and throw you in the stocks or worse. I *have* to go."

Darren looked away unhappily but nodded in agreement.

Kyle clapped his hands together and laughed, then turned and smiled wickedly at Iris. "Alright, then the princess comes with us tonight, men."

"Kyle, if you know what's good for you, you'll stop calling me that." Iris glared at him again.

He bowed his head in mock sincerity. "My apologies, lady. I suppose you prefer the title of queen then?"

"I have shown you no disrespect. Why do you disrespect me so? Your quarrel is with Darren, not me. You don't even know who I am!" she shot at him with growing fierceness.

Kyle paused for a moment, the smile fading from his face. He glanced over at Darren, who returned his gaze with a scowl. Finally he sighed and raised his hands in the air in mock surrender. "Okay, okay. My apologies. You are quite right. Perhaps we can start anew, Iris." He looked at her solemnly and offered her his hand.

She looked at it and then at his face. *He appears to be sincere. But I still don't trust him.* Iris nodded and clasped his hand. "Agreed. Thank you."

Darren stiffened beside her as she shook hands with Kyle. Apparently this contact between them infuriated him. *Maybe that's why Kyle did it, just to make Darren mad.* When she looked back at Kyle, he wasn't paying any attention to Darren.

"Right, then, when do we go?" Bryant asked after downing the mug he had swiped from Darren and ordering a third.

Iris grimaced. How much could he drink in one sitting?

"Why not right now?" Kyle shrugged. "The rest of the town is occupied with the festival, and the guards will be too busy making sure a drunken riot doesn't break out here to be worried about what happens at the lord's home."

"But what if he's not there?" Iris queried.

Kyle smiled mischievously in response. "Then we wait for him!"

Darren signaled for one of the serving girls to pay their tab, though most of it belonged to Bryant. As soon as that had been taken care of, they all left their table and prepared to go back through the chaos of the town center. Before leaving the inn, Darren pulled Iris aside at the door.

"Maybe you should leave your pack in the room," he suggested, motioning to the bag on her back. "You have enough to worry about right now without having to watch for every little pickpocket here."

"I'll be just fine."

"But I really think—"

"I said I'm fine!" she snapped at him, hoping he'd let it be.

"Fine then! Don't say I didn't warn you!" he barked back and walked outside.

She sighed thankfully. She didn't want to be rude, but Darren wouldn't understand. This pack on her back allowed her to conceal the short sword; otherwise they would have seen it as soon as she removed the saddle from her horse. Keeping the pack with her let her continue to carry the blade for her own safety. After all, she didn't trust any of these men; she couldn't risk being unable to defend herself. She knew that she couldn't match any of them in strength, and her speed would only last for so long.

Darren was right, though, about not wanting the added distraction of pickpockets through the town, but she would either worry about that or worry about not having it with her. In the end, she would have to deal with a troubled mind, no matter what she did. Yet maybe focusing on her pack was better than focusing on what was ahead. She couldn't imagine that the lord would be willing to listen to them when he found out that they had broken into his home. She just hoped that she would be able to convince Kyle and Bryant to not hurt anyone.

Iris forced herself to focus on her surroundings. It wasn't hard to do considering that if she didn't pay attention, she would easily lose sight of the others. So many people were in Saunskirt right now! At least this wasn't her first time here; otherwise she would have been lost for sure. But rare visits did little to help her navigate through the crowd. On more than one occasion, she'd have to stop and scan the crowd, making sure she wasn't following the wrong people. Darren stopped often to wave his hand above everyone's head to help guide her.

As they neared the lord's home, the activity on the streets progressively thinned out. All the festivities were focused on the center of town, so the people had no reason to pay attention to the outskirts. The heat of the day was beginning to rise as they continued their trek farther from the city. Sweat formed on Iris's brow, forcing her to rub it away before it rolled into her eyes.

On hot days like this, she longed for a heavy storm. It hadn't rained in a little more than a year now. She had heard stories of how the lands to the far east, thousands of miles beyond even Alaster, had been dealing with a drought for almost ten years. She hoped that this lack of rain they now faced wasn't a sign that the drought was moving in their direction. The last thing they needed was to have all their crops die off. If this whole skirmish escalated into any sort of true battle, food would be a necessary reserve. A breath caught in her throat. *It is possible a war may break out over this.*

The scope of the effect of the massacres would be great. An unprovoked attack on a kingdom, a country, as large and far-reaching as Fitsengea would not go unanswered. *Am I bringing war to these people?* The townspeople passing by them suddenly became very real to Iris. Their faces were overlaid with pain and sorrow, flashing between reality and gruesome possibilities in the future. Her thoughts raced out of control. She couldn't stop them!

A barrage of sickening, vivid images flooded her mind. Blood flew everywhere as the men tried to protect their homes; shrieks of pain and horror rang in her ears. Suddenly she was transported back to the decimation of Throansburrough. Glass shattered, and houses were engulfed in flames. Their eyes filled with terror. Their cries—the very cries of her own family—pierced to the core of her being. Iris threw her hands over her ears as if to block out the sounds in her head.

She shook herself, trying to make her mind stop. She couldn't think about this! If she did, she would go crazy for sure. The more she tried to force herself to think about something else, the more relentless the gruesome memories became. Her mind couldn't fight her pain; she was far too tired to even try. She struggled to breathe as fear coiled tightly around her chest. Iris's legs grew weak, and she suddenly collapsed on her knees. Tears streamed down her dirt-stained face.

"Iris!" Darren shouted from ahead. In an instant, he was kneeling by her side. "Iris! What's wrong? What happened? Are you okay?" He placed his hands on her shoulders to help her focus on him.

"I . . . just . . . I can't . . ." Iris tried to form the words but could barely talk. She moved her hands from her ears and covered her eyes.

"Take a breath, Iris. Slow down. It's okay; I've got you." Darren gently brushed away her hair from her face.

Iris inhaled a few times and wiped the tears from her eyes. She had to get a hold of herself! Now wasn't the time to drop her guard. *Just suck it up and move on!* she angrily chided herself. *Just hold out a little longer. You can break down later. Now isn't the time!* After taking another deep breath, she looked up at Darren and forced a weak smile. "Sorry. I didn't mean to worry you. I guess I'm just—just tired or something."

"Are you sure? I could take you back to the inn instead. Maybe you should go back and rest up a while?"

She shook her head stubbornly. "No. I'll be fine. I want to go with you."

"But I really—"

"Please, Darren?" she whispered in soft determination.

Darren sighed and finally nodded. He stood and then helped Iris up as well. "Alright, but stay in front of me from now on, okay?"

She smiled at him. "Deal."

Bryant and Kyle stood waiting and watching a few feet away. "I could always carry her the rest of the way!" Bryant called out.

"No!" Darren and Iris cried out in unison. They looked at each other, surprised at their shared reaction.

"I . . . uh—mean, no, I'll be fine walking, thanks," Iris called back, her gaze still fixed on Darren.

Bryant shrugged. "Suit yourself."

The small ragtag group spent the rest of the long trek to the lord's manor in silence. As it came into view, Kyle stopped them in an alley a few yards away from the front gates in order to scan their surroundings without arousing suspicion. He went on by himself for a closer look.

Massive gates protected the home, which was practically a castle.

Apparently Saunskirt had been doing very well in recent years so that the lord could maintain such extravagance. A few sentries were placed up front, but farther down, there was no one, not even a guard stationed directly in front of the actual home. *You would think that with such a grand estate, they would want it more carefully guarded,* Iris mused. Kyle quickly returned to report his findings.

"So? How do we get in?" Darren blurted out before Kyle could speak.

He glared at Darren for a second and then turned his head to address Iris and Bryant directly. "It's just as I thought. The lord isn't here right now. He's taken most of his guards with him into the town. If we walk a little ways down to the side of the estate, we should be able to get in without a problem."

"Don't you think it's a little odd that he would leave his home so horribly unguarded?" Iris suggested.

"If it had been any lord other than Lord Valomeer, I would say yes. But you see, Lord Valomeer is known throughout the land for setting an assortment of booby traps all over his property. He loves seeing how many would-be robbers or kidnappers he can maim or kill with them. It's impossible to know where they are because he always moves them. Even his most trusted guards don't know. They are simply given the strictest orders to never leave their post for the day. Those who don't listen often find themselves missing body parts or worse."

Iris looked at him with disbelief and disgust. *This man is insane!* "How in the lands are we supposed to get through unharmed?"

Kyle smiled. "Simple, we switch off the traps. Every one of them is powered with an electrical current. Inside Lord Valomeer's study is a switch to turn them off."

Darren glared at Kyle with mounting annoyance. "That still leaves us on the outside needing to get in!"

Kyle's smile turned mischievous. "That's where my little trick comes in. You see, for as smart as Lord Valomeer is, he has an odd soft spot for birds. All of the sensors on each trap allow a small bird to land on it unharmed. So the traps aren't as sensitive as one might think."

"You sure seem to know a lot about this guy." Iris frowned uneasily.

Kyle ignored the remark and continued explaining. "What we need is a little bird to fly into his house and flip the switch for us." He turned directly to Iris. "You feel up to it, little bird?"

"Wait! What? Me!" Iris blinked, utterly confused.

"No way, Kyle! There's no way I'll let you make her do that!" Darren growled and took a menacing step closer to Kyle.

"It's the only way!" Kyle snarled back. "She's the only one here small enough for it to work!"

"It's too dangerous! What if it wears off before then?"

"It won't!"

"You don't know that!"

"Wait a minute!" Iris cried out, holding up her hands. "Don't *I* get a say in all this? And besides, what would I be doing anyways?"

Kyle glared at Darren a little longer before he turned his attention back to Iris. "Glad you asked. The plan is that we make you light as a bird."

Iris scrunched her brow in confusion. "And how, exactly, would we do that?"

Kyle reached into his pockets and pulled out two discs just slightly smaller than his palm. "With these."

"Okay . . . what are *these?*"

"They're Floater's Discs, a little invention I happened upon a few years back. I have no idea how the technical details work. But I do know *what* they do! They make the wearer extremely light-footed, briefly making them weigh one-eighteenth of their usual weight. This gives the wearer a sensation of floating, hence the name."

Iris tilted her head to the side as she inspected the little discs. A purple crystal set inlaid at the center of the golden metal objects. Small ventilations holes along the top revealed small turning gears inside. The slightest glow emanated from it, concentrated near the edges of the crystal. A faint etching of the initials R.D. sat on the outer rim in between the rivets. Iris twisted her mouth at the purple geode. *They're not inherently evil, don't fall for that old anti-Sylphaenian superstition,* Iris chided herself.

"They really work?"

"They've helped me out of a number of sticky situations. Just take some stone light dust, spread a thin coat on your shoes and the discs will adhere." Kyle patted his hand on a tiny leather pouch tied to his side.

"Wouldn't it just be easier to wait outside the gates for Lord Valomeer's return and try to speak to him *then?*" Iris noted as she crossed her arms. In her opinion, all this was much more trouble than it was worth.

"No. Lord Valomeer hates to have strangers around his home. Everyone knows that if they're found even standing by his gates, they'll instantly be thrown in jail. Why else do you think we haven't run into any commoners out here?"

Because I assumed that most of them were at the festival. Man, this Lord Valomeer is eccentric!

"Iris, no one will make you do this if you don't want to." Darren stated kindly, casting a glance at Kyle. "I, for one, think it's too risky and that we should find another way."

"There is no other way!" Kyle raised his voice in exasperation. "Don't you think I would have mentioned it if there was?"

"Maybe, maybe not. Depends on how much fun you're having." Darren frowned fiercely.

"It's safe to say that in the present company, I have nothing but a foul taste in my mouth."

"Boys, please!" Iris sighed, stepping between them. "What are you? Five? You hate each other; we get it! But can we please focus here?"

Kyle and Darren held each other's stare. Finally Darren sighed and turned to look back at Iris. "Sorry, you're right. But Kyle, make no mistake! When this is over, I'll be sure to settle this once and for all."

"You're welcome to try." He smirked in return.

Iris groaned and massaged her forehead. She had to remind herself that she shouldn't get into the middle of their disagreement, no matter how badly she might want to.

"Right then!" she stated, popping her head back up and looking at Kyle. "Let's get this show on the road then, hmm?" She smiled and held out her hand for the discs.

Kyle smiled, surprised at how quickly Iris agreed to his plan but thrilled that she had listened to him instead of Darren. He knew it must drive Darren crazy. He took the Floater's Discs and put them in Iris's hand. "Let's go."

Chapter Nine

"Careful . . ." Darren whispered under his breath. He hated just standing there and watching Iris go off to her possible death. At least Kyle had explained to her in greater detail how the Floater's Discs worked. He was pretty sure, though, that if he hadn't pressed Kyle, Kyle would have left out the extra information.

Along with the benefits, the Floater's Discs came with a few side effects. For one, the use of each disc had a time limit of approximately ten minutes before they used up their power and needed to be recharged. Normally this would be plenty of time to do what was needed, but the devices required the user to move slowly, which was an added problem. With the sudden change in weight, a person's initial balance was thrown completely off. If you advanced too quickly, you could very easily fall, causing the device to short circuit. They could be useful for moving short distances, but making it across the expanse of Lord Valomeer's lawn in time was beyond risky for Iris.

Darren grit his teeth and clenched his fists as he watched, every muscle in his body tense. It was all he could do to keep himself from scaling that fence and running to her side, but that wouldn't do either of them any good. He probably would just end up getting them both killed. In the meantime, he had to settle for watching out for patrols and for making sure that the few guards that were left didn't notice her tiptoeing through the grounds.

Darren's grip tightened on Iris's pack. After some bickering, Iris relinquished, and eventually Darren's logic won out. Even the smallest amount of extra weight could be disastrous. When he took it from her, he realized why she had been clinging to it so. It made sense, really. Why wouldn't a person want a way to defend themselves when stuck with a group of dangerous and complete strangers? He couldn't help but feel badly for her. At least he knew what he was getting himself into. Iris, on the other hand . . . He hated Kyle for this. It would be just like him to place her in danger as if she hadn't been through enough already! He just hoped that she wouldn't pass out in the midst of this. He could tell how exhausted she was. It wasn't just her earlier break-down. Her face was tired; her whole body looked ready to collapse. He knew for certain that she had gone at least two days without sleep because they had been together that long and he hadn't slept either. Even before they met, she hadn't slept, though. She had walked all the way from Throansburrough, which was no short journey from Jaralynx. Then there was the horse ride to Saunskirt. Yet she was much stronger than she looked as she was still standing now. And not just standing but actually coherent, able to come up with quick responses to counter him. He wondered if he had ever met someone as stubborn as she was.

"How long has it been now?" Darren questioned Kyle curtly.

Kyle shrugged.

"Kyle!" Darren snapped.

"Alright, alright! Five minutes," he answered disinterestedly.

"Five minutes! But she's not even halfway there yet!"

"Don't you think I can see that?" he responded gruffly.

"If she gets hurt, Kyle, so help me . . ." Darren clenched his jaw and glared at him with murderous intent.

"There's nothing either of us could do for her now anyway," he stated, not taking his eyes off Iris. "If you're truly worried, you could always pray to that Holy Father of yours."

Darren glanced down at the ground. *That was a low blow*, he thought bitterly.

"She tripped!" Kyle cried out, taking a step out of the alleyway and toward the fence.

Darren's heart stopped as he jerked up his head. "What!" He rushed to the iron bars, grasping them in fear.

Iris stood across the expansive lawn, teetering dangerously trying to regain her balance.

"Come on, come on. You can do it, Iris. Don't fall." Darren whispered, willing her success with his words.

"Darren, back away from the fence. If the guards see you, they'll know something's up!" Kyle hissed at him.

Darren watched Iris closely, not releasing the bars until he was satisfied that she wouldn't fall. Finally she regained her balance. He backed a couple of steps away from the fence, sighing heavily and reminding himself to breathe again.

"Good. It'd be a shame for such a pretty thing as her to get damaged now, wouldn't it?" Bryant commented from Darren's right side.

Darren's temper flared. He ached to punch Bryant square in the jaw.

"You really are a pig, you know that, Bryant?" Kyle snarled, half in jest.

Bryant shrugged. "I just like to admire the finer things of life, and she happens to be one of them. Still, she could do with a little cleaning up. It's funny, though; I could have sworn that I've seen her before."

"Bryant, that's enough." Darren warned dangerously.

Bryant raised an eyebrow and studied Darren for a second. "My apologies. I didn't realize she was already spoken for."

"She is, so drop it." Darren stated harshly. It would probably be better if Bryant thought that Iris was promised to Darren rather than to correct him. Otherwise Bryant would consider her fair game. Labeling her as taken probably wouldn't stop him as it never had in the past, but it might at least slow him down a little.

"Funny," Kyle interjected calmly. "I remember she stated earlier that she wasn't even sure if you were friends. Or did she pick up that nasty little habit of lying from you?"

Darren refrained from looking at Kyle. "It's . . . it's none of your business." But Kyle was probably right. After lying to Iris, there was little chance that she'd be willing to trust him, and she didn't even know the half of it. But he knew. He knew if he told her everything, she'd hate him even more. He didn't know what it was about her, but he couldn't bear the thought of losing what little friendship they had. He ached inside at the thought of the look of disgust on her face, the look everyone had when they discovered the truth.

"Three minutes left," Bryant called out shortly.

Iris needed to pick up the pace. If she didn't, then she would be stuck on the lawn about a quarter of the way from the house. *Curse these retched nobility and their need to show off their wealth through their landscaping!* Darren fretted. Did Iris even know how little time she had left? He couldn't stomach the thought of what would happen if the discs ran out and she stepped on a trap.

"Please . . . come on, Iris . . . make it!" he whispered desperately.

An odd *whirring* suddenly sounded all around the lawn. Darren gazed over its expanse, searching for its source. A thousand tiny little devices, each about five inches tall and only two inches wide, ascended through the ground. The circular metal structures were spaced in a random arrangement. The whirring was obviously the noise of some device used to raise them. Once they reached the established height of five inches, the noise ceased. Iris stood deathly still. Darren's heart beat faster.

He jerked his head in Bryant's direction and hissed, "You said she still had three minutes left!"

Bryant looked on, bewildered. "She does."

Darren turned his anger toward Kyle. "If she still has time, then why have the traps gone off? I thought you said the sensors wouldn't pick up her movements!"

Kyle simply rolled his eyes. "They haven't."

"But those—"

"—*aren't* the traps," he cut in coolly.

"Well then, what *are* they?"

Kyle smirked. "Bird feeders."

Darren looked at him dumbfounded and then turned his head back to the devices. The whirring had started again, and sure enough, birdseed was being spouted from each little metal object. The sound was soon cut short by the thunderous calls of a swarm of birds in the sky. They swooped down onto the property and began their feeding frenzy. Apparently the birds knew the feeding schedule.

Hundreds upon hundreds of small birds covered the ground, completely surrounding Iris with only a few patches of green left in between. Iris looked about, taking in all the commotion. Slowly she bent down and lifted up one of her feet to her hands.

"What is she doing? She's wasting time!" Bryant called out, annoyed.

Darren squinted his eyes and moved closer to the fence to get a better look at what Iris was picking at on the bottom of her shoes. His eyebrows shot up, and he let out a gasp of horror. She was removing the Floater's Discs! Kyle had noticed as well.

"What does that girl think she's doing? Is she insane? She'll be killed for sure without those on!" Kyle spoke in rising panic.

Darren continued to stare, wide-eyed, barely able to breathe. Once she had completely removed the discs, Iris sprinted toward the house, weaving across the lawn, dodging birds and plant life alike. Twice she stopped briefly and allowed the birds around her to resettle and continue their feast. As soon as they touched down, she took off again. Was she really that crazy, thinking that blind luck would see her through unharmed? *Fool! You irresponsible fool!* Why would anybody do something so reckless? Did she really care so little for her own well-being? Darren clutched at the bars as if he were holding onto his own life, not even caring anymore if a guard noticed him. His mind screamed at her with all his might: cursing her stupidity, pleading for her success, and berating himself for allowing her to be put in this situation. Once again, she abruptly halted her run so that the birds could settle. Suddenly a thought struck Darren as he watched. Not daring to take his eyes off Iris, he spoke to Kyle without moving.

"Hey Kyle, is it possible that the traps become visible once something touches them?"

"What are you—" Kyle cut himself off as he grasped Darren's train of thought. "Oh, I see now! Yes, it is possible, that is, if something too light to set them off completely were to land on them. The ground in that area would give off a faint blue light."

"So that's what she's doing then. Iris must have realized that she didn't have much time left."

"And she's using the birds to tell her where and where not to go?" Bryant queried.

"Precisely," Darren answered.

"Smart girl, smart girl." Kyle smiled to himself.

"And she's in!" Bryant announced victoriously.

At that statement, all three men sighed collectively. The most dangerous part of the plan was complete. Now all Iris had to do was get into the library, find the switch that controlled the traps, turn it off, and signal for the rest of them to enter. That was the easier part of this plan, because when Lord Valomeer was out, he allowed no one to remain inside his house. Just another one of his little quirks.

Darren turned back to the pack lying on the ground where he had dropped it and hoisted it up over his shoulder, careful to maintain the secrecy of Iris's hidden short sword. If Kyle or Bryant discovered that he now had a weapon, there would be a fight for sure. The question remained as to whether he should give it back to Iris. Would it be wise to return it to someone who didn't trust him? A frightened person with a sword was rarely a safe combination. Was she the type of person to attack first and ask questions later? Reflexively, he touched the side of his head. A chuckle escaped as he recalled their first encounter. She may not even be properly trained. In that case, she would just end up hurting herself and not her attacker. On the other hand, if he didn't return the short sword with the pack, then he would all but solidify her assumption that she couldn't trust him.

"There's the signal," Bryant called out, disturbing Darren's thoughts.

"That didn't take long," Kyle mused suspiciously.

Bryant shrugged. "Well, she's better than I gave her credit for."

Kyle shook his head as if to discard a troublesome thought. "Right then, time to go!" He clapped his hands together once, made sure the guards weren't looking, and easily scaled the fence.

Bryant followed suit, a little slower but with relative ease. Darren glanced toward the guards once more before proceeding with his ascent. Landing as quietly as possible on the other side, he shifted the pack on his shoulder a bit and then followed after Kyle and Bryant toward the castle-like mansion. His mind was made up. He'd rather pay a small price to win back Iris's trust instead of seeing her hurt. Maybe this way, she would listen to him more readily. Darren shook his head and sighed mentally. No, even with a weapon in hand, he was certain Iris would argue with him. It took some effort to keep himself from laughing out loud at that mental image. If she wasn't careful, that little characteristic could get her into a lot of trouble. Your greatest strength is your greatest weakness, after all. Where had he heard that phrase before? The answer was on the tip of his memory, but right then, he didn't have time to stop and analyze it. They had reached the steps to the house and would soon be inside.

Now he had to figure out how they would approach Lord Valomeer. What would they say to him? How would they convince him to listen? How long would it be before he even returned? They couldn't wait too long, which meant they would have to find some way to draw him back to his home. Did it have to be so complicated just to have a lousy conversation with the man? Perhaps they shouldn't have listened to Kyle. After all, his ideas always led to unnecessary trouble. No fun in doing something easy, as he used to say. Darren wondered if

Kyle still said that. No, probably not. That would only remind him of how things were before. Kyle had probably done the same thing he had: erased every trace of Darren from his life. But really, why should Darren even care? Kyle was a despicable human being, a backstabber, not worth the effort. *Just forget about it,* Darren thought, once again pushing his feelings and the past to a dark corner of his mind.

"All this for one man?" Bryant asked in awe upon entering Lord Valomeer's mansion.

"Yes, but I assure you, this place will seem rather cramped as soon as the *great* Lord Valomeer arrives."

"What? I don't—"

"He means the man has a big ego, Bryant. Not unlike someone *else* we know." Darren smirked at Kyle.

"Now, now, we know it's always admirable for one to admit their faults, but really, Darren, save the confessions for later. In the meantime, we must find where our little bird has flown off to."

I really hate you, Darren glowered but decided to let it go and look for Iris. Why wasn't she there to meet them at the door? Something didn't seem right.

"Iris? Iris where are you?" Darren loudly whispered.

"Why are you whispering?" Bryant asked, looking at him as if he were a fool.

"Something's wrong. Why isn't she answering?" Darren queried aloud, more to himself than to anyone else.

"Darren, you—"

"In here!" Iris's voice cut in from a small distance away. "In the study."

Darren sighed and turned toward her voice.

"In where? Which one's the study?" Bryant called out, confused.

"This way," Kyle motioned toward one of the open doors.

How does he know where the study is? Has he been here before? "Kyle, what are you not telling me?" Darren asked suspiciously as he followed him across the hall.

"Nothing. You don't need to know."

On edge, Kyle held himself stiffly. Not because he was annoyed, it wasn't that kind of strain. He was on guard, preparing for some unseen danger. A mixture of anger and apprehension washed over Darren. Furious at the idea that Kyle would hide any information that might jeopardize their safety and apprehensive at whatever had made Kyle so anxious. True, Kyle usually kept his guard up, which was necessary for his line of work. Still, Darren had learned early on that whenever Kyle was on edge, he should be as well.

They crossed the hall and entered the doorway of the study. The size of the room seemed more appropriate for a library rather than a simple study. The ceiling's height resembled that of an old church building, rising for what seemed like forever. Bookshelves so high that one needed a ladder to reach them towered over the group. The last time he had seen a study of this grandeur must have been—what was it now? Eight years ago? Taking a few steps farther in, Darren looked around the room for Iris. She stood by a desk to the right of the doorway. His smile at finding her soon faded away at her rigid stance.

"Iris?" he called out cautiously.

"That'll be far enough," came a chilling voice from the shadows directly behind Iris.

Kyle, Darren, and Bryant froze in place.

"Who's there?" Kyle questioned calmly.

"I'm hurt, Kyle. Don't you recognize the sound of my voice?"

Kyle remained still, waiting for his answer while peering into the darkness.

"Show yourself!" Bryant growled in frustration.

The man in the shadows sighed and took a couple of steps forward. "I suppose I must. Truly a disappointment. Thought I had taught you better, Kyle. Apparently I was wrong."

Darren's eyes caught the glint of metal in the light, the tip of a sword, pointed low, but still angled toward Iris. As the man walked farther from the shadows, he stepped closer to Iris, eventually standing directly beside her. As soon as the man's face was visible, Kyle sucked in a sharp breath through his nose.

"Ah, so *now* you recognize me. Well, at least I know that your eyesight isn't as poor as your hearing." The man smiled wickedly.

Darren's right hand moved slowly to the pack he carried for Iris. With Kyle distracting that man, whoever he was, he could use it as an opportunity to pull out the short sword. Midway through his movement, though, he locked eyes with Iris briefly. She seemed to read his thoughts and gave him a very slight shake of the head while her eyes screamed no to him. Confused at her reasoning, he paused for a second then lowered his hand again. As if breaking out of some sort of stupor, Kyle cleared his throat and then breathed deeply before speaking.

"Bryant, Darren, Iris . . . allow me to introduce"—he paused and gave a half-smile—"Lord Valomeer."

Chapter Ten

The stranger held out a small loaf of bread in his hand, offering it kindly to Lori. "Here, take it." He smiled at her.

His short cropped brown hair and sparkling gray eyes gave the man an almost boyish look, contrasting with the firm lines of his face hinting he was in his thirties. Lori nervously looked at the bread in his hand. Dropping her gaze shyly, she shook her head no.

"Oh, come on now. I know you're hungry, I think even the horses heard your stomach moan when you saw my lunch. Go ahead, really, it's okay." He nudged it toward her a little, again smiling as warmly as possible.

Lori's tiny fingers danced on her lips as she considered whether this man was trustworthy or not. Her mommy had told her to never take anything from a stranger unless she told her it was okay. But mommy wasn't here, so maybe she shouldn't, just to be safe. Then again, she *was* really hungry, and the man seemed nice enough. She had to think about Jacob too. He was still back in that cage. He'd be hungry too. Maybe she could show the food to Jodie or Sara. They could tell her if it was safe to eat or not. Older kids were always smart about stuff like that, especially Jodie. He had always known what berries were safe to eat and which ones made you sick. So why wouldn't he be able to tell if the bread was bad?

"Come on now kid, take it. My arm's getting tired of waiting." He sighed.

With her eyes on the bread, she bit her bottom lip and then looked at the stranger's face. He had happy eyes, she liked that. They reminded her of her daddy's eyes that had always seemed to be smiling at her. She couldn't help but smile back at her daddy just as she couldn't stop herself now.

"Ah, there now! There's a smile," the man said happily. "Can you tell me your name, little girl?"

"Lori," she barely whispered.

"Pleasure to meet you, Lori. I'm Fred."

"Nice to meet you, Mr. Fred," Lori said softly while playing with her lips again.

Fred stretched out his right hand in place of his left one that held the bread. Lori smiled broadly and shook his hand like she had seen her parents do many times before. Fred matched her smile and chuckled to himself.

"Do you know what I like to do when I make new friends, Lori?"

She shook her head no.

"I like to give them gifts. So would you please take this bread as my gift to you?"

Lori smiled shyly. "Mommy did say it was rude to refuse a gift from a friend."

"What a smart mommy you have!"

Lori giggled and reached out her little hand to take the bread.

"Hey!" Fred lifted confused eyes at the furious shout from behind them.

"What do you think you're doing!" the irate man demanded as he stomped toward them.

Lori turned her head fearfully to see one of the mean men who had forced her to go on errands with him. Her lower lip quivered, and her hands trembled a little.

"Can I help you, sir?" Fred asked calmly as he stood to his full height, which was about a hand higher than the bad man.

"Yeah! You can mind your own business!"

"Excuse me?"

"This here is my property!" he stated gruffly as he clasped his hand down on Lori's shoulder and then jerked her roughly behind him. "And I'll not be having some stranger mess with *my* property!"

Lori wanted to cry. She knew that she'd start any second. Well, if she hadn't been too scared to do so. Crying made the bad men even angrier.

"My apologies, sir." Fred spoke sincerely as he put his arms up to show he was backing off. "But if you don't mind my saying so, your—err —*property* could do with a little extra nourishment. Just like a good horse can't work well without food in its belly, neither can a child." He smiled a little as if to prove his statement was only out of concern for the man.

"I said keep out of my business! The girl will be just fine! Come on!" He growled as he turned and yanked Lori after him.

Fred's smile faded quickly as the two of them left. His eyes grew sad, and he sighed as he put the loaf of bread back in his pack. He suddenly wasn't hungry anymore.

Lori chanced a glance behind her as they left the stables. She wished she could have spent more time with that kind man. It seemed like forever since an adult smiled at her. The bad man dragged her behind him until they reached the end of the stables, and he whirled her around to face him.

"You stupid brat! What do you think you were doing? What did you tell him!"

"N–n–nothing," she stuttered, shaking all over.

"Don't you care about your brother at all?"

"Y–yes. Yes, I do!" She hated being yelled at; it scared her.

"Then don't *ever* do something so stupid again! If you even walk three feet away from me, I'll make sure you *never* see your brother again!"

Tears rolled from her eyes as she nodded.

"Good, now make yourself useful and carry that!" He barked at her, pointing to a pile of supplies nearly as big as she was.

Quickly she complied, trying to move everything as best she could. Yet most of it was too heavy for her to budge.

"Hurry up!" he shouted and then sighed to see what little progress she made. "Give me that!" He angrily snatched up some of the bigger items. "Pathetic. Now get the rest and come on!"

Wiping the tears from her face, Lori breathed deeply and struggled with her burden. She couldn't move that quickly because of her awkward load. It didn't help that they were in such a crowded town. She struggled even more to keep up with the bad man. Lori wished that she could just run away and knew that she could easily escape here. But if she did, she might lose Jacob forever.

Suddenly the bad man came to a stop. Lori scooted closer to him. She couldn't let herself become lost in this big scary town; then she'd never make it back to Jacob! The bad man stood talking to one of his cruel friends.

"—in the stables."

"Are you sure?"

"I know a stone light when I see one."

"So there might be some Alastrians here then. That could cause some problems."

"In a place as crowded as this, I don't think we have to worry about them much."

"Just the same, we'd better hurry and warn the captain." The man stopped for a second, noticing Lori for the first time "What is she doing out?"

"Being useful."

"But she's not even chained! You idiot! Do you have any idea what would happen if she escaped?" he raged.

"Relax, the kid's not going anywhere. We still have her brother back at camp. Besides, she promised me she wouldn't leave my side. Isn't that right, girl?" He smiled cruelly at her.

Lori nodded her agreement, much too scared to speak when *two* bad men were around.

"Well, she's gonna have to break that promise then because the captain will want to hear of your little discovery straightaway."

"But what about the supplies?"

"I'll take care of them. You'd just better intercept the captain before he reaches the lord."

"Right. I'll report back to camp as soon as I do. I leave the girl to you."

The men nodded at each other. The first one left quickly as the second man turned to Lori. "Well? What are you waiting for? Get a move on!"

Lori struggled to pick up everything and follow the new bad man. He walked faster than the first one had and carried even less for her, making her progress all the more slow. At the same time, the crowd grew increasingly dense with people. Every few seconds, someone bumped into her, causing her to drop something. The bad man grew angry each time he stopped and waited for her to pick it up.

"Come on! Stop being so clumsy!"

"S–sorry." Lori whispered.

Finally they got through the worst of it when a drunken man suddenly smashed straight into Lori, sending everything flying.

"What now!" the bad man yelled, turning around at this interruption. At the sight of supplies everywhere, he grew furious. "You mangy dog! What have you done?"

"I–I–I . . ."

"Hold on there a second, sir!" cried out the drunken man, still sitting on the ground. "'Twasn't the girl's fault. It's these darned rolling streets!"

"What?"

"The streets. They roll, made me roll right into her." The drunk smiled dumbly.

"Get outta here, you lazy bum!"

"Now wait a minute, wait a minute. I made the mess. I should clean it up. Mom always told me—*hic*—I said, mom always told me—"

"I don't care *what* your mom said! If you're going to clean it up, then get busy!"

"Right you are, right you are!" The drunk smiled and nodded, then rose onto wobbly legs to help Lori retrieve the rest of the items.

The bad man coldly glared at the drunk until he made sure that every item was back in place. Once her pile was organized again, he shoved the drunk away and forced Lori to pick up the pace. This time, Lori found it a little easier to keep up. The way the drunk had arranged the supplies had made the load much easier to carry. And besides, she had to hurry back to see Jacob. She wanted to share the loaf of bread with him she had hidden in her dress pocket now. She was glad she had made friends with a man like Mr. Fred. After all, he was very funny when he pretended to be drunk.

Chapter Eleven

Iris snapped her head to the side to look at Lord Valomeer, mouth agape. She studied him closely. He was tall with long blonde hair pulled back into a ponytail that rested on his shoulders. The random streaks of silver in his hair and beard showed his age. His beard was shorter than most and trimmed into a sharp point at the end. The regal bone structure of his face and his erect posture alone spoke of his great importance, but his clothes—well, his clothes looked like a basic commoner's outfit. Why would a man who was so powerful, so rich, be wearing such ratty attire?

"But I thought you said he was in the town center, watching all the activity," Bryant blurted out, completely confused, as was everyone else.

"I did, but apparently"—Kyle kept his eyes on Lord Valomeer—"James had other plans."

James? Who's James? Oh! That must be Lord Valomeer's first name. But how dare he talk to this man on such familiar terms? Iris pondered, as her gaze danced between the two men.

"Just what exactly is going on here? Kyle, how do you two know each other so well?" Darren fumed.

"We'll just say that for some time, James and I had a partnership of sorts."

Valomeer let out a disgusted grunt. "More like master and apprentice if you ask me."

"No one did." Kyle smile ruefully at him.

Great! That's just what they needed. Of course, Iris would end up between another unsettled grudge, and the man they needed help from the most right now would be the one against them. Really, should she expect anything less at this point? Lately the only sign she had that things were going to get worse was when things started to get better. She was becoming more and more certain that the world truly did hate her. But now wasn't the time for pity parties. She had to try and diffuse the tension before this situation went really wrong. She could start by removing the sword aimed at her back.

"Please, Lord Valomeer, we meant no harm in coming here. Quite the contrary, really." Iris angled her head to look at him, trying not to move too much so that he didn't consider her a threat. "If you'll just allow me to explain."

Valomeer studied Kyle for a few more moments before finally replacing his sword in his scabbard. "I'll listen under one condition."

He agreed to that rather quickly; maybe this won't be so bad after all. "Name it!" Iris smiled to see that the conversation was finally headed in the right direction.

"The rest of your friends here have to willingly turn themselves over to my guards to be put into the dungeon for breaking into my home."

"What? You can't be serious!" Bryant blurted out unhappily.

"Then and only then will I listen to whatever you have to say." Valomeer continued, ignoring Bryant entirely.

"But you—you can't do that!" Iris pleaded desperately.

"Oh? And why can't I? You *did* break into my home, did you not? Even under regular circumstances, this act renders severe punishment. You should be grateful that I'm being this lenient."

Stupid response, Iris! Of course he has every right! But still, you can't just let this happen! "Okay, so maybe we went about this the wrong way! But please! Believe me! We did it only because we didn't know how to reach you faster!" Iris begged despairingly

Valomeer raised an eyebrow at her. "Would you rather I simply throw *all* of you in the dungeon?"

"I don't know why we're just standing here listening to this!" Bryant spoke up. "Okay, so the guy had a sword, but it's still three to one! Four to one, if the missy here decides to join in." Bryant pounded his right fist into his left hand as if to emphasize his point and took a few steps forward.

No! This is just what I was afraid of!

Before Bryant took another step, Kyle held his hand up, gesturing for him to stop. Bryant paused, confused. "No. Even five to one, we would still lose against James. Maybe if I had a weapon . . . but I think it's best if we complied for now. We'll let Iris speak her piece. I'm sure she's more than capable of handling herself." Kyle smiled, winking at Iris.

"Iris, I don't care about getting locked up, but are you sure you'll be okay with this guy by yourself?" Darren asked with growing concern.

Iris nodded. She had no trouble talking with Valomeer, but she was still struggling to believe that she was sending the other three to prison by agreeing to his terms. But really, what choice did she have? This was the only way that she could be assured of at least warning Saunskirt. That was her sole reason for coming here, after all. Maybe her companions would be released after she explained everything. If only the answer were so simple!

Inhaling deeply, Iris nodded again "Alright. Okay, Lord Valomeer, we agree to your terms."

"Like hell, we do!"

"Bryant, stop!" Darren commanded.

"No! I'm not going to prison while this little tramp lives it up with this guy here! I don't care how good you think this guy is, Kyle, I'm not going down without a fight!"

Bryant squared his shoulders and stepped forward menacingly.

"Bryant, don't!" Darren broke in again, following him.

Iris's panicked, glancing from Bryant to Valomeer who stood firm, unwavering but ready. She couldn't let this happen! They came to help this man, not to attack him! Iris quickly stepped in front of Valomeer, raising her hands in front of her to ask Bryant to stop. *Thwack!* Bryant froze mid-run and then in an instant, crumpled to the floor. Behind him, stood Kyle, his right arm still in the air. Kyle smiled sheepishly down at Bryant.

"Sorry about that pal, had to be done. You can thank me for saving your life later." Kyle grimaced slightly as he massaged his hand.

The room grew deathly still. It had all happened so fast. Iris looked down at the hand now resting softly on her shoulder. She turned and saw that it was Valomeer. He moved her gently aside.

"My apologies, James. But I believe this is our cue now."

Valomeer grimly nodded as four guards burst into the room. *Where did* they *come from?*

Two men retrieved Bryant from the floor while the other two each grabbed an arm of Darren and Kyle. As she watched them get taken away, her conscience pricked with guilt.

Once they were gone, Valomeer motioned for Iris to take a seat on the other side of the desk. She complied readily, as a healthy dose of nervousness built up inside her. Something told her that if she couldn't convince this man of the danger ahead, even worse calamity would come. She sat at the edge of the chair and looked across the desk at the leader of all Saunskirt. *Holy Father, help me!* she whispered in her heart. Despite her anger and hurt toward the Holy Father, she just couldn't seem to stop herself from constantly calling out to Him. Really, she had nowhere else to turn. Valomeer's presence was so foreboding that Iris found herself wishing that he wouldn't look at her.

"Well?" Valomeer finally said. "For a person with such dire news, you sure take your precious time in sharing it."

Iris cringed at the rebuke and then forced herself to speak "There—there is a threat coming toward Saunskirt." She paused for any interjection he might have. Instead, he waited for her to continue. "An army has been attacking and completely obliterating towns for no apparent reason, and I believe—*we* believe that since Saunskirt is the next town along the main road, this army will target it next."

"And how can you be certain they'll attack us too?" He spoke with little enthusiasm.

"Well, I–I can't, really, but we didn't want to take that risk! Both Throansburrough and Jaralynx have been decimated already. If I didn't at least *try* to warn you, I–I know full blame would be mine if–if something *did* happen. I don't know if this force will continue its bloody actions. All I know for sure is that I can't allow it to happen again!"

Iris looked down at a sharp pain in her hand. She had been clenching her fists so tightly that she had pushed her nails into her palms.

"So I see." Valomeer spoke shortly and then paused again.

"If you don't believe me, I can—"

"No, I know you speak the truth. In fact, I'm certain you witnessed it yourself, right? And I'll even wager that you're from Throansburrough, eh? Sole survivor, no doubt."

How did he . . . ?

"But the thing is, dear girl, this whole ordeal here has been a waste! Our society thrives on war here in Saunskirt. No manner of mysterious army forces or unknown foe could scarce dream of ever taking us down, with or without advance warning." With this, he smiled at her patronizingly.

Frustrated, she lashed out. "No, you don't understand! These guys know what they're doing; they're strong and ruthless. You were right when you said I witnessed the attack, which is why you need to take my warning seriously! If anyone knows what you're up against, it's me. Yes, I know of Saunskirt's warring abilities. I know that you and your people are at the top of your class, but trust me, unless you allow me to describe in detail what could be coming, the losses you face will be worse than anything you've ever witnessed on the battlefield before!"

Valomeer simply smiled at her and then shook his head. "Throansburrough . . . They were quite the peaceful town, weren't they? A very kind, welcoming place. I also hear that a number of foreigners even settled there, due to its openness. A great shame that it's gone now. The people in your town didn't believe in executions, right?"

Where is he going with this? "Yes. And . . . ?"

Valomeer nodded knowingly. "I thought so. And exactly how many wars has Throansburrough participated in, in say, the past twenty years?"

Oh, I see now. He's trying to discredit the severity of what I saw! Anger bubbled dangerously close to the surface. "Just because Throansburrough hasn't experienced many violent, bloody situations doesn't mean that I'm incapable of judging just how dangerous this truly is."

A bemused smile annoyingly plastered on his face, Valomeer looked at Iris as if she were a child playing politics. Iris wanted to scream but instead bit her tongue and then willed herself to continue speaking calmly.

"Please, Lord Valomeer, at least consider what I'm saying here. If you don't think this threat is even worth your time, then fine. But is it not your duty as a lord to report any possible threat, no matter how seemingly insignificant, to the King of Fitsengea in Alaster? Yes, I originally intended to simply come here and report what I've seen, hoping that somehow I could stop it all. I don't know what I expected to happen after meeting with you. I know now that my actions have been poorly planned, but if you continue to refuse to hear my account, then I ask you to allow me *and* my three companions to move on to Alaster and describe in detail what I have seen. I don't mean to imply that you would not complete your duty in contacting the king; merely that if you truly think this is all a waste of time, then why not get us out of your hair and send me and the others to complete this task for you? Could you grant me at least this favor?"

Did she honestly just ask a favor of a lord? Was she crazy? What had possessed her to speak to him in such a manner? Her stomach tightened in anticipation of Valomeer's outburst in response.

Valomeer looked at her calmly, not moving, barely even blinking.

The silence was quite unnerving. Finally Valomeer leaned slightly toward Iris. Staring into her eyes, he spoke.

"Why?"

Iris blinked a couple of times, confused. "Ummm . . . why what?"

"Why do you need Kyle and his partners?"

Come on, girl, think of a good excuse! "Well, I would like some sort of an escort to Alaster because it *is* such a long way away."

"I could always send some of *my* men with you."

"Uh—yes, but . . . wouldn't that defeat the purpose of me going in the first place? After all, I intended that *we* go so that you would not have to part with any of your men."

"Really, now?" He smirked at her. "And are you sure that you would feel safer with Kyle and his men instead of my own?"

Iris hesitated. "What . . . do you mean?"

"Well, was it or was it not dear Kyle's idea to break into my home?"

"Well, I—"

"Quite a dangerous situation he put you in, no?"

"He informed me of the risk, but at the time, we felt it was the only course of action we could take."

"I see, so then I assume he *didn't* tell you that I never go out in public on festival days and that he *knew* that I would more than likely be home, dressed as a commoner in order to fool anyone who might see me."

Iris's heart skipped a beat. *He wouldn't. He couldn't have, but he—he . . .* "But he was just as surprised to see you as we were!"

"An act," he shrugged. "Or perhaps he was surprised to see me but not merely because he thought I was in town as he led you to believe. He had simply assumed that he was going to surprise me instead of the other way around. The end result is the same. Kyle placed you and those other two men in a situation that was bound to get you thrown in jail just because he wanted to win our little wager that he'd never be able to break into my home."

At Kyle's selfish actions, Iris's blood began to boil. But still, she couldn't just leave him in that dungeon. After all, if she couldn't convince Valomeer to let *him* out, then she would be doomed at trying to release Darren. *Honestly I wouldn't feel too awful if Bryant had to stay in there a little longer.* Iris shook her head and sighed. *All this because of a stupid wager? I wonder . . .*

"What were the conditions of this wager, if you don't mind my asking?"

Valomeer smiled at Iris, somewhat surprised at her question. "The wager was that if Kyle could manage to break past my traps and enter my home, then I would grant him one favor. If he tried and failed, that is, if he physically survived, then he would spend the rest of his days in my dungeon. An eternal guest, you could say. Which is why I can't allow those men to leave my prison even if I wanted to let them go. For it was you, not Kyle, who made it past my defenses, and I am a man of my word. A wager made is a wager kept."

"But Kyle *did* make it past your defenses. *He* had the idea of how to get in here!"

"Yes, *you*—not Kyle—actually did all the work."

"Fine, then grant the favor to me!"

Valomeer gave her a bemused look "Grant it . . . to you?"

Oh, Holy Father, convince him, please! "Yes, me. Otherwise people might question if you're truly a man of your word. I mean *I* believe you and follow your reasoning as to why Kyle didn't win, but others might not. They might say that since it was Kyle's idea and because he did indeed make it inside, then he actually won the wager with Lord Valomeer. They also might say accuse Lord Valomeer of an inability to lose to someone of a lower class. They'll say that he therefore balked on his promise, trying to come up with any excuse to get out of it."

"People talk and misunderstand all the time. Why should it bother me?"

"Because people of all social levels would be talking, and some of them might be rulers you trade with. We all know how jumpy foreign parties can be under the best of circumstances. But when they are fed rumors about the leader they wish to do business with, it's even worse. They might think that this man's pride would prevent him from maintaining his honor by keeping his word, even in something as small as this."

With that, Iris stopped, her heart racing in anticipation of Valomeer's response. He remained stone-like, his face etched into a frown as he processed all that Iris had dared to say. An eternity of waiting seemed to pass as the silence in the room bounced off the high walls of the study.

"Hmmph . . . heh heh . . . hahaha . . . hahaha! *Ahahahaha!*"

Iris's eyes grew two sizes in confusion as she witnessed what she could only assume was Valomeer's mental breakdown. She didn't think anything she had said was so funny, and yet there he was, sitting in front of her, roaring with laughter. She was caught completely off guard with no idea of how to respond. The only thing she could do was to stare at him blankly and wait for his laughter to subside. Finally it faded into a few sporadic chuckles.

Valomeer rubbed his eyes and shook his head, smiling as he looked at Iris. "You are quite the character, my lady. You have some nerve to lecture let alone try to manipulate someone as high up as I am. Your little speeches might have worked on a lord with less intelligence than I, but as you see, I can see right through your little antics, however amusing they might be."

The blood drained from Iris's face as her stomach tightened from nerves. She didn't like where this was going and prayed that she hadn't just dug her own grave.

"You sure do have some fire in you. Iris, was it?" Iris nodded stiffly as he continued. "Yes, fire indeed. To think a woman would be willing to throw herself into danger not once but twice just to deliver her message. Both acts unnecessary, I assure you, but the gesture remains impressive all the same. You risked your life walking on my grounds, your first brave but stupid act. And then you moved to protect me from that one brute that surely could not have done a thing to me. But to you, the end result would have been much more severe. I see that you are a woman who does not merely speak for the sake of speaking but also acts when needed. Iris, you intrigue me. Tell me, dear girl. Why would you put yourself through all this for people you have no connection with? What do you hope to gain?"

Iris looked at him, slightly insulted. "What do I hope to *gain*? Is that the only reason you think people do things? So that they might gain some sort of prize from it? I want nothing in return! And I mean that, not the kind of nothing people claim they want when they hope to be offered something anyway. No, I've only come because I can't let such a slaughter happen again. With all my power, I *won't* let it happen again. So maybe what I'm after is a clean conscience, to know that I have done what I could to help."

"Do you not wish revenge upon these monsters who butchered your loved ones?"

"I–I did at first, but . . . vengeance isn't mine . . ." Iris's voice lowered slightly as she reminded herself of the lines from the Sacred Texts.

"I see." Valomeer paused, turned his head to the side, and stroked his beard for a second, deep in thought. Turning back to Iris, he looked at her solemnly. "Iris, I do like your fire, but in the end, *someone* must spend some time in my prison for breaking the law as all of you have."

Iris's heart sank. She had hoped they had finally moved past this part of the conversation. Hoped that he would just be a good sport about it all and release them.

"But! I do believe that we can come to some sort of an arrangement."

Chapter Twelve

arren peered into the darkness around him, his eyes slowly adjusting to this sudden lack of light. Their cell was sparse of any sort of furnishings: no beds, no benches, no stools, not even chains on the walls to attach the prisoners to. The walls, floor, and ceiling were made of stone. The door was a solid wooden structure with only a tiny slit cut out of it so that a guard could glance in to check on the status of his current prisoner. The cell was small but large enough to house the three of them and possibly a few more.

Darren sat against the wall facing the door. He leaned his head back and sighed. How long would they be left here? Would they be released after Iris finished speaking with Valomeer, or would they be stuck down here for years to come? *I wonder how her conversation with him is going. Will we even be told what happened? I sure hope she can convince him to free us.*

Darren turned his head lazily toward Kyle, who had shifted his position on the wall to his right, now leaning on his right shoulder instead of his left one. In between them, on the ground, lay the unconscious form of Bryant. Darren pictured the scene that would erupt once he awoke. Bryant would be ready to throttle Kyle. And everything considered, Darren didn't feel particularly inclined to intervene. He didn't know how, exactly, but he was pretty certain that this entire situation could be blamed on Kyle. He considered joining in a fight against Kyle if one started.

"What?" Kyle said at last, annoyed. He didn't even bother to turn and look at Darren.

"I didn't say anything," Darren stated, matching his tone.

"No, but that glare you're throwing my way is shouting volumes."

"I'm just trying to figure out how this is all your fault. I know that you're to blame, but I don't know the details."

Kyle grunted in disgust. "Right, and it was my goal to end up locked up in here forever with you two."

"We both know that it would be just like one of your plans to fall apart like this."

"And yet you still listened to me, didn't you?"

Darren turned his head away angrily, staring instead at a tiny crack on the wall opposite him. His vision blurred in and out of focus, not really paying attention to what was in front of him. Kyle was right; he *had* been dumb enough to listen to him, a mistake he swore to never make again. Still, he had a lot of questions that needed answering. Turning back to Kyle, Darren narrowed his eyes in distrust as he spoke.

"How do you know him? You said you worked together for a time. What did you do? Why were you here?"

Kyle turned his head slightly, looking at Darren. For a second, he contemplated whether he felt like disclosing any information to him.

"Come on, Kyle, just tell me. It's not like we have anything better to do." The bitter sarcasm saturated Darren's reply.

Kyle flipped over on his back to face Darren. Still leaning on the wall, he crossed his arms and looked Darren in the eye. "Five years is a long time to be away from home, isn't it, Darren? A lot can happen in that time."

"It wasn't my fault, and you know it." Darren retorted menacingly.

"What I know, Darren, is that it had *everything* to do with you! You just refuse to face the facts. You ran away five years ago, and you're *still* running even though you're right in front of me!"

Every hair on Darren's body bristled as he stood. "I had no other choice! If it hadn't been for *your* betrayal, your greed, then—"

"Then what! We wouldn't be here right now? We would've lived happily ever after? That's how fairy tales end Darren, not real life! Don't preach to me about betrayals! All of it rests on your head!"

"What do you mean it all rests on my head?" Darren yelled, heart pounding in his ears. "I did what had to be done! I couldn't have lived with myself if I had done nothing!"

Kyle took a few steps forward as he shouted back, "No? But you can live with causing her death! Marriam died because of what you did! You *murdered* her!"

"Her blood is no more on my hands than it is on your own! I warned you; I pleaded with you. I tried to reason, but you were too thick to get it! In fact, you *still* don't get it!"

"Would you just shut up! Stop making excuses for yourself! Face the facts! No matter what you say, it was all your fault! Do you even know how many lives you ruined that day? Michael is still in prison; his wife left him; they took his children! Aaron's family has disowned him; he's lost all business from his shop. He spends more than half his days in a drunken haze just to forget his pain! Our families were questioned, humiliated, and outcast. None of us can even enter Alaster now, save under a disguise, or else we'd be locked away forever!"

"And yet here we are, in prison anyhow!" Darren cried out, throwing his arms in the air to emphasize the space around them. "Don't forget, Kyle, you're not so innocent yourself! I can't help what happened. I even fought against it! I risked everything to help you!"

"I find that hard to believe! Tell me, Darren, what kind of a deal did they make with you in order to sell your soul so that you betrayed those who had been loyal to you? Was this the type of behavior condoned by your Holy Father? Your faith sure has gotten you far! What a gracious Holy Father you have that He'd help you destroy all those around you just so that you could sleep soundly at night!"

Darren had had enough talking. Kyle was too dense to understand, to listen. He clenched his jaw and squeezed his fists. He really wanted to punch him, but what would that gain him? He'd feel better, sure, but he had promised himself that he wasn't going to be that man anymore. It was the last promise he had made to Marriam before she died. Darren glared at Kyle with an intense hatred before he forced himself to turn away.

"Did I strike a sensitive chord there, Darren? The truth too much for you to handle?"

"I'm done with you."

"What did you say?"

"I said I'm done with you, Kyle! There's no point in arguing with you further. You'll never get it; I'm just wasting my breath. And I refuse to waste any more time on you! I'm done!"

"You're done when I say you're done!" Kyle shouted furiously.

Darren ignored him and walked back to the other side of the room. Before he got there, Kyle cried out from behind him and rushed toward him. Darren turned around just in time to lose his breath as Kyle smashed straight into his torso and both of them crashed to the ground. Kyle proceeded to pummel any part of Darren he could reach. Darren quickly blocked some of the blows and then returned his own as he shoved Kyle off him. Darren moved so that he would have the upper hand and continued to fight back.

Darren threw two punches into Kyle's face but then suffered a heavy blow to his ribs. Kyle hit him under the jaw, knocking him backwards. As he fell, Kyle lunged at him. Darren readied himself and kicked Kyle away with his feet. Darren took advantage of the small break to jump up and rush Kyle. At the same time, Kyle rose and swung wide. Darren dodged and swung back. Kyle caught his arm and held on as Darren grabbed Kyle's other free arm. They locked in a wrestling stance as they tried to pull each other down. Kyle relaxed his arms momentarily to pull Darren in closer and then kneed him in the stomach to break free from Darren's hold. He then grabbed Darren from behind in a chokehold.

Darren moved quickly to try to break free but was trapped. Instead, he used his own weight to fling Kyle into the wall behind him. Kyle's right shoulder smashed into the hard stone, forcing him to relax his hold on Darren. Darren once again slammed into the wall, this time, causing Kyle to hit his head. Kyle completely let go to shove Darren away so that he could escape this precarious position. Kyle's quick move caught Darren off guard as he flung backwards for the third time. Darren struck the wall, dazed, and leaned against it for a second. Kyle grabbed Darren's shirt collar with both hands and threw him to the floor. Kyle tried to deliver a rib-crunching blow to the side. Instead, Darren knocked Kyle's legs out from underneath him, just in time. Both men were back on the ground, rolling around as they punched, kicked, and tore at one another. So engrossed they were in their fight that they didn't even stop when they ran into Bryant, who, by now, was slowly waking up.

When he finally sat up, Bryant looked at the scene before him in a haze. His neck and his head were throbbing, and he struggled to recall exactly what had happened. As the pieces fit together, the door to their prison cracked open. Ignoring the fight momentarily, Bryant stood to see who or what was coming in. Four guards entered, who, once they realized a fight had broken out between their charges, quickly ran to separate Darren and Kyle.

"What in all the lands is going on here!" cried an angry female voice from inside the doorway.

The men all stood still and looked toward the sound.

"Iris?" Darren perked up in surprise. He started to smile at seeing her but stopped as a wave of shame passed over him. As his fury at Kyle subsided, embarrassment washed over him that Iris saw him like this.

Iris stormed into the dungeon, marching right past Bryant and stopping in front of Darren and Kyle. Her eyes flicked over the various wounds they had given one another. Concern flashed across her face for just a moment but was quickly pushed away. Iris was ticked.

"What in the lands do you think you're doing? No! Don't answer that! I mean, come on, guys! Thirty minutes! I've only been gone for thirty minutes! For crying out loud! After I go through all this trouble to make sure no harm falls on *any* of you, what do I find? You're trying to kill each other! You have *got* to be kidding me!" She threw her arms in the air in disgust, groaning in frustration.

"If it makes you feel any better, we haven't been fighting the *whole* time." Kyle tried pitifully.

Iris simply glared at him for a second and then shook her head. She rubbed her eyes and then let her hand slide down her face, attempting to wipe away her annoyance and calm herself down.

I'll never hear the end of this! Darren winced.

"Fine, okay, sure, whatever! Let's just go!" She turned to leave but then spun back around, pointing at them like a scolding mother. "I didn't get you guys out of prison just so that you could beat the ever-living snot out of each other! So grow up and shape up! All three of you are to act as my escorts. How can I expect you to help or protect me if I can't trust you to be left alone for even thirty minutes? Good grief, you guys!"

"Wait? You got us out? You got Lord Valomeer to release us? *All* of us?" Darren asked, amazed.

Iris sighed. "Yes, under certain conditions. And one of those is that you must act as my escorts to Alaster. So come on, now, we need to get going. That is . . . *if* you can handle being around each other a little longer."

Darren looked at Kyle out of the corner of his eye, then sighed and nodded. "Okay. I promise. No more fighting." He turned to the guard holding him. "Really, I swear. You can let go now."

"Same here," Kyle told the other guard.

The men looked at their charges, at each other, and then at Iris, who nodded her approval. They released Darren and Kyle simultaneously and then stepped back. Iris shook her head once more and then turned to leave. Walking past Bryant, with his mouth agape, she couldn't help but smirk.

"You coming, Bryant? The tramp has a transport vessel waiting to cart you home to Alaster."

Bryant closed his mouth and looked down as she walked by. The guard behind Darren gave him a slight shove to get him moving. Soon all men, including the guards, followed Iris from the dungeon. They were immediately led upstairs and out of the building. They walked in silence until they came to a carriage that was to bring them to the transport station on the outskirts of the town. Saunskirt was much larger than Jaralynx. If a person were to walk from one side of Jaralynx all the way to the outskirts, it would take only seven or eight hours. Saunskirt took about twenty hours, even more now because of the festival. They would have to ride around half of the perimeter of the town to reach the transport station before dark.

Darren held open the door of the covered carriage for Iris and offered his hand to help her up. She took it absentmindedly and stepped inside. She was tired; he could see it all over her face. He had hoped that she could rest here a little as he went on to Alaster. Things rarely ever went as initially planned, at least, that seemed to be the rule for him. Bryant and Kyle followed after Iris, sitting on the bench facing her, neither wanting to sit next to her after she chewed them out only moments ago.

Darren started to enter as well, pausing to look back toward Lord Valomeer's home. Across the way, he could barely make out a group of well-built strangers—three men—approaching the gates. They seemed to be wearing foreign-made clothing. The man in the middle stepped forward; even from this distance, Darren could tell he was larger than the other two. Apparently the man had spoken to the guard, for the gate was promptly opened. The strangers entered confidently. The man carried the air of someone who knew he was untouchable, not one who just pretended but one who really had the strength to do whatever he pleased. Darren wanted to watch a little longer but was interrupted by the impatient cry of the guard who sat ready to drive the carriage. Darren stepped up into the carriage reluctantly, still watching as the men entered the house. Something about them unnerved him, espe-cially since they seemed to have a meeting with Lord Valomeer. The entire situation was rather suspicious to him, but he couldn't put a finger as to just why.

Upon entering the carriage, he looked at Iris sitting to the far side on the left, leaning against the carriage wall deep in her own thoughts. She didn't move, gazing out the window, as he sat down next to her. *Better lost within her mind than verbally berating me!*

Darren smiled, relieved. He glanced at her and then turned to look out his own window as they began to move. All four remained silent for the five-hour ride, perhaps a little more.

They came to a stop right outside the station. Not many people were in this area of town, which was not that surprising because of the festival and because of the high expense of transport travel. For the most part, only merchants used this technology for trade between towns; no one else could really afford such a luxury. It was a necessary cost, though, because it took a lot of money to maintain a transport vessel. They had a very short working lifespan and regularly underwent repairs. This wasn't surprising considering the distances these machines traveled and the speeds they reach. Transports had been around for about fifty years now, but only within the last fifteen had areas other than Alaster begun to own some or even manufacture their own.

As they came to a complete stop, Bryant and Kyle moved to exit. Iris had dozed off, so Darren reached over to wake her. His hand had barely brushed her shoulder when she jerked up with a screech, recoiling at Darren's touch. Startled, he jumped back as well.

"Woah! Iris, calm down, it's just me." Darren spoke gently, leaning back, holding his hands in front of him to show he meant no harm.

Iris breathed heavily as she looked at him, eyes wide with terror. All color had drained from her face, and she was on the verge of tears.

"Hey, it's okay. Everything's fine. We're at the transport station now." Darren did his best to soothe her though he didn't touch her, fearing that he would only frighten her again.

Iris blinked a couple of times and then let her head fall into her hands. She sat there for a minute longer, then breathed deeply. She shook her head and sat back up. A smile now covered her inner turmoil.

"Sorry. I–it was a bad dream. I didn't mean to react that way." She looked at him sheepishly and laughed nervously to break the tension.

Concerned, Darren frowned. "Are you going to be okay?"

She giggled in embarrassment. "Yeah, I'm fine. It was just a *really* bad dream."

Darren looked at her for a second longer, but he knew she wouldn't willingly discuss it with him, at least not now. He exhaled and nodded. He knew exactly what was happening; he had seen these kinds of reactions from a few severely traumatized soldiers he trained under back during his life in Alaster. He knew better than to push the issue.

"Well, okay then. We probably should get going before Kyle and Bryant start complaining."

Iris smiled at him and nodded. Exiting from the carriage, Darren looked around him. Apparently the station itself was undergoing renovations as a number of construction platforms were set up. No one was on them at the time, probably taking a break to enjoy the festivities. Currently a simple platform with a cover on top protected customers from the weather while they waited for the next transport. The flimsy shelter was only temporary, soon to be replaced by a much more elaborate stone structure to show Saunskirt's new growth in wealth. *It seems that Saunskirt has made another weapons deal with a foreign investor,* Darren concluded. Saunskirt often underwent physical changes whenever they found a new trade partner.

Iris stood beside him, gawking at the station and the transport vessels parked there. This was probably the first time she had ever seen one. The construction of stone roads had not yet reached Throansburrough. The new plan to bring transports throughout all the land would take some time. The first places to undergo construction were the towns directly around Alaster that connected to the bigger cities, ones of more importance and trade value. Transport vessels were rather large metal machines, though some swore they were made of silver because of their shine. This was only due to the special plating covering them to protect them from weather corrosion and possible falling debris.

Many transports had to run through or around the Phaen Mountains now that they more frequently traveled between Alaster and Saunskirt. In a few instances at the start, avalanches interfered with the transport's progress, but now with the aid of this new paneling, transports could better withstand such conditions without being knocked off course. The problem now was that a number of less-than-intelligent bandits were trying to steal the transports, hoping to make some money off what they assumed to be silver. But in an often bitter discovery, they found out they would not have even been able to sell the transports back to other towns. Everyone knew that only the king could grant permission of the use of this technology, and surprise visits from his personal guards made sure that everyone followed these regulations. How a small group of thieves could ever hope to take down one of these contraptions was beyond Darren's imagination. The machines were just too massive and bulky, usually taking no less than thirty men to do the smallest repair. Saunskirt was currently outfitted with only three of them.

Considering that their main purpose within Saunskirt was to transfer items for trade, the transports were practically gutted, save for a few bunks attached to the walls for the men who traveled with their goods. Each transport was equipped with a bathroom and enough water to cleanse oneself between the checkpoint stations. If you became hungry or needed to refill your water along the way, you had to wait until you came to one of the supply stations. Transports did cut a trip in half, but even then, it would probably take them close to four days to reach Alaster. Still, four days *was* better than two weeks by horse. Though the idea of being stuck in the same room with Kyle for four days didn't sound too wonderful to Darren, Bryant wouldn't be much of a thrill either. Perhaps he could pass the time by getting to know Iris better; maybe he could convince her to open up a little bit more. *Doubtful . . .* he sighed. Glancing at Iris as she walked past him and toward the transport, he realized that of all people, *she* would be the one to find this situation the most uncomfortable, spending three to four days with three strange men. Too bad he had already lost her trust.

"So how does it work?" Iris asked as she surveyed their surroundings.

The guard who had driven them here called out a response from the back of the carriage. "It uses the power from the stone lights of Alaster and a special kind of stone from the Smallman Mountains." He appeared from around the carriage, holding some traveling packs. He handed a couple to Darren and the rest to Kyle and Bryant. "I'm not exactly sure on all the details, but as far as I know, the road is made up of stone from the mountains, and the underside of the front and back ends of the transport are made up of the stone lights, which have been melted and reshaped to form a thin crystal sheet molded to fit the transport's shape. The stone lights component is what causes the underside to have a slight glow to it at night."

Darren looked at the packs in his arms, which looked oddly familiar.

"Hey, this is our traveling gear! How'd you find it?" Bryant questioned the guard suspiciously.

The guard gave him an annoyed look and continued to walk up to the transport beside Iris. "Don't take us too lightly here in Saunskirt. We have a wonderful information line." He turned to Iris and continued speaking. "Anyway, what basically happens is that the stone lights are drawn toward the mountain rocks, at least slightly to a natural degree. This ends up pulling the transport forward."

"So then how does it come back if this attraction causes it to move in only one direction?"

"An automated switch inside releases a chemical spray underneath that will change the reactive properties of the stone lights on the road, causing the transport to push itself away from the mountain stones instead of pulling. These chemicals are at either end of the transport, making it easier to change both the strength of the pull and the reaction of the push. It is quite impossible to try and turn a transport around due to its size, which is why the stone lights are focused along the front or back or vice versa, depending on which way you're facing. They have also been used throughout the transport in other ways to create a lighting source within and as the general power supply that moves all the other features. Stone lights can be used in a number of ways, probably even in more ways than they are currently used, which is why the king still has his people researching them. But you can only find them in Alaster, which is why you don't see them used much outside of Alaster itself aside from being on transports that travel from place to place."

"What a wonderfully boring lecture," Kyle observed as he approached the transport. He slapped the guard on the back and laughed. "Perhaps you're in the wrong profession; seems you would be much more suited to the position of a teacher." He laughed again and walked through the open doors of the transport.

"Certainly dull enough and full of useless information," Bryant added as he followed Kyle.

Iris shot them a look as they passed by and then smiled apologetically at the guard "No, I appreciate the explanation. I found it very interesting. I've always been curious about this stuff as they haven't been installed in Throansburrough yet. So thank you." She smiled broadly at him.

Darren walked up to them and added, "And thank you for delivering our stuff to us. Though what will happen to our horses?"

"Your horses? Oh, they will be sent to you in the next animal shipment to Alaster. We have to use a different transport for livestock."

"Don't bother!" Kyle cried from inside. "Malachi and Aaron will retrieve them for us. Just make sure to take care of them properly until they do."

The guard shrugged. "Fine, it would cost more to send them by transport anyway." He pulled out an official-looking scroll from the back of his shirt and handed it to Iris. "I was instructed by Lord Valomeer to give this to you."

Iris took the scroll and held it between her hands curiously.

"It's a letter with Valomeer's seal and signature giving you and your escorts permission to meet directly with the king. This should make getting around Alaster a lot easier and much more welcoming for you."

"Thank you—um—forgive me, but what was your name?"

"I am Lieutenant Fredrick Maythan, but you may call me Fred, miss." The guard smiled, his gray eyes sparkling kindly at her.

Iris smiled and nodded. "Thank you, Fred, and please convey my gratitude to Lord Valomeer as well."

Fred nodded. "Will do. Well, I was informed that you people were eager to be on your way, so I won't keep you any longer. If you two would please step aboard, I will get this thing running."

Darren followed Iris through the doors. It had been a while since he had ridden in one of these contraptions. Saunskirt's transports had few decorative features and were much more spartan than Alaster's. He looked around for the wall straps that were used when a transport first started up. Finding a section of them to his right, he walked over and locked himself in place. Iris continued to stand by the doors, looking at everything around her.

"Hey, Iris," Darren called out. "You're going to want to get into one of these." He indicated the straps beside him.

Iris walked over and cocked an eyebrow. "What are they for?"

A slow hiss erupted as the heavy doors slid closed. They locked into place, echoing loudly across the room. Iris jumped at the sound and turned to look at the doors. Darren tried to get her attention again but was cut off by the noise as the chemicals released from their containers underneath. The transports went from zero to ninety knots in an instant. If she didn't brace herself, she would go flying.

As he knew they would start moving any second, Darren unlatched himself from the wall, rushed over to Iris, and grabbed her arm, pulling her quickly over to the straps. She flew in close to him, and he wrapped his arm around her back and reached for a strap with his left hand. Just as he grabbed ahold of her, the transport took off. The motion nearly jerked his arm out of the socket, and it was all he could do to just hold on. Iris squeezed her eyes tightly shut and latched onto him. Darren threw his legs under him and braced himself, knowing that they would decrease to a speed of fifty knots in a few moments.

The initial burst propelled the transport forward, which would maintain the fifty knots for the remainder of the trip, save for the times they stopped at checkpoints. The sudden deceleration lurched them forward, but Darren kept them from falling by holding tight and keeping his right foot firmly planted in front of him. Once the transport reached fifty knots, he released his hold from the strap and relaxed. His left shoulder throbbed from the harsh movements; he was thankful that he hadn't jerked his arm out of the socket. Now that they were at a constant speed, they could easily move around. He looked at Iris who was still holding onto him, waiting for the next sudden movement.

He smiled down at her. "It's okay; it's over now. Transports are great for speedy travel, but they haven't quite figured out how to start them more gently."

Iris looked at him and smiled weakly. "Thanks. For keeping me from being flung around, I mean."

Darren chuckled. "No problem. First time I ever rode a transport, I didn't know to strap in either. Broke my arm in two places because of it. I didn't think you'd want that type of initiation."

Iris laughed. "No, not really."

Kyle cleared his throat from behind them, unlatching himself from the wall at the other end. "I think it's safe to let her go now, Darren."

What? Oh, crap! Darren clumsily moved his arm off Iris's back. "Uh —s-sorry 'bout that." He winced with embarrassment

Iris quickly turned away from him but not before he caught a glimpse of the blush rising in her cheeks. He wanted to hit his head against the wall a couple of times.

"No really, it's okay." Iris responded but kept her back to him.

He couldn't make this situation more awkward if he tried.

"Think we should leave them alone for a bit?" Bryant teased maliciously from the other end of the room.

"Bryant!" Darren growled and turned around to face him.

Just then, Kyle stepped in his path and help up a finger as if he were scolding a child. "Now, now, Darren. Remember! We promised Iris. No more fighting." He grinned cruelly.

Darren turned away and dismissed him with a wave of his hand. "Yeah, yeah, whatever." He sighed and walked around Kyle. "I'm just gonna put the packs away."

As he left, he couldn't help but glance back at Iris. She had moved to check out the rest of the machine, stopping in front of the large window that looked over the road they traveled on.

Stupid, stupid, stupid! Darren shook his head as he walked. He glanced at Bryant as he passed him. Bryant roared with laughter. Darren glowered at him but didn't stop. He grabbed all the packs that had slid to the back wall and proceeded to go through them as he decided which items needed to go where. A number of extra supplies were included in the bunch, probably added by Lord Valomeer for their travels. Most of the new things were pieces of clothing and other such items for Iris, which made sense, considering she didn't have anything with her at all. Grateful to find a few more of his Mantriok leaves, he chewed on one to ease the pain in his left shoulder.

After he worked for a while, sorting and putting away things in the built-in storage slots, he stopped and looked around. No one had said a word in a really long time. *Oh yeah, this is gonna be a* fun *trip,* he thought sarcastically.

Chapter Thirteen

Iris stood with her arms intertwined across her chest. She absentmindedly gazed out the window in front of her. The night sky seemed to swallow her whole. She pulled the blanket more tightly around her shoulders and played with the Askgan fur. Others back home had mentioned the softness of the great Askgan's coat, that rare creature bred in the mountains beside Alaster, but she had been unable to judge it for herself until now. The tips of her fingers registered to her brain how gentle it was to the touch, but her heart focused elsewhere.

She thought how uncomfortable she was as the only female on this giant machine. How revealed she felt in her nightgown when standing next to Bryant even though the dress showed nothing. She grabbed the Askgan blanket from one of the bunks to use as a clothing shield, anything to protect herself from his prying eyes. Iris had to admit it had been wonderful to wash all that grime off her. She considered the silence around her. It was one that only metal could create. The very absence of sound echoed off those cold walls. Looking around a bit her eyes led her head to take a glance behind her.

At the back of this building-like machine slept her three escorts. Transports were much bigger than she thought they would be. This one was about two stories tall and the length of almost two homes put together. Darren said that was so that Saunskirt could cram more products in for trade, which was also why most of the seating had been removed, save for the five or so chairs bolted into the floor along the length of one side. Her eyes rested on the sleeping bunks. *I hope Darren's arm will be okay.* Her brow stitched into a frown. He had clearly pulled a muscle when he was thrown about hours earlier. If only she hadn't been so stupid!

Sure, he claimed he was fine after finding those leaves, but she still felt guilty. She shouldn't have been gawking at everything like that. If only she would have listened. Maybe then they could have strapped themselves in the way they were supposed to. *Then again . . .* A smile threatened to escape as she thought, *if I had paid attention . . . he couldn't have grabbed me like that. He was so strong—wait, stop it! What are you thinking?* She shook her head violently. Now wasn't the time to focus on his strength. It was stupid, really. For goodness' sake, she barely knew the man! *I don't even know exactly how old he is. He might be twenty-four like me, but still, it's not like he's offering up the information. I don't even know his last name! No, he won't* tell *me his last name.*

Iris sighed and dropped her head sadly. That was right, he wouldn't tell her. She had tried, but he didn't *want* to be honest with her. All she knew about him was that he was from Alaster and that he held some terrible secret in his heart. It wasn't like she should concern herself with matters of romance anyway. More important matters than that were at hand.

"And besides," she sadly whispered to herself, "It's not as if our relationship would go anywhere. It *can't* go anywhere." She lifted up her left wrist and looked at the delicate bracelet now encircling it.

She fingered it mindfully with her right hand and then touched her fingers over her heart, the metal cold through her night gown. Funny, all the things she wore right now were because of Valomeer. Her heart beat hard in fear as she fingered the contraption on her chest.

"Guess Darren's not the only one who isn't being completely upfront and honest."

She sighed heavily and crossed her arms as she adjusted the blanket once more, attempting to comfort herself. She looked out the massive window in front of her, the only true window in the transport except for a few portholes along the walls. This was the only one with a really nice view. Darkness cloaked the sky, the only lights those given off by the transport itself and the stars. They were quite brilliant tonight, even easier to see because the trees had been cleared away from the stone road, pushed miles back so that roots wouldn't ever threaten to break through. Looking at the vastness of the sky above Iris felt small.

Holy Father, where are You? Why are You letting this happen? Why are You punishing me? Have I not done all that I'm supposed to? Whatever happened to Your love? Your mercy? Your grace? All I see, all I know is pain, so much pain, to the point that I don't think I can even breathe. You've stolen everything from me! I know You could make things right, and that's why it hurts so much! You have the power, the strength. You are Holy Father after all, are You not! I can't even sleep anymore because every time I lay down and close my eyes, all I see is death, their deaths. Do You really hate me this much? Why have You abandoned me!

"Where are You?" She spoke through trembling lips as the tears escaped her eyes and fell to the ground.

She hugged her arms around herself tightly, hands grasping the blanket, as she battled to keep her cries in check. She didn't want to wake the others; she didn't want them to see her breaking down. She didn't feel safe enough to let them see. She had never felt safe enough to let anyone see her tears. She had hated how she had been so vulnerable in front of Darren that night in Jaralynx. For as long as she could remember, she had cried at night when she was alone so that no one would accidentally hear or see her. Only three people in her whole life had witnessed her tears. Well, excluding the times that they had gone to a play with some tragic scene that left the whole crowd weeping, but that didn't really count. No, only her sister, her mother, and her father had ever seen the tears that came from the deepest parts of her heart. They were her safe place.

Everyone in life plays a certain role, and the part Iris played was the smile. For anyone else, she was the listening ear, the shoulder to lean on, the one who made others feel better. The tragic part of this role was that she was forever pigeonholed into it. Her only job for others was to comfort them, not to receive comfort. Some of her friends had even refused to believe that she was capable of any other emotions. And for the most part, Iris had accepted this. She couldn't change people, she found that out at a young age, but it was okay, because she could always trust her family to be there to hold her tightly. Tight enough so that she could completely let go. But now . . .

Iris clasped both hands over her mouth as she tried to choke back her moans. She shook with the effort, jerking each time a cry arose, was cut off, and threatened to come out even more loudly than before. The blanket slid from her shoulders to the floor; she let it fall. An emptiness clawed and ripped through her being, trying to tear her apart. She didn't understand; she just didn't understand why this was all happening. She didn't know how much more she could take.

The soft shuffle of feet approached her from behind. Panic rose at the fear that she might be found out. She had spent years listening for sounds so as not to be caught mid-tears. At the tiniest sounds, she shoved her feelings to the back of her mind, cutting off the flow. She quickly wiped her eyes in a practiced fashion, looking as if she was only rubbing away sleep. She breathed deeply to calm herself down so that her voice would not quake and give away her true emotions. Just in time as Darren came up beside her.

"Iris, what in all the lands are you doing up?" he questioned in concern as he leaned over to retrieve the blanket from the floor. He casually threw it over his right shoulder.

"I–I couldn't sleep." *Well, that's partly true, I guess.*

A sad frown crossed his face. "Iris . . . come on, you've got to be exhausted. You really should get *some* sort of rest."

"But I—"

"Come on, I think I might have something to help you sleep packed away." He smiled gently and put his hand on her arm to lead her.

Iris stood firm. "No, Darren, I can't"

He stopped, confused. "What?"

"I—I can't, I mean, I don't want to. I mean . . . I'm okay. I'm really not that tired."

Darren crinkled his brow. "Iris, are you okay?"

"Yeah, I'm fine." She nervously pushed a piece of her brown hair behind her ear. Still slightly damp from her shower, the coolness chilled her skin.

Darren wasn't buying it. "Do you . . . do you want to talk about it? Whatever that's bothering you, well, keeping you awake, that is."

Iris turned away from him and bit her bottom lip. She was desperate for a soul to confide in; she yearned for it more than anything. But . . . she just didn't trust Darren. How could she let go of something so personal with someone who couldn't do the same with her?

"Iris . . ." he pleaded.

Iris stood still for a moment and then turned back to him. "Your last name."

"What?" Darren balked.

"Tell me your last name . . . please."

"Well I—um . . ."

"You want me to talk to you. You act as if you care. You say you'll listen. Darren, we're still strangers. All that I know of you is what I found out before we reached Jaralynx about two nights ago. And you, you don't know *anything* about me."

Darren reached out and placed his hand tenderly on her right shoulder. "Then tell me. I *want* to know who you are."

"Share my heart with a man who can't even be honest and forthright with his own name? Could you be so selfish?" Iris asked, looking him directly in the eyes.

Darren let his hand slide off her shoulder as he looked away, cringing under her unblinking stare. "You just don't understand—"

"I'm not asking for your life story, Darren! Though I could if you'd rather! I just want your last name! Just a name, that's all! Why can't you give me that, at least?"

"I . . ." Darren trailed off and then looked into her eyes.

Iris was shocked at how much pain, how much fear, was in them. She waited for him to continue.

"I don't want . . . I can't . . . I don't want you . . ."

"You don't want me to what?"

"I don't want you to . . ."

Iris bit her tongue, dying to scream at him. But she knew an outburst would only shut him up faster. Why was this so hard for him? She inhaled before speaking. "Out with it already!"

He turned completely away from her and ran his fingers through his hair before whispering, "I don't want you to hate me . . ."

"*Hate* you . . . but why?" Iris knit her brow in concern and confusion.

How could a last name make someone hate a person? She pressed her lips together firmly and looked at him sadly. He really was afraid that he would push her away. No, he was afraid that she would run away. That if he opened up, she would never understand, possibly even treat him cruelly.

"Why do you think I would hate you?" she asked, but Darren only remained still, refusing to look at her.

His silence only made her more curious. She wanted to know what happened! Should she be afraid of him? She was nervous, yes, but that was only because everything she did now was scary to her, unknown and uncertain. But even though she didn't trust Darren, did she fear anything about him? No, they didn't know each other at all, but she did know her own heart. And time after time, she had found that some people, those that one should fear, would stir her up on the inside. Something just seemed off about them. But Darren? She *wanted* to trust him if only he would let her. But right now, he was a closed book, a book with a lock, and he firmly held the key in his hand. He wasn't letting *anyone* in.

"Look, Darren, I'm not asking you to give up your deepest, darkest secrets. I won't force you to explain yourself to me, but just so you know, I am not the type of person who is quick to hate. In fact, I've *never* hated anyone before. The only people I hate are those who massacred my town, destroyed my home. Even then, I have to work through that and . . . forgive them someday." She sighed at that thought, then continued with a playful smile. "And unless you magically became two people and caused all of that while the other you stayed in the woods miles away, I don't think you have to worry about me *hating* you."

He turned and looked at her, a little incredulous. "You've *never* hated anyone before?"

Iris shrugged. "Well before now, no. But like I said, that's something I'm still working on."

"Why?"

"Why what?"

"Why are you trying to forgive them, whoever they are? You have every right to hate them. Honestly, if I were you, my only thoughts would be of revenge."

Iris released a heavy sigh and turned away, closing her eyes for a second. "Please Darren, don't encourage that. I am having a very hard time with all this. It's part of my beliefs, my religion, to forgive, even love my enemies. Pray for those who curse me, do good to those who spitefully use me . . ."

"That's . . . that's a Sacred Text isn't it?"

Iris's heart skipped a beat as she spun back around. "Are you a Follower too?"

"I—uh—"

"I mean, do you follow the Holy Father? Follow Holy Beloved, the Holy Wisdom?"

"I—um . . . no." Darren cast his eyes downward.

"Oh . . . well, that's okay. . ." she replied softly, somewhat surprised at how disappointed she was. She really could have used some spiritual guidance right now or even just a little support and reassurance.

"I mean, I did once, but . . . I . . ."

"No, really, it's okay, Darren. You–you don't have to explain your-self to me. You don't have to explain anything to me if you don't want to. Just please understand that if you don't feel comfortable telling me about yourself, then I might have the same problems as well. I'm not saying this to force you to open up to me. It's just how I am. If I don't know anything about you, then I can't feel truly safe enough to share everything with you. Well, where matters of my heart are considered, at least."

They stood together silently as Darren had nothing to add. Iris turned back to the window to stare at the stars. Darren moved beside her and surveyed them with her.

"Turner."

Iris glanced at him out of the corner of her eye, waiting for him to continue.

"My last name, it's Turner. I am Darren Turner."

Iris tilted her head toward him and smiled. "Thank you, Darren Turner. That means a lot to me."

Darren nodded, obviously waiting for her to blow up in some way or to press him for more information. But she wasn't going to, at least not tonight. It had taken a lot for him to give her his last name, and she knew that if she pushed him any further, he would completely close up. The last thing she wanted to do was annoy him further. No, she'd only pester him about his past if it ever seemed to be of vital importance. Right now, she was just trying to make a friend. She desperately needed a friend.

Darren playfully nudged her with his elbow. "Your turn now." He smiled at her blank expression. "I told you my name. Now it's your turn to tell me something."

"Oh, so we're taking turns now is it?" Iris laughed.

Darren nodded. "Exactly."

"Haha, okay. Ummm . . . what do you want to know?"

"Why you aren't asleep right now?" he asked with a playful frown.

Iris's smile faded as she looked away, focusing on a distant star. "Because I don't want to sleep. I can't sleep." She sighed and dropped her gaze to the floor. "Remember earlier today? When you woke me in the carriage?" Iris caught Darren nodding gently from the corner of her eye. "My dream, my *nightmare* was witnessing the murders of my family again. And I'm scared—I'm afraid that if I—seeing it once in life was more than enough. It replays itself in my mind while I'm awake, but then it's easier to ignore. When I'm sleeping, I can't shut it off. There are no convenient distractions. I'm terrified that when I close my eyes in sleep, those will be the only things I see." Iris stopped, still staring at the floor. Darren's hand touched her shoulder. She raised her head to meet his gaze.

"You'll have to rest sometime."

"I know . . ." she sighed.

Darren brushed Iris's hair back from her face. Iris remained still to allow his touch.

"I wish I could take away the nightmares for you, but—" He dropped his hand and cut himself short, fidgeting uncomfortably.

Iris's pulse quickened at his tenderness. She rubbed her left arm nervously and turned to hide a blush. She had never experienced such intimacy with a man before. But maybe she was imagining it. She forced out the words at his sentiment. "Th–thank you."

"In the meantime . . ." Darren spoke at last. "If you'd like, I can keep you company for the rest of the night."

Iris smiled appreciatively at him. "I would like that very much."

Chapter Fourteen

D arren's head bobbed lazily as he drifted off to sleep. He forced himself to jerk back up and opened his eyes. He and Iris had sat under that window for most of the night. He looked down at Iris, who slept with her head in his lap. She was stirring again, a sign that her dreams were taking a turn for the worse. He picked up his hand and softly stroked her hair. With each touch, Iris's breathing slowed as she once again fell into a peaceful and deep sleep. She had said that she didn't want to go to sleep, but she couldn't stay awake for days on end. It wasn't healthy. He didn't plan to trick her into sleeping, but as the course of the night drew on, both of them nodded off.

Iris jolted awake a few times as horrors flooded her mind, waking up Darren as well. At one point they had both been asleep for quite a while when Iris woke up crying. Darren had tried holding her for a bit to comfort her. Iris didn't reject him but had attempted to stifle her tears. Apparently Iris didn't like showing her pain. Finally stilling from her terror, Iris readjusted herself to lean against Darren's arm. Eventually her head slid down to his lap as exhaustion won out. Darren adjusted Iris's hair to help her as she rested across him. He continued to play with the locks like his mother had when he was a boy; and slowly she drifted into a deep sleep once again. He discovered that by playing with her hair, Iris seemed to sleep dreamlessly. He didn't understand why, but he was glad she was resting. Besides, he was already more rested than she was, so he wasn't complaining. He was actually quite comfortable in this position.

He looked back down at Iris as she slept, happy to see that peaceful expression return to her face. She looked so beautiful. His fingers gently ran through her long, soft hair. It glistened in the moonlight from being recently washed. Iris had been thrilled to find a shower in the bathroom on the transport. Her smile brightened her whole face. She told him she felt so much better cleaning up. There was something to be said for taking a hot bath after traveling for days.

Darren recalled Iris exiting the bathroom wearing a new pale green nightgown. He had struggled not to stare at her. The simple yet becoming gown flowed gently around her, emphasizing her shape. She seemed awkward in it, hiding herself under one of the blankets until the others had gone to bed. Transports were kept at a comfortable temperature, and she hadn't really complained about the cold. It had to be because she wanted to stay well covered. He had offered the blanket back to her while they stood watching the stars. She only took it after they spent some time lying on the cold floor.

Iris adjusted herself into a more comfortable position in her sleep. Her left arm moved out from underneath her body and angled up slightly, resting on Darren's leg. As she moved, the blanket slid down a little, uncovering her left arm. Darren carefully pulled up the blanket around her, doing his best not to wake her. He glanced down, his brow furrowing at the sight of the thin bracelet on her wrist. *Hmm, didn't notice that before. She didn't get that in Saunskirt, did she? What else did Valomeer give her?* Darren appreciated the change of clothes that Valomeer had given her, but he couldn't help but feel a little jealous at the thought that he was giving her jewelry. But was it from him? Maybe she had been wearing it before, and he just didn't remember. He rarely paid attention to the trinkets women carried. Why did he feel so defensive about the situation, anyway? He didn't have any claim on Iris. Like she had said before, they barely knew each other. It's not as if a relationship between them would go very far even if he tried.

His family would see to that. He could just imagine his mother crying at the impropriety of it all. Darren stifled a chuckle at the thought of the horror his mother would express if she saw them now. "And not a chaperone in sight!" he could practically hear her say. His small grin quickly evaporated into a stern frown. No, his station in life, his *sentence* made it impossible. And then there was Iris herself . . . she wouldn't want him. He knew that for certain after talking to her tonight. She believed in the Holy Father and not just the kind of belief that many Alastrians feigned. She believed to the point that she would even forgive those people—those who had wickedly ruined her life. He just couldn't wrap his mind around that depth of forgiveness. What she said proved how very different they truly were. He knew how this religion went; he had partaken in it once, after all, and with that knowledge, he knew that Followers were not to attach themselves romantically to non-believers. Darren had known many Followers who had conveniently ignored that section of the Sacred Text. People like that convinced him to turn his back on the faith. But since Iris was still committing to her Holy Father after everything, Darren knew she was certainly not the type to bend the rules.

His mind spiraled down another track as he remembered his bitter involvement with the church of Alaster. They were hypocrites, the whole lot of them! His heart stirred with anger at the memories. Because of them, his life was as horrible as it was now. If anyone other than Kyle had been to blame, it was that church, the one corrupt leader who had worked so hard to destroy him. He almost succeeded too.

Darren squeezed his eyes shut for a moment, willing himself to think about something else. As he opened them again, the light crept in through the window. Had that much time passed already? The sun was rising, and in a couple of hours, the automated internal lighting system would kick in.

In order to conserve power on a transport, a timer was set for the lights to turn on in the morning and off at night. Both Kyle and Bryant would get up before long. Part of Darren felt a little sad that the night was over. He liked spending time with Iris when it was just the two of them. In the few days he had spent with her, they had very little time alone. It refreshed his heart to just relax with someone who didn't hate him. Darren sighed as his head fell against the wall behind him. He was getting ahead of himself again. *Too much time in the woods.* Five years alone would make anyone desperate for personal connection. He reminded himself to be careful, to not simply throw himself into this connection just because he was lonely. But still . . .

Darren looked back down at Iris. It just felt so right. Darren leaned his head backwards again and stared at the ceiling. *You feel protective of her, that's all. She's in a bad place, and you pity her.* After a while, he focused his attention on the sunlight climbing the wall as it continued to rise. All his thoughts faded away, absorbed in the encroaching light. These were the moments he enjoyed best, when he didn't have to solve problems, brood on the past, or fear the future. He could shut off his mind and simply exist, just use his five senses to take in his surroundings, to not process any of it to find its deeper meaning. Life was filled with too much thinking. Here and now was the perfect place, the perfect time, to switch off his brain temporarily. He could be happy just being. He cherished this time the most because it was often gone in an instant and rarely achieved again. It never lasted long enough.

Darren's tranquility was broken by Bryant's blundering toward the bathroom in the distance. The sunlight had fully lit up the room; it was firmly in place in the sky. The internal lights of the transport clicked on while the outer ones switched off. Apparently the timer was set to go off a little sooner than he had thought. Darren squinted at the brightness of the lights as his eyes tried to adjust. The lights weren't really much stronger than the natural lighting outdoors, but he still blinked a few times at the difference. With the lights came Kyle, who always woke up easily. Stranger still, Kyle was a morning person. Normally, early risers didn't bother Darren, but Kyle's version of being a morning person was to be as loud as possible, forcing everyone else awake as well. Darren, on the other hand, *wasn't* a morning person, and a cacophony this early put him into one of his more foul moods.

Darren glared at Kyle and Bryant, hoping they would keep it to a dull roar so that they didn't wake Iris. The poor girl could do with a few more centuries of sleep. To his dismay, Kyle spotted them and walked their way. Darren signaled silence by raising a finger to his lips. Kyle stopped, glancing between the pair with a malicious grin. He turned back around. *Well, at least, he wasn't going to wake her up, though I could have done without the suggestive look.*

"And what do we have here?" Bryant shouted from across the way. He had just returned from the bathroom and had finally noticed Darren and Iris.

Both Darren and Kyle cringed at Bryant's shout. *Idiot!* Darren looked down at Iris whose eyelids had begun to flutter. *I could kill you, Bryant!* Iris slowly turned her head to look at Darren, still not entirely coherent. A confused look crossed her face as she looked up at him.

"I fell asleep?"

He smiled down at her. "Yeah."

Iris sat up slowly, resting on her knees. She glanced toward Bryant, drawing the blanket close around her. She stretched a little and focused back on Darren. "For how long?"

"About five hours." Darren shot a glance over at Bryant who was making his way toward them. *Would have been more if it hadn't been for that lout!*

"I don't remember dreaming," Iris spoke up. "Maybe that means I'll be okay to sleep again." A smile spread across her lips but then stopped as Darren stretched. "Did I sleep in your lap the whole time?"

Darren replied as he stood. "Yeah, but don't worry about it." He offered his hand to her. She took it and stood as well.

"You didn't get *any* sleep, did you?" she asked apologetically, her eyebrows knit together with guilt.

Darren shrugged. "Like I said, don't worry about it."

"Nonetheless, I'm sorry."

"It's okay, really. You needed it more than I did, and I can always take a nap later."

Iris sighed. "Okay then, and Darren . . . thanks." She gave him a shy, sad smile.

"Now what were you two up to all night?" Bryant burst in, wickedly interrupting their conversation.

Annoyed, both Darren and Iris glanced at him.

"Just looking at the stars, Bryant." Darren replied curtly.

Bryant crossed his arms and smirked. "Facing the wrong way to be looking at the stars, weren't you?"

"We fell asleep, that's all. *Nothing* happened, and I don't appreciate your implication otherwise," Iris stated firmly, eyes narrowing at Bryant. "Now if you'll excuse me, I'm going to get dressed."

Bryant and Darren watched as Iris walked briskly away. Kyle sidestepped quickly to let her pass and then went to join the others.

"You know, I'm beginning to get the idea that she doesn't really like me much." Bryant stated, still watching her.

"She's not the only one," Darren muttered under his breath.

Kyle strode up casually with his hands in his pockets "I see you're as good with the ladies as ever Bryant." He laughed, jerking his head back toward Iris.

Bryant grunted as if it didn't really bother him either way. Kyle shook his head and rolled his eyes, then shifted his attention to Darren.

"Seems like you're doing pretty well for yourself, though."

"What's that supposed to mean?" Darren bristled.

"First yesterday, with the whole coming-to-her-rescue bit as the transport took off. And then last night. Sleeping in each other's arms after gazing up at the stars. A little over the top for my taste, but who am I to judge?"

"It wasn't like that!"

"Really? But I thought you said you two were already a couple." Bryant interjected.

"I–I did, but it was just—I was just—"

Kyle held up a hand to cut him off. "Say no more. After all, enemies don't share personal matters." Kyle finished, a serious look replacing his lighter one.

"Then why'd you come over here Kyle? Other than to torment me?" Darren rolled his eyes.

"It's not like I have a lot of people to pick from to converse with here," he observed. "And we have some more serious matters to discuss."

Darren raised an eyebrow suspiciously. "Like what?"

"Like how the three of us are going to get into Alaster."

"Isn't that what that paper thing Iris got from Valomeer is for?" Bryant asked.

Kyle smiled. "Yes, but an Alastrian guard might not take the time to read a scroll first and then act later."

"So what do you suggest we do?" Darren asked, bored and not really ready to hear another one of Kyle's ideas after so many problems with his last one.

"We'll probably have to alter our appearances a good bit."

"How so?" Darren queried, narrowing his eyes.

"Well, Bryant, for one, will have to shave off that beard of his."

"What? No! It's a part of who I am."

"That's the point!" Kyle sighed. "We're trying to *change* who you are!"

"How do you know they'll even recognize us?" Bryant huffed.

"Because they've placed us on the *list*."

"Right, the *list*...I tried to forget about that thing. 'Fitsengea's utmost reprobates and vilest threats.' Our greatest claim to fame." Darren sighed in annoyance. "What all *else* have you been up to for the past five years?"

Kyle shrugged. "A few odd jobs here and there. Separately, not really that big of a deal. Together, done by the same people . . . could say we're a little infamous now."

Darren ran his hand through his hair. "And I'm, what, guilty by association?"

"Rumor has it that you're still part of the crew," Bryant informed him.

"What?"

"Believe me, that's not *my* fault," Kyle stated. "The last thing I'd want is to be attached to someone like you."

"At least we agree on *something*," Darren flatly affirmed.

Ignoring Darren, Kyle continued, "Do you have anything to get rid of that forest on your face, Bryant?"

"Maybe. Somewhere, I think."

"Good. Now, Darren, you should refrain from shaving all together. You're already well on your way to a beard right now."

Darren ran his hand over his growing stubble. He hadn't been able to shave for a while. He hated having a beard; it was always so itchy, especially when it first started out.

"What about you?" Bryant asked Kyle, wanting to make sure that he wouldn't get out of this scot-free.

"I'll think of something. Maybe I'll grow a beard and change my hair. You might want to think about changing your hair as well."

"Ummm, Darren?"

Darren looked past Kyle at Iris who was calling him from beside the bunks.

She was now dressed in a dark-green fitted blouse and a pair of dark-brown pants with matching lace-up boots. Her hair was tied back into a loose ponytail that rested against her neck. She held a long piece of clothing in her hands with a quizzical expression.

"Has the dress code become stricter for women in Alaster recently?"

"Not that I know of, why?"

Iris responded by holding out the article of clothing she was looking at. "Because as far as I can tell, when I put this on and button it up, the only thing visible on me will be my eyes."

Kyle stepped toward Iris and beckoned to her. "Could you bring that here, Iris?"

Iris readjusted the fabric in her arms and walked over to him. "I don't know how I'll move in this thing. It's much too long for me. I'm bound to trip all over it."

When she reached them, Kyle held out his hand to grab it. "May I?"

She handed it to him. Kyle took it and studied it for a second, a smile sneaking across his face. As he looked it over, he questioned Iris. "Did James give you this in your pack?"

"Lord Valomeer? Yes."

"Did you happen to notice how many of these were packed?"

"Three, including that one, I believe. Is there some special reason for them?"

"Oh there's a special reason, alright. But they're not for you."

"They're not?" Iris titled her head quizzically.

Kyle bunched up the garment and tossed it over to Darren, who caught it with a questioning look. "I believe that's your size, Darren." He nodded at Bryant. "Looks like you won't have to shave your beard after all, Bryant." Kyle turned to Iris to explain. "These are the clerical robes of the Diviners of Saunskirt. James knew we would need more than just a scroll to be allowed back into Alaster. Looks like he's thought of everything."

"Diviners?" Iris asked.

"They're the advisors to all in Saunskirt. They're said to have mystical powers to foretell the future," Darren elaborated.

"Fortune tellers?" Iris exclaimed, scrunching up her face.

"Basically," Kyle nodded. "But they are also the official escorts for messengers to the king from Saunskirt."

"But why would you need to disguise yourself? Why wouldn't you be allowed back into Alaster?"

Kyle looked at Darren out of the corner of his eye. "Interesting. I see you haven't told her yet, have you?"

"Told me what?"

Darren's heart raced as he glared at Kyle. *Don't you dare Kyle!* Kyle looked between Darren and Iris, greatly amused. A look of evil glee danced in his eyes.

"Interesting indeed." Kyle smirked at Darren. "Don't worry, I'll let you have fun explaining that one. But know that if you mess with any of the details, I *will* correct you." Kyle motioned to Bryant with a hand. "Come on, let's go look at the other robes and see which ones will fit. We'll leave these two to have their little discussion." Kyle chuckled as he walked past them, back over to where Iris's pack lay.

Iris looked at Darren who couldn't bring himself to meet her gaze. He did *not* want to talk about this. Not yet. Part of him hoped that if he stayed quiet long enough, she'd just leave it be and move onto something else. But with Iris, he knew that wouldn't be the case.

"So . . ." Iris started. "I guess this means it's your turn." She smiled at him, trying to lighten the mood

Darren couldn't help but halfheartedly smile back. He kept quiet, not really sure how to start.

Iris sighed when he wouldn't say anything "Look Darren, if there's something that happened with you guys that could cause trouble once we reach Alaster, I need to know."

She was right. She had to face the king, after all. He knew that things could go wrong quickly if she unintentionally misspoke. Darren took a deep breath before starting.

Chapter Fifteen

"Okay, you're right. You do need to know. It's kind of a long story, though. Maybe we should sit down?" He gestured to the chairs along the side wall.

Iris followed him promptly and sat down. Darren sat next to her and kept his eyes on his hands as he tried to think of what to say and where to start.

"Okay, so . . . A number of years ago, I was part of the Brethren of Five, a group that Kyle and I formed. There was me, Kyle, Aaron, Bryant, and another guy named Michael. As kids, we pretended like we were heroes or something. At first, we were just joking around, but as we grew older, we realized that we could actually do something with it. At the time, our families were starving. So we decided to change that." Darren paused and glanced at Iris. She was listening intently, absorbing his words, with kindness in her eyes.

He sighed before continuing. "We stole food for a while but never told our parents where it came from. They wouldn't have accepted it otherwise. Well, as time went on, we became pretty good at what we did, and as we grew older, we realized that the only way to get our families out of the poor house, so to speak, was to give them money instead of just food. That's when we started really stealing. After a while, though, it became less and less about getting what we needed and more and more about what we wanted. I became someone who I didn't even like. We entered into a dark world. We made deals with unsightly characters, and at times, *we* were the unsightly characters. This went on for years. I–I'm not proud of that time of my life." Darren stopped again, the flood of memories threatening to drown him.

For so long, he had kept this all at the back of his mind. He appreciated that Iris wasn't rushing him; instead, she waited patiently for him to continue.

"Finally, five years ago, some of us decided enough was enough and tried to convince the others to do one last job. I was just twenty at the time; Kyle, twenty-two. Kyle said we were still in our prime, but Michael said he was getting too old for all this. He was thirty then and married with three kids. On top of that, he was now a guard for Alaster. He wanted us to stop because he just had too much to lose if we ever got caught. Well, actually we had been caught a couple of times before, but they could never pin any of the charges on us. Anyways, Michael was ready to quit as was I. Bryant and Kyle wanted to keep going, and Aaron, who was only eighteen at the time, followed anything Kyle told him. Kyle was kind of our leader, you see, so he wasn't too pleased when Michael and I approached him on the issue. But he told Michael he understood and let him out completely. Me, on the other hand . . . Okay so, no, Kyle didn't *force* me to stay; he wasn't like that, but Kyle and I . . . we were like brothers. So I made a deal with him to do one last job. That one came and went.

"That score should have provided for us for years, enough to satisfy *anyone*, but then Kyle came back one day ecstatic. He had received a tip about a job to end all jobs, stealing the crown jewels. When he told me about it, I knew it was a trap. There was no way that kind of detailed information about the security would have been leaked so carelessly. I tried to persuade him otherwise, but Kyle refused to listen. He even tried to convince me and Michael to join back up, but we both refused. Kyle felt betrayed by me because he thought that of all people, he could depend on me. But I couldn't do it. I had promised . . . someone that I was done with that stuff, that I wouldn't be a part of it anymore, that I would fight against wrongdoings . . . In the end, I couldn't stop Kyle and the others from going forward with their plan. I had to find another way to stop them; if I didn't, they were sure to be killed. So I gave them up before they could even get into the chamber."

"How did you know they would be killed?"

"Because . . . I had been warned . . . Kyle found out that their capture was my doing; needless to say, he was furious. I admitted my involvement with the group, hoping that I could somehow lessen their sentence. It did help a little and kept them from banishment. They were put on trial and sentenced to ten years imprisonment. Because of my position, I put my family name on the line to vouch for their character and was even in the process of trying to lessen their sentence. But Michael helped them escape, and because of this, was eventually thrown in prison instead. Kyle knew I was doing whatever was possible to get them out; he knew that I was putting my honor on the line by standing up for him. When he escaped, he showed that he cared nothing about my honor and wanted only to destroy me and my family.

"I already had to deal with the fall out when I admitted to being a member of the group and with their escape even greater crimes were pinned on them . . . In the end, I had to leave Alaster because of the scandal. I had hoped to just disappear from the world as time passed, but apparently people still believe that I am involved with the Brethren and that I left just to meet up with Kyle and the others. And also it seems"—Darren glared over to where Kyle and Bryant were standing, removing some of the food in their packs— "that they remained in and around Alaster, up to their old habits. So now none of us are allowed in the city. If we were to be recognized, we would be imprisoned on the spot." Darren stopped, waiting for Iris's response.

Darren had told her everything—almost. He wondered what she would think about his vile past. He was sure by now that she would finally recognize his name and all the related associations. He agonized as he waited. *Will you please just say* something, *anything Iris?* He couldn't even bring himself to look at her. He raised his head when Iris rested a hand on his shoulder. He looked her in the eyes, their sadness mirroring his own pain. She smiled in sympathy.

"Darren, just so you know, I appreciate you telling me all this. I know it must have been hard for you." She let her hand fall off his shoulder as she focused on Kyle and Bryant. "I think I remember hearing about this crime, but I'm a little fuzzy on the details since it's been so long and since our leaders of the Holy House tended to shelter us from much of the outside world. Which I'm seeing how much of a detriment that was now... It sounds to me like you have made a great effort to change yourself. You had a bad past; you made some poor choices, but really, no one's perfect. No one ever can be." She glanced back at Darren. "I won't ask you to tell me all that you did before, and I can't claim any right to judge your decisions or actions. So basically, I guess what I'm saying is that . . . no, I don't hate you." She nudged him playfully with her elbow causing Darren to break into a grin. Relief flooded his heart so that he couldn't help but release a small chuckle.

Iris smiled. "Well, looks like I have three fortune teller, or—um—Diviner escorts then. Maybe you can fill me in on any other specifics I might need to know about this stuff later."

Darren smiled back, sitting a little straighter now. "Sure."

"Great! But for now, I say we go find out what foods Lord Valomeer packed for us. I'm starving, and I know that the checkpoint stop is a day or so away, so let's get something to eat." With that, Iris stood and motioned for Darren to follow.

Darren rose and walked beside her. "So . . . now it's your turn you know?" He winked at her.

Iris fiddled with the bracelet on her wrist briefly as if pondering something and then popped her head up. "My favorite color is blue."

"Blue?" He frowned at her playfully. "That's all you're going to tell me? After all I just shared with you, all I get is that your favorite color is blue?"

Iris rolled her eyes jokingly. "Fine then! My favorite color is *sky* blue. There, is that better?" She couldn't keep herself from laughing

Darren laughed as well. "Much."

As he walked with Iris and retrieved some food, his heart felt much lighter. She didn't hate him for what he had been, for what had happened. But then again, he hadn't told her everything. He would tell her soon, within the next couple of days. He wouldn't talk about everything at once, though, for fear that sharing it all would completely frighten her away. At the same time, Darren knew that Iris was holding back something rather important from him.

He thought again about the night before. She had said they didn't know each other. But it took time to get to know a person, and they were on the right track now. He smiled again at the thought of it. Darren wasn't normally a man who liked to share his heart or to just chat in general, but he was finding that he actually liked to talk and share his heart as long as it was with her.

Chapter Sixteen

Iris and Darren were nearly inseparable for the next twenty-four hours. She had spent almost all day inspecting the facets of the transport as Darren explained each part. She didn't mind it, though, because she had a lot of questions. Darren's extensive knowledge came from repairing transports in his younger years.

They shared many stories about their childhoods, staying up late into the night just talking. Although they had numerous similarities, sometimes Iris struggled when talking about her past. Her heart often longed for her family. But Darren was always very patient with her and didn't press her too much. He realized when it was time to change the subject, or he just let the silence slip in. Merely sitting in his presence comforted her.

With just two days left in their journey, Iris chatted once more with Kyle in the open area. She understood the betrayal he must have felt when Darren gave them up, but Kyle knew Darren had only done it to save their lives. She was sure Kyle blamed Darren for something else, that there was more to the story that he hadn't told her yet. But due to the sensitive nature of the subject, she couldn't bring herself to pry. If she dug too deep too quickly, she might inadvertently spark another fight between Kyle and Darren, similar to what she had witnessed back in the dungeon. Or worse.

Instead, she focused on getting to know Kyle as a person. He was very smart and apt to find the humor in any situation. But why did Darren tense up whenever he saw the two of them together? She didn't want to create further conflict, but it was honestly impossible to avoid anyone on a transport, not to mention rudely obvious.

At the same time, she didn't feel guilty for finding ways to avoid Bryant, considering that he had tried to harass her the very first time she met him. She didn't offer any excuses, not even for her conscience's sake. She hadn't gotten around to sharing that yet with Darren. She wanted to tell him, but at the same time, she didn't know how he'd react. He might even try to fight Bryant, and since they were all stuck together for another few hours, she just couldn't see how pushing the issue would do anything but end badly.

She did have to admit, though, she was beginning to become a little stir crazy and was ready for a change of scenery. They would stop at the checkpoint today, which normally took a couple of hours, depending on how thorough the inspections were. They were not only checking for illegal shipments but inspecting the machine itself, making sure that all the parts were in proper working condition. According to Darren, checkpoints were very interesting places. Up to five different transports could be at these stops at once. Since each transport could carry many people, the stops could become quite hectic. In fact, checkpoint stations had become towns in and of themselves because of the huge traffic flow. People had set up many taverns for their various foods and some real beds, unlike those on a transport, to sleep in. Sometimes the inspections could take over a day if the transport needed any repairs, giving these traveling inns plenty of business.

Iris grew excited about all she would see because people from all over Fitsengea would be there. Even though all those people lived in the same country as her, Fitsengea was a huge land. With such an expanse, people were bound to be rather different from place to place.

To her amazement, King Zaerin kept all of Fitsengea united. He had been ruling from Alaster for forty years now.

The thought that she would have to speak with such a man face-to-face made her more than just nervous. Iris forced herself to put her fears to the back of her mind. Fretting about it now wouldn't do her a lick of good. Instead, she would focus back on the clock and count down how long it would take to reach their next destination. She looked around to find Darren securing the packs into the slots in the wall, keeping them from flying about when the transport came to a sudden stop. Iris went up next to him, handing him the last pack.

"Thanks." He smiled and then pulled down the cover and locked the latch to the slots.

"So how much longer?"

"Until we stop? About fifteen minutes, actually."

"Good, I'm more than ready to get out of this thing for a bit."

"I'm ready to get myself a hot meal!" Bryant called out as he walked toward them. "And I'll be able to get my fill there dressed like this."

Iris turned her head to see what he meant. Bryant was already dressed in that odd fortune teller's garb. She couldn't help but make a face. "Why are you wearing it now?"

"Well, *my* reasoning is that they always give officials special treatment. But Kyle," he said, pointing out Kyle behind him with his thumb. He had just exited the bathroom and was also dressed in the uniform. "Kyle says that we should go ahead and get into character now, considering the soldiers here often report back to Alaster."

Iris looked at Darren for a better explanation.

"If Diviners suddenly showed up at Alaster without being spotted at least once at one of the checkpoints, the king would know something was up. If we are to truly play the part, then we'd better start now. Diviners are known to be rather ostentatious and will take any opportunity to be revered by others."

"Oh," Iris said simply. "Guess that means you better get dressed then, if we only have a few minutes till we reach our stop."

Darren nodded and went over to one of the bunks on the wall to retrieve his Diviner's outfit and stepped into the bathroom to change. When he stepped out again, it was all that Iris could do to keep herself from laughing. The Diviner's outfit had looked odd on Bryant and Kyle, but for some reason, it looked incredibly comical on Darren. Maybe that was because he was standing there so awkwardly. She couldn't really blame him for that, though. She probably would have felt the same way if it had been her.

Darren had also completely buttoned up the garb. For the time being, the other two had left the buttons around their mouths open to make it easier to talk. He pointed out to Bryant and Kyle the buttons left undone. Bryant sighed and fastened his unwillingly while Kyle followed suit. Considering the short amount of time they had left, they didn't want to risk being seen dressed improperly by a guard's watchful eyes.

They really look strange, Iris thought as she surveyed the trio. The Diviner's outfit consisted of a long cloak that touched the ground. Large metal buttons ran up the middle all the way up to where the bridge of the nose would be, closing the coat to cover the face. No skin could show. An angular hood was also attached to the coat and covered the head entirely, leaving only enough room for the eyes to peer out. Even the sleeves were too long so that the hands couldn't accidentally show. The whole costume, gaudy in design, included far too many golden symbols stitched all over its turquoise fabric. At the bottom of the coat were tiny silver bells, used to announce their presence, so that no one could miss them.

Darren had told Iris that Diviners were not permitted to speak to anyone save the people they were supposed to deliver their message to. The bells also acted as a warning for people to move out of their way. The get up was really odd, but at the same time, the pure audacity of the uniform was awe-inspiring. Iris didn't know if she wanted to laugh or run away and hide when she saw it. But since she knew who was under the weird clothes, she found herself more inclined to the former.

"Time to strap in," Kyle's muffled voice called out through the fabric.

Iris complied readily this time, not wanting to repeat the previous fiasco. First she had to help strap in Darren, Bryant, and Kyle because their outfits limited their movements and use of their hands. Iris then moved to strap herself firmly in place.

Within the next few minutes, the transport drastically decelerated. Iris's body strained against the straps at the rapid change in motion, making her glad that she was in place this time. She didn't even want to know what would have happened otherwise. The transport's wall vibrated slightly as it finally slowed to a complete stop. Iris started to release herself from the wall when Darren, who was strapped in beside her, stopped her. Confused, Iris looked at him but did as she was told. Darren opened his mouth to explain when the harsh mechanical *clunk* of the doors opening interrupted him. Darren quickly focused ahead, but Iris couldn't help but turn and watch the doors lift.

As soon as they were opened, in marched five soldiers, each equipped with a sword. They entered the transport uniformly, years of practice and routine showing in the precision of their movements. Once they saw only four passengers aboard the transport, they turned to face them and stood at attention.

Iris watched their movements, confused. *What should I do now? Am I supposed to announce who they are, where they came from, or what they are doing? Am I supposed to release the straps? I wish Darren could help.* But he couldn't tell her; after all, Diviners weren't allowed to talk to anyone. Would their ruse work? This was a vital moment for all four of them.

Iris looked around at the different soldiers to see if any of them would give some indication of what to do next. But each pair of eyes was instead trained fearfully on the three Diviners standing before them. Iris couldn't help but roll her eyes. *Fat lot of help you are!* One of the soldiers cleared his throat as the others refocused and stood at attention. A very portly man of obvious higher rank passed through the transport doors. He wore a different uniform than the rest of the men. The soldiers each wore a metal breastplate and a silver helmet that covered their brow down to the back of their heads. This other man wore no armor whatsoever. Studying him more closely, Iris didn't think this man was part of the army at all. From how he held himself and then came and unstrapped each of them, he must have been some kind of an official greeter or in a head position at the checkpoint.

He undid Iris's straps with the finesse of someone who had repeated the same movements many times. He lessened the pomp of his posture as he undid Darren and the rest, relaxing more with each Diviner he passed. As Iris watched, she couldn't help but think about how truly sheltered she must have been and how many things she knew nothing about: Diviners, transports, and other elements that played a huge role in the more advanced towns in eastern Fitsengea. All she really knew were the customs of Jaralynx, Throansburrough, and the places to the west of it. It was almost as if she were a foreigner to this land. And now she had to pretend as if she knew what she was doing. Too bad she had always been a horrible actress!

"Welcome to checkpoint X32," the head man announced at last, stepping back. He turned his head to the Diviners with a deep, formal bow. "We are greatly honored to have men such as yourselves at our humble checkpoint. To what do we owe this unexpected pleasure?"

Oh, Holy Father, help me! Iris cried as her stomach became all butterflies. "Excuse me, good sir." She stepped forward, in an effort to boost her confidence and appear sure of herself. She squared her shoulders and looked sternly at the man. "But I am more than certain that you are familiar with the customs of the Great Diviners of Saunskirt, and you should therefore know that they are bound by tradition to speak to no one other than the person who is to receive their message. Why we are here is our business and ours alone! Furthermore, the Diviners would appreciate it if you didn't address them directly." Iris put her hands on her hips to show that she meant business, though really she was trying to hide her trembling hands.

The man raised his head slowly with a satisfied smile. "Well said, my dear. If you will forgive me, I had to test and see if you were truly a party of Diviners. Too many times, wanted criminals have come through checkpoints dressed in official robes so as not to be recognized by the guards."

If you only knew! Iris did her best to feign annoyance and insult. "Well, you can *obviously* see that these men truly are the Great Diviners. Look at their clothes! Are they not the genuine item?"

The man examined the clothes as Iris continued. "If you are still not persuaded, we have with us a scroll from Lord Valomeer himself. You may verify the seal, but the contents of the scroll are not for wandering eyes. Now if you're done insulting our character, we will be moving on to acquire a meal at one to the best taverns of checkpoint X32. You will be sure to aid us in any way possible, will you not?" *Heh, it's kind of fun playing a stuck-up aristocrat!* Iris fought a smile by intensifying her frown. She crossed her arms in front of her chest and acted as if she were waiting impatiently for an answer.

The man smiled respectfully at her. "Yes, yes, you are indeed a Diviner's party. My men here will see to it that you receive whatever you desire while my workers will put off all other duties so that you can go promptly on your way."

"Good, speed is everything. I expect you to be finished within two hours."

"Certainly, miss." The man bowed deeply again, stepping aside to allow Iris and her escorts to exit the transport.

Oh blast it, do I let Darren and the others walk ahead of me, or am I supposed to lead the way? Dang you Darren, why didn't you tell me all of this stuff before when we had time to talk about it? We really need to work on our communication skills!

Iris wanted to glance at Darren for some sort of direction, but the head man was watching them closely, and she knew he'd notice instantly. *Blast all this deceit! It only brings more problems!* Iris finally decided to lead the way because it would be far more suspicious if they just stood there. Just as she was about to start moving, Darren approached her from the side. Bryant stepped up directly to her left, and then Kyle took the central lead. *Okay? So apparently, they have a special method of walking too? Gee, thanks guys, for telling me all of this* ahead *of time!* Iris set herself on giving them a piece of her mind when they were all done with this. Truly, they couldn't have been less helpful if they tried!

All four of them exited the transport solemnly, the soldiers following them out. Stopping outside the transport, Iris directed the soldiers to go and retrieve some food supplies from the town. They received directions to one of the best taverns to eat at. Along the way, they walked down the small dirt streets as if they were royalty, royalty who thought they were better than anything or anyone in the universe, not even paying attention to the remarks made to or about them.

Iris did her best to not let her eyes wander. *Pity . . . I had been looking forward to doing a little sight-seeing. I guess I'll have to wait until my next trip.* The sun reflected off her bracelet, and she glanced down, once more aware of the metal around her wrist. *Oh, that's right. There may not be a next time. I wonder how long it will be. Surely not for forever . . . I hope.* At the thought of what awaited her, her heart beat with terror anew. But now was not the time to fret about something so far in the future. She had plenty enough to be nervous about at the moment. They entered the tavern that the soldiers had directed them to.

An unnerving silence washed over the crowd at seeing the newest arrivals. Kyle stepped aside rigidly as Darren and Bryant remained in place beside Iris. *Guess that means I'm on again, eh?* Iris stepped forward and tried to keep her voice from wavering. Her eyes scanned the room until they rested upon a stout old man who looked as if he was the owner.

"This your place?" Iris asked firmly, nodding to him slightly.

"Y–yes, miss."

"Good, we'll take your best hot meal and—"*Oh no, are Diviners allowed alcohol?* "—your purest water." *Better to be safe than sorry! Why did we waste so much time talking about nothing instead of going over more important details?* Iris lamented to herself as they moved uniformly over to one of the unoccupied tables and sat down.

The noise within the tavern crescendoed, this time with a slightly different undercurrent to it, a song that focused on wild speculations as to why Diviners were here in their precious semi-town of X32. Not all gossipers were locals as plenty of odd characters were within those walls, and each seemed to need to now share their stories about their encounters with Diviners. The whole situation probably wouldn't have bothered Iris as much if she had someone to talk to, but since Darren and the others were limited by this new vow of silence, she had to instead just sit there and bear all the wary glances. Some people outright stared and pointed at them. What was worse was that the conversations were now shifting from speculations about the reliability of the Diviners and instead were focusing directly on what role Iris played in all this. Iris couldn't remember the last time she had felt so horrendously awkward. On top of it all, she had to pretend as if it didn't bother her, as if she didn't notice. Not because she was unaware but because she was obviously above them, and such lesser people didn't deserve her attention. At least that's what her character demanded.

Short interactions with the wealthy visitors docking at the western coastline ports had taught Iris how people with power typically held themselves in public. She didn't know if she was just simply feeding into a stereotype, but it was best not to question it, save her actions be questioned. Instead, she would maintain this self-superior façade a little longer and try her best to ignore the crowd and just enjoy their wonderfully fresh-cooked meal.

That was another problem for Iris. The food was truly delicious, and she struggled to restrain herself while eating. She didn't know what kind of meat she was eating or what was in the stew or how the bread had so many colors yet was still so tasty. She longed for the ability to just sit and chat with the owner and ask him all sorts of questions.

She was also trying not to burst out laughing while she watched Darren, Bryant, and Kyle struggle to eat. It really took quite the amount of maneuvering as they were not supposed to show their faces to anyone. They instead had to work around the limitations of their clothes, only unbuttoning a few buttons here and there, and try to hold their utensils through the long sleeves that covered their hands. Iris had to force herself to look away as she knew she wouldn't hold back much longer if she did. She couldn't help but wonder how real Diviners survived similar situations on a day-to-day basis. The mental picture of a thousand Diviners trying to eat as Darren and the others were now threatened to leave her rolling on the floor with laughter. Iris sucked in her cheeks and bit down on the inside of her mouth to maintain her composure.

"Here you go." One of the waitresses brought over a fresh round of water and set down the glasses with shaky hands. "Oh, and the mister says the meal's on the house." She gathered up the empty dishes, gave a slight curtsey, and then left without once raising her eyes from the floor.

What is it about Diviners that terrifies everyone so? They're just fortune tellers, not fortune changers. But I suppose people do tend to equate any coming disaster with the messenger who foretells it. Not like they really *have any control over the outcome, but people are suspicious, and they want a face to blame for unexplainable travesties.*

People are so odd sometimes. Not like treating these so-called Diviners better was going to make their lives more favorable. But I wouldn't doubt that the Diviners don't make much of an effort to alter the public mindset. Especially not with the way they apparently expect to be treated. I mean, for goodness' sake! They're just messengers, after all. I hope I never have to meet a true Diviner; I don't think I could stomach it!

When they had all finished their food and water, Kyle rose from the table as Bryant and Darren followed his lead. Iris stood too, curious to see where they were going now. They only had a little over an hour left. Iris had no idea what they would do next as they couldn't just roam around the town like normal travelers. The other travelers and residents parted in waves whenever they noticed them coming their way. Being the center of attention felt so awkward. After a while, Iris just wanted to hide under a barrel, hide *anywhere*, just to escape their unwavering stares. She wondered how people in important positions could stand such continual gawking. *Though I suppose some of them like it, don't think I ever could.*

Iris focused again on the present just in time to see that Kyle had stopped abruptly in front of her. She halted and tried to see around him. In front of them stood a large elaborate tent with two guards, still as statues, watching. On their armor, each wore an emblem that looked similar to one of the decorations on the back of the Diviner's uniform. Did Diviners have their own army? That seemed rather silly to Iris, a little too much fanfare for mere fortune tellers.

Kyle made some kind of motion to the guards, which apparently worked as they were promptly allowed inside. Iris followed the others, glancing at the guards as they passed by. *Now* that *has got to be a boring job! Standing there all day, doing nothing. No, thank you!*

Inside, the tent was like a fabric building; patches of cloth hanging from floor to ceiling acted as dividers for different rooms. All around were lavish pillows for reclining, and in the center of each seating arrangement was a spot for burning incense upon a shallow bronze plate. Various carpets were used to cover up the dirt ground, each richly embroidered with the same designs on the Diviner's clothes. Iris curiously looked around the immediate entryway; the whole experience seemed strange to her. Where were the Diviners who usually inhabited this place, and why, if they were so important, did they only receive a temporary set up instead of some monumental building? She had assumed that such a structure was more suited to their tastes, depending on what she had gathered of a Diviner's character so far.

Kyle moved to the back and off to the left, going through a fabric divider with a large symbol stitched onto the center. Bryant followed Kyle while Darren paused to move the fabric aside so Iris could go through.

Iris gave Darren a friendly smile and whispered a thank you to him, not sure if she was allowed to talk to him yet. Upon entering the room, both Bryant and Kyle had thrown off their cowls, rolled up their sleeves, and unbuttoned what covered their faces. Darren came in behind Iris and followed suit.

"Now, that's better." Bryant sighed contentedly, shaking his head and scratching his bearded chin. "I don't know how those chaps can stand it for so long; it's stifling in there!"

"Hah! You think that's bad? Try wearing it for weeks on end while traveling to villages on foot!" Kyle boasted as he plopped down on an overstuffed pillow.

Iris sat down on a pillow across from Kyle with Darren sitting next to her and a pillow in between them.

"Why were you dressed as a Diviner for such a long time? Did you actually become a Diviner? Is that how you know so much about them?" Iris asked.

Kyle chuckled. "No, I never became one officially. Really, my only reason for traveling with them was because they often traveled with wealthy parties. I'll admit that I was able to take more than a few valuable items from right under their noses. In addition, the overall treatment I received wasn't too shabby, either."

"Admit to? Sounds more like bragging if you ask me," Darren scoffed.

Wanting to avoid any bickering, Iris quickly changed the subject. "So, Kyle, what is this tent for, and why isn't there a more permanent structure?"

Kyle completely ignored Darren and focused on Iris. "This tent is a place for Diviners to stay in between their visits from town to town. Diviners refuse to stay in any of the inns within a checkpoint or even in the towns for long periods of time. They feel that it is beneath them and also fear that prolonged exposure to outsiders might end up contaminating their visions. Diviners are to live only within Saunskirt, which is why there are only tents in place at checkpoints, because they are supposed to be temporary. They should deliver their messages and then return to Saunskirt as quickly as possible."

"Do Diviners constantly travel?"

"Not normally, which is why it is often a big event when they are seen in other places. It tends to mean that something huge is about to happen."

"So that means we don't have to worry about running into any others. In that case, we can talk freely here," Bryant interjected as he reclined farther back on the pillows, obviously comfortable.

"Have Diviners ever been wrong?" Iris queried Kyle.

"Well, it's hard to say. A Diviner's message tends to be rather vague."

"In other words, people can interpret it to mean anything, which means that someone is bound to be right sooner or later." Iris smirked.

"Pretty much." Kyle shrugged. "Which is why not everyone believes in their abilities, but at the same time, many remain superstitious about them and won't write them off, just in case."

"Well, do *you* believe in their—um—*abilities*?"

"Oh, heck no!" Kyle laughed. "They're *completely* full of it!"

Iris chuckled in spite of herself. The Diviners were quite possibly charlatans, but she also knew better than to completely dismiss the supernatural. Oh, these Diviners were not in line with the Sacred Texts for sure. Holy Father would not share a word this way with His children. Prophets and prophecies were strewn through His writings, but they were never to be used for self-gain. Still, Iris was somewhat relieved to know that Kyle wasn't wrapped up in the Diviner's practices. Groups like these often fell into relationships with the Great Deceiver far too easily.

"Kyle thinks all religions, mystics, and what have you are completely full of it," Darren added.

Iris's smile faded. "You don't believe in the Holy Father at all?"

"Nope. But I take it that you do?"

"Yes."

Kyle cocked his head to the side a little. "Interesting."

"Why is that . . . *interesting*?"

Kyle shrugged. "I don't know. It's just that if most people had witnessed what you had, one of their first reactions would be to reject any notion of the existence of God."

"Because if there truly was a Holy Father, then how could He allow such evil to exist? If the Father is supposed to be good, all-knowing, and all-powerful, why wouldn't He have stopped it from happening? That's what you're getting at, right?"

"More or less."

"That's the age-old question, isn't it? Why do bad things happen? Even more so, why do bad things happen to good people?" Iris paused, taking a deep breath. It was surprisingly difficult for her to talk about all of this. "Why . . . it always comes down to that. Why . . ." she sighed thoughtfully. "The thing is, Kyle, if I don't believe in the Holy Father now, if I turn from Him, I have nothing left to hold onto. My life . . . it becomes meaningless. I have no connections; I have nothing. The point remains that at a time like this, I *have* to hold onto Him."

Iris raised her eyes to meet Kyle's intent look when she finished, wondering at the expression on his face. Kyle didn't seem like the type of person to take many things seriously. He could be attentive, but he always seemed to be on the verge of making some sort of snarky comment. But no hint of budding sarcasm remained in his eyes right now. What could he be thinking?

Shifting lazily on his cushion, Bryant interjected, "What I don't get is how you people say you follow the so-called only God when you clearly have three. I may not have been the best student, but I can do the math!"

"Bryant, you never went to school," Darren threw out in annoyance.

Bryant simply waved him off. Iris took a deep breath; she knew this conversation all too well. It was one of the first lessons she learned in their evening worship times. She briefly contemplated whether or not she should try to explain the answer or just ignore Bryant to the best of her abilities. But the urge to show him the truth won out. Iris glanced around the room, her gaze resting on some flowers in a clay vase upon a small stand along one of the tent walls. She cleared her throat to gain Bryant's attention and then pointed to the pot.

"You see those plants over there, Bryant? What would you call them?"

Bryant perked up his head slightly and followed the direction indicated. "Flowers?"

A half-smile danced across Iris's face. "Exactly. The Holy Father is just like a flower. A flower usually consists of three main parts, right? The petals, the stem, and the leaves. Each section fulfills a specific role. In the simplest of terms, that is how my faith works. The Holy Father is also made up of the Holy Beloved and the Holy Wisdom. All three have separate titles and more specific roles, but all three are actually one. So in the end, we worship one God, not three separate gods. Just like that plant is considered one flower and not three separate plants."

"Right . . ." Bryant responded skeptically.

"And yet, through all those parts, whole and separate, none of them were able to protect your home, were they?" Kyle spoke bitterly.

Iris looked at him, her pain stealing her voice. Seeing how Kyle's words had hurt Iris, Darren grabbed a small rock from the ground and threw it at him, hitting Kyle in the back of the head. Kyle snapped his head around and glared at Darren. Catching the hurt spread across Iris's face he realized what he had just spoken out loud. Guilt rose in his eyes momentarily, and he shifted away once more.

The group faded into an uneasy silence. Iris had thought that she would be able to avoid uncomfortable silences this time. She was wrong. She let her eyes wander over the details of their room, her mind drifting into a hazy state of partial awareness.

Well, this is fun, Iris thought sarcastically. *I'm actually longing to be back on the transport. At least there, I could look out the window.*

At that moment, off in the corner of the tent, behind where Kyle sat, a breeze was blowing so that the tent edges slightly flit open. Tired of simply sitting and staring around the room, Iris got up and walked over to that corner. Darren and Kyle both watched. Bryant, on the other hand, lay sprawled out across several pillows snoring. Iris knelt down at the corner, turned her head back to them, and shrugged her shoulders.

"What? I'm bored! I can't wander the streets of X32, so I might as well just watch what I can see from here." With that, she turned her gaze to the edge of the fabric and pulled it back just enough to peek out.

Iris sat there for a few minutes, enjoying the bustling scene before her. People hurried about, selling items from all over at different carts. She could easily spot who had made their home at the X32 checkpoint. Due to the dress and the way that some of the other people carried themselves, she could just as easily see which ones were distant travelers. Different groups of people reacted in their own ways: some pleasant, some far from it.

Every one of these souls had a life story, some just beginning, some with many chapters past. Each had their own families and friends; each had experienced some form of love, hate, heartache, and joy. Iris played with the idea of taking part in those different lives. Thousands upon thousands of people all over Fitsengea were just like Iris in one way or another. They were doing their best to live their lives, and yet she would never meet, never know, more than half of them. It would be as if they never existed to her, and when they died, she would feel no loss, for she would not know what she missed. Sure, their respective families and friends would mourn, but unless they did something to affect others outside their typical sphere of influence, they would pass from this life relatively unknown. *And yet we consider ourselves to be of such great importance when really, most people won't even know that we were ever alive.*

"How long have you had that bracelet?"

Iris nearly jumped out of her skin at Kyle's words; she hadn't even noticed him kneel down beside her. She placed a hand over her heart and laughed.

"Good grief, you scared me!"

Kyle smiled. "Sorry, wasn't my intention. But about the bracelet, where did you get it?"

Iris looked down at her wrist, wiggling it so that the bracelet spun around. "I—um—got it while in Saunskirt. I—"

"Why?"

"Why? Well, because I—um—I don't know, why not?"

Kyle lowered his voice, not wanting to draw Darren or Bryant's attention. "Why are you set to return to Saunskirt as a prisoner?"

Iris looked at him in shock.

"Remember, Iris, I worked closely with James for over a year. I know all the ins and outs of Saunskirt. So I also know what he used to indicate a messenger who is to be returned back to Saunskirt and serve out their sentence in the dungeons. I want to know why you are bound to such a fate."

Iris lowered her voice as well. "When I met with Lord Valomeer back in Saunskirt, he told me that in order to maintain the respect of his people, to maintain his honor, and to hold to his legal system, *someone* would have to remain in the dungeons for the crime committed against him. He told me that if I would become his prisoner, then he would let you and the others go."

A grim expression crossed Kyle's face. "Did they place that little metal badge over your heart?"

Iris nodded.

"Did they explain what it would do?"

"They told me that if I do not return within two weeks, the timer within the device would go off, electrocuting my heart and killing me painfully."

"Did they also tell you that if you try and tamper with it, it will cause it to go off prematurely?"

Iris nodded again.

Kyle cast his eyes to the side, his low voice rattled with anger. "I can't believe James would force that on you."

Iris reached out and placed her hand on his arm. "Don't be angry with him, Kyle. It was *my* idea. It was the only thing I could think of so that he would be willing to let you all go."

"I wondered why we were released so promptly."

"Kyle, please don't tell the others yet. I don't want Darren to feel responsible in any way. I don't want *any* of you to think it's your fault or to try and stop it from happening."

Kyle looked at her unhappily. "I will let you tell them in your own time, don't worry."

Iris smiled at him. "Thank you, Kyle. You don't know how much I appreciate that."

Kyle nodded shortly, then moved to stand up, bringing his voice back to a normal level. He spoke to get Darren and Bryant's attention. "Alright people, I do believe we have passed the two-hour mark. Time for us to suit back up, get out there, and act like stuck-up jerks once again. A task that's a little easier for some than others," Kyle announced, unable to resist taking a shot at Darren.

"I know, but I do it so well!" Iris jumped up, wanting to diffuse the situation before it could even turn into one.

"I didn't mean—"

"Ah! Now, now Mr. Diviner! We shan't go breaking our vow of silence now shall we?" Iris winked at Kyle who made a face at her. "Good, now shut it, or I guess more appropriately button it! And let's be on our way. It really is far too boring in here!" She made an overly dramatic sigh and then giggled.

Iris passed Darren as he held back the fabric flap. He bit the side of his cheek, about to burst from holding in his laughter. *Good, better it be laughter than anger. Well done Iris, another crisis averted!* Kyle, Bryant, and Darren returned to their previous positions and all exited the tent to make their way back to the transport, making sure to resume the somber character befitting of their position as Diviners.

With Kyle directly in front of her, Iris couldn't help but think about their conversation from moments before. So now Kyle knew, and she had to say, she was a little surprised at how upset the whole situation made him. But maybe he was just angry because he thought he had won that bet with Valomeer, and so no one should have had to stay in the dungeons. That idea made the most sense. Yes, he was upset that he wouldn't receive that favor from Valomeer, not because he was genuinely concerned for her safety. Or was he? Iris shook her head to dispel the thought.

No, I'm just overthinking things as always! Anything Kyle does toward me has to be just to make Darren jealous. Right? Wait, what am I saying? I don't even know if Darren likes me that way. I mean, I can make my assumptions, and the way he acts around me does make a girl a little suspicious. Oh, just shut up brain! It wouldn't work anyway! So forget about it and move on. Oh, look, we're here, perfect time for a distraction. Alright Iris, think. Show time!

Kyle once again took a step to the side to allow Iris to move forward. Iris looked at the soldier in front of them and began her little act.

"Where is the man who met us at the start?"

"He is inside the transport, miss."

"Well, bring him out then!"

"Yes miss." He dropped his head slightly and then turned to go fetch his boss.

Iris looked around and saw one of the soldiers they had talked to earlier about getting supplies for them.

"You! Are we all set with our things?" she called out to him.

The man jolted to attention and nervously stuttered his response. "Y–ye–yes miss. You're good to go!"

He seemed awful young to be a soldier, barely even eighteen, if not younger. Poor kid, he was scared out of his wits at having to deal with a Diviner's party.

"Good." Iris nodded curtly to him and then shifted her focus back on the transport as the leader walked through the doors.

"Ahh, welcome back Great Diviners! You are right on time. As to be expected."

"Are we ready to depart?"

"Well, yes and no. If you will allow us but a few more minutes, we have some new developments that we wish to add to your transport. For who better to be honored with such advances in technology than the Great Diviners? Sure, it will cost a little price but still it—"

"No."

"No?"

"No."

"Alright then, we'll just go ahead and remove those items. Don't worry, the transport will be ready in a few moments."

"It's ready now." Iris spoke coolly.

"Or it's ready now! Yes, yes. Very good." The man laughed nervously. He stepped aside to allow them to enter.

Kyle took the center once again, and they all stepped onto the transport. Upon entering, they saw that the interior of the transport was sparkling clean. Four guards stood at attention before them. Iris and the others walked over to the straps on the wall. The leader followed them and began the process of strapping them each in. As he came toward her, Iris felt a prick at her heart. She was going from place to place to warn all of a secret enemy. Would she pass through here without giving them such a warning as well? They had a right to know. X32 may just be a checkpoint for transports to pass through, but it had developed into its own sort of village. The impression grew so strong to speak that she didn't think she could live with herself if she remained silent. She decided at last to take a chance and warn this head of X32 once he reached her and began the process of locking her in place.

At first, he didn't even raise his head to look at her as he went through the routine. Just as he was about to latch the last strap, Iris grabbed his hand to get his attention. He raised his eyes up slowly to greet hers, not really sure what was going on. A bit of fear flashed across his face, fear that he might have done something wrong to upset the Great Diviners.

"Beware a foreign attack form the West," Iris whispered to him, holding his gaze with her eyes.

The man's face lost a few shades of color. He swallowed a couple of times as his mouth became suddenly dry. "W–when?"

"I don't know. Just be prepared to either defend yourself or flee. For if you cannot take out this enemy, they will not leave one of you alive. But do not attack first! Simply maintain a watchful eye, for they might even pass without confronting you."

He nodded solemnly to her, indicating he understood and would do as he was told. He finished latching her in, beckoned his soldiers to him, and then all left. As the mechanical door clicked shut, Iris exhaled heavily. She was glad she told him not to attack first or else he might have become too zealous and run out any and all foreigners. The last thing she wanted was to cause an unjust persecution. Hopefully her warning would help them in some way.

Iris's body again strained against the straps as the transport took off. They were on their way once more. Only two days left before they would be in Alaster. Only two more days before she would have to stand before King Zaerin—alone. What would she say to him? She knew that she could no longer shove this issue to the back of her mind. She had to prepare; she had to know what to say. She had to review every single detail of what happened in Throansburrough. She would have to picture it all again. She couldn't run from it anymore. She would *have* to face it. Once she had delivered her message and made her plea, she could clasp back onto her comforting denial. Iris wasn't certain how long she could force herself to not think about these things, but she had to try. As soon as she fulfilled her purpose, she would do whatever possible to just shut down entirely. Her hope that anyone else had survived ebbed with each passing hour. She saw no signs otherwise. These last days, hours even, before meeting with the king would be the longest of her life. Maybe the others could instruct her on how to present herself before the king.

"Iris, you realize you can move around again, right?"

Iris snapped back to reality at Darren standing in front of her. She looked down and saw that he had already unlatched her from the wall.

"Oh, good grief! Did I ever zone out or what?" She laughed wearily and rubbed her face with her hands.

Darren chuckled in response. He then took off his Diviner's cloak and put it with the rest of their stuff.

"I have to say, missy," Bryant called out from across the way, "you were down right hilarious out there today!"

Panic rose within Iris. "What? Do you mean I didn't act as I should have?"

"Haha, no, no! That's not what he's getting at, Iris." Darren laughed.

"Actually, you were the perfect picture of a messenger in a Diviner's party. You handled yourself beautifully," Kyle praised.

"That's what was so funny. You were so great at it! The way you snapped at people was wonderful!" Bryant laughed, coming over and slapping her on the back.

"Umm . . . thanks . . . I think?"

"I thought you didn't know anything about Diviners."

"I don't. Everything back there was just me going with the flow. We're lucky I didn't do something to completely blow our cover! Which reminds me—from now on, we *really* need to communicate better, all of us! If you don't want me to screw up, then I need all of the details."

"Okay." Darren returned from putting away his uniform. "What do you need to know?"

Iris pursed her lips for a second as she thought. "Well, really I know practically nothing. So . . . tell me about Alaster!"

Chapter Seventeen

The transport doors once again locked into the open position. Iris and her three Diviners maintained their stance against the wall. Five soldiers immediately marched through the doorway, two stopping in front of the passengers with hands held ready on their weapons. The other three ran around to check the transport for contraband or hidden passengers. Within five minutes, they concluded their search. They then moved to stand next to the other two soldiers, mimicking their rigidity.

"Check complete!" a soldier called out loudly, keeping his eyes trained on the passengers.

At that, a man strode purposefully into the transport, stopped in front of the passengers and studied them intently. Maintaining his serious frown, he gave a deep bow.

"Welcome to Alaster, Great Diviners. I am Flyn, Master of the Transports." He rose from his bow and directed his gaze to Iris. "For what purpose has your party come to Alaster?"

"We have come to meet with the king," Iris answered and held out the scroll from Saunskirt.

Flyn motioned to one of the soldiers, who stepped forward and retrieved the scroll from Iris. Flyn took it, unbound the leather tie around it, and unrolled it just enough to inspect the seal at the bottom. He took his time reviewing it, angling it in the light in different ways, bringing it close to his eyes and then holding it back again. Finally, he seemed satisfied with its authenticity and raised his eyes back to Iris and nodded.

"Very well." As he spoke, the soldiers moved forward and unstrapped each of them. "You will be escorted immediately to the palace by carriage."

The five guards proceeded to stand around Iris and the others as they got into position. The soldiers then moved to guide them from the transport and to the carriage. This time, Iris felt a little surer of herself as she had a better idea of what to expect. Even so, upon exiting the transport, no manner of description could have prepared her for the awe-inspiring sight before her. To put it simply, Alaster was *massive!* Yet even that word didn't capture its amazing ornateness. The transport station consisted of a consecutive series of enormous pointed stone arches that stood over the road that the transports passed through and were a good twenty feet higher than the transports themselves. A platform sat level to the transport door and ran the length of the station. As the group walked past the arches, they came to a gigantic gate, one of the four entrances through the wall that encompassed all of Alaster. Each gate was placed at one of the cardinal directions.

Do not gawk! Do not gawk! Do not gawk! In vain, Iris commanded herself to act calmly as they approached the gate. The gate stood three stories tall while the wall was about six stories. The wall was made entirely of white stone but was smoothed perfectly down so that no one could ever hope to scale it. At the sight of such a massive defensive structure, Iris almost felt silly coming all this way to warn them. Maybe it *was* unnecessary, but she was here now, so she might as well report what had happened to Throansburrough and Jaralynx. Despite the size of Alaster, she couldn't help but feel within her heart that she needed to be here. She didn't know if her words could make any difference, but really, what else did she have to do?

"Open the gate! Diviners coming through!" the soldier at the front called out as they stood before the doors.

A series of shouts echoed the command to "Open the gate!" The cries were followed by the slow creaking of chains and pulley systems being moved as the doors inched their way open. Iris swallowed nervously as she took in the sight. She couldn't help but allow a small "wow" to escape through her lips as the entire land of Alaster appeared before her. A wide stone road stretched out before them. Lining the road were large stone buildings, white like the wall and just as smooth. They ran for miles and were placed together closely. The city was a flurry of activity. People ran to and from buildings, walked along the road, or simply sat upon a doorstep, conversing with other citizens. The stone road held a large variety of carriages, wagons, and sometimes people just riding the horse itself. It was sparkling clean and full of color. People wore many different types of clothes with such an array that it was next to impossible to stand out. That is unless they were dressed dully. Iris couldn't even dare to try and take it all in as there was just so much to see.

They promptly moved forward and to the side where a silver uncovered carriage awaited them. Two large black stallions danced their hooves upon the ground, anxious to be on their way. The three Diviners stepped upon the carriage first. Iris took the hand one of the soldiers gave her and followed. As soon as they were seated, the man driving the carriage slapped the reins on the horses so that they were quickly on their way. As they pulled out on the road, all other vehicles and people moved aside, allowing them to proceed rapidly down the middle. As they flew by, all other carriages were either brown or black and were enclosed. Theirs was the only silver ride and the only one with two black stallions leading the way. As the wind whipped around them, Iris was thankful that she had tied her hair back. She couldn't imagine how badly knotted it would have been. Still, the refreshing wind on her face also carried different, lovely aromas from the shops along the street. Even if a smell wasn't pleasant, they soon passed it so that it no longer plagued them. The sight of the palace ahead of them in the distance took Iris's breath away. She had never seen anything so spectacular!

The monumental palace stood out even more as it was placed high atop a large hill so that it overlooked the rest of the land. Unlike all the other buildings, the palace was made from some sort of glistening silver material with golden accents throughout. It shone brilliantly in the sun and was accentuated by the contrasting expanse of lush green vegetation with a few trees surrounding it. It was some of the best-looking vegetation she had seen in months. No other buildings were erected around the bottom of the hill by the palace for at least a couple of miles. The trees and the grass were faded green from going too long without water, but the land looked so much healthier than anywhere else they had been. *Could they somehow water parts of it? But with such a huge area, that would be impossible! Unless they depleted their own water supply, which would just be stupid.* Iris shrugged slightly, realizing that she would probably never understand and let it go. Instead, she continued to study the surroundings.

The only road that led up to this grand palace was the one they were currently racing down. Looking at all these things—the grandeur of the palace and the awe-inspiring greatness of the land—Iris became more aware of her own insignificance. *It was ridiculous to come here.* There was no way any enemy could ever dream of destroying Alaster. Sure, they wiped out Throansburrough and Jaralynx in a matter of days, but Valomeer was right: those towns weren't used to war. Of course, they were decimated. She wanted to turn back, to tap their driver on the shoulder and tell him never mind. It was too late now. Her stomach twisted tightly into a number of knots; she knew she was going to be sick. Iris shot a look at Darren. Why had he been so panicked when she first told him all this? He should have known that Alaster would be fine in any kind of an attack. If she were him and had someone tell her that Alaster was in danger, she would have outright laughed at them.

So why did he react as he did? And why was he still concerned? He had to know something, something important. Something that made him fear for his family. What was he not telling her *now*? Didn't she make it clear to him that he needed to tell her any helpful information immediately? Was he *trying* to make things difficult for her? Or maybe, maybe Darren was just the kind of guy to overreact. Maybe he hadn't been here in so long that he had forgotten what it was really like. No, that couldn't be it, because how could *anyone* forget a sight such as this? It was far too spectacular to behold. What did it matter now if he was hiding something else from her? Not like she could do anything about it now. She wouldn't have enough time to ask Darren about it, much less be able to do so freely without blowing their cover.

Their cover . . . she would have to deal with that too. She would have to tell the king sooner or later that they weren't actually a Diviner's party. She prayed that he wouldn't be furious at their deceit. Should she give up Darren and the others or not? Sure, the scroll she had in her hands stated that they should all be allowed to approach King Zaerin freely and tell him all they had to say, but the scroll didn't ensure their safety after they had delivered their message. For all she knew, King Zaerin might order the guards to throw Darren, Bryant, and Kyle into jail as soon as they completed their tasks. Yet if she didn't tell King Zaerin who was hidden underneath those Diviner's cowls and why they remained hidden, he would surely become suspicious. She could always tell him that they dressed as such to make sure to arrive as speedily as possible. That was somewhat plausible. But would he believe it? He *was* the leader of all Fitsengea, after all. If he couldn't see through such a thinly veiled lie as that, then she didn't see how he had lasted this long. She wished she knew what to do or had some idea what she should say! She felt so lost. Her heart pounded with worry.

Iris threw her eyes up to the sky, not wanting to look at the palace in the distance any longer. The sun was beating down today. If it hadn't been for the breeze from their carriage ride, she would have been sweating miserably. But at the same time, the sky *was* a brilliant blue with not a cloud in sight as far as the eye could see. The peacefulness of the scene calmed her heart momentarily. Iris closed her eyes and soaked in the combination of the sun's warmth and the wind upon her face. She had to relax. If she didn't calm down just a little, she couldn't present herself as confident or coherent, two traits she needed to display above all else right now. Iris forced herself to inhale deeply and then slowly release her breath. She opened her eyes again and glanced around at the others. She couldn't tell if they were sleeping or awake. They all sat so stiffly, and she couldn't really see their eyes due to their outfits, which was frustrating. It was impossible to read what they were thinking because there was no way to see their facial expressions. Maybe that was why they dressed that way in the first place.

As she looked up, they finally reached the foot of the hill. It was only a matter of time before they were at the front doors. Fear and worry—the same emotions she felt the minute she stepped off the transport—overwhelmed her with renewed fervor. Iris bit her bottom lip as each movement drew them closer and closer to that palace. It seemed to take an eternity to reach, but at the same time, it was happening all too quickly. Iris longed for a hand to hold, the reassuring touch of someone she loved. Never before had she done something so big without her family to back her up. Of course, her family hadn't always been there physically when she faced such challenges, but they had given her some sort of a pep talk beforehand, and she could count on them to pray for her the whole time. She no longer had the one thing that had given her such confidence. She couldn't do this without them. *But I have to. I have to do this* for *them!*

Oh, how she longed that her father were still alive! He always had the answers for these things. He was her spiritual advisor, the man who knew the Sacred Texts from front to back. He could make sense of anything. He explained things in a way that made them clear and just made life right. He had a way of helping her find the answer within herself. He encouraged her like no one else could. She was lost without him.

She had always known that she relied heavily on her family for support, but she didn't realize to what extent until now. How could she stand on her own without them? Could she stand without them? *Stop it! Stop thinking like that. Stop thinking about it at all! The last thing you want is to be caught crying right now.* Iris's gaze dropped to her hands in her lap as her focus blurred in and out of consciousness. Her thoughts were swallowed up by the wind rushing around the carriage and those within.

The carriage slowed down, forcing Iris to look up again. They had reached the palace gate, which was almost as large as the doors they had initially come through. The driver pulled the horses to a complete stop a few feet from the metal structure. The gate was made of heavy wood with a strong metal grate in front of it and seemed impenetrable.

"Who goes there?" a shout called down from the other side.

"Diviner's party to see the king!" their driver bellowed back.

"Identify yourself."

"Marcos Flent, soldier of the third regiment, West Gate."

"Open the gate!" the voice ordered after a moment's hesitation.

At the directive, the metal grate in front of the wood rose slowly, the wood door soon following suit. Once they were raised as far as possible, the driver spurred the horses onward. As they entered the official palace grounds, Iris's jaw dropped. Was there anything in Alaster that *wasn't* amazing? The horses pranced up a ways on the stone courtyard, directed easily through stone arches and past the connecting buildings. They came to a stop in front of the most central and largest building of the complex. Two soldiers stepped down from beside the front doors and opened the carriage door. They stood at attention at either side as the Diviners stepped off and then offered a hand to Iris to help her down. As soon as they exited, the driver flicked the reins to move the carriage onwards, leaving them behind. Kyle immediately directed the others into their positions around Iris and then marched forward. As they climbed the steps, the remaining two guards by the doors blocked them.

"Present your papers," one perfunctorily called out.

Kyle promptly stepped aside, and Iris moved forward to hand him the scroll as she had rehearsed while on the transport. The man took it, unrolled it, and read the whole document carefully. He paused to confirm the validity of Lord Valomeer's seal and raised his eyes to Iris, looked back at the scroll, and then back at Iris again. He nodded his head once, rolled up the scroll, and spoke at last.

"Follow me."

With that, the other soldier opened the door, allowing the soldier with the scroll to pass through first and then the Diviner's party before he closed the door again. Upon entering, Iris stifled a gasp at the stunning elegance of the entryway. The high, vaulted ceilings were covered with detailed paintings that depicted various scenes: from history, mythology, and even from the Sacred Texts. On the ground ran an enormous ornate carpet covered in designs of vibrant colors. The walls held a series of portraits of the past rulers; in between each one were built-in stone lights placed upon intricately formed bronze stands. The array of lights gave a beautiful glow to the room, which had no windows in the immediate entryway.

Iris wanted to laugh as this was only an entryway. She had seen entire homes that were smaller than this room! She didn't have much time to stare, though, for they were led rapidly forward through the next open doorway. This space was apparently a hallway to the king's throne room and was much brighter than the last room, for the walls were almost entirely made of stain glass. The colors that danced off them as the light poured through was almost too much for Iris's eyes to bear although it was beautiful, to be sure. The floor in this hallway was made of smooth tile that also captured the light and reflected it, adding to the intensity of the light. *I wonder if anyone has ever nicknamed this place the rainbow room?* Iris mused.

Kyle halted in place, bringing Iris to a stop as she focused on what was ahead. They now stood before the throne room. The only thing that separated them from the king were those solid wooden doors before them. Well, that and the two guards who stood at attention in front of it, but at the sight of their fellow soldier leading this group of strangers, they quickly moved aside. A nervous sweat broke across Iris's brow. She swallowed a couple of times as her throat grew dry. *You can do this. You can do this. Keep it together, now. You'll be okay. Just don't panic!* The doors were pulled open slowly for them. They stepped through them and stopped again as the soldier went forward a little ways, knelt on one knee, and bowed his head deeply. Iris still couldn't really see the king because Kyle stood directly in front of her, blocking her view. But that didn't bother her, and she honestly wished that they could stay standing like that.

"Your Majesty, I present to you a Diviner's Party sent by Lord Valomeer of Saunskirt." With that, he held out the scroll above his head and waited.

An attendant standing behind the king's throne quickly stepped down to retrieve the scroll. He then brought it back to hand to the king. All stood silent within this vast room as they waited for the king to review the scroll. Iris wondered if anyone else could hear her pounding heart.

"Messenger, come forward," came the deep regal voice. Iris supposed it was the king.

At that command, Kyle stepped aside once more, allowing Iris a full view of the king. He was terrifying to behold. Sunlight streamed through a skylight above directly upon him and the throne. The detail of his attire put even the Diviner's robes to shame. He had a thick and neatly trimmed beard with short hair slicked back from his face. Both his beard and hair were raven-black with distinct silver streaks throughout. Wrinkles crinkled at the corners of his eyes and permanently creased his brow, but they only furthered his distinguished appearance and fearsome gaze. Even from a distance, his piercing black eyes bore through Iris. They seemed to know everything and be surprised by nothing. His frown was permanently etched into his face and intensified by all the other features: the distinctive wrinkles, the strong eyes, the heavy, arched eyebrows, the dark hair. His wrinkles didn't soften his face like most other elderly people Iris knew, for his were not from years of smiling but were created by a face frozen in anger with a permanent scowl. Had he *ever* smiled before?

Iris walked forward to the spot where the soldier remained kneeling. She came to his side and bowed respectfully as well.

"Return to your post, soldier. And all other attendants leave the room. The Diviner's messenger and I have important matters to discuss."

Chapter Eighteen

Iris stayed kneeling with her head down. A number of different feet walked past her, through the front door, and out a servant exit she hadn't seen while coming in. Once the doors closed, she knew she was alone with the king. She wondered if he would let her get up any time soon, because according to the others, she couldn't move until the king said so.

"Messenger, stand before your King and speak the truth."

Iris rose slowly to her feet, her eyes meeting the king's. *The truth? Oh, Holy Father, help me!* "Your Majesty, we thank you for agreeing to meet with us today." Were her knees shaking? If so, she hoped he didn't notice "If I may be so bold, Your Highness, as to request the safety and protection of myself and these men once the message has been delivered?"

King Zaerin stared at her with unblinking eyes. Had she just offended him, or was he simply thinking over her request? She prayed that he believed that they were truly Diviners and that he would agree. Once she told him the truth and shared their true identities, he might throw them in jail. She hoped not. Maybe he would stay true to this sudden agreement and allow them to leave with ease. Otherwise she would be downright angry at going to prison to keep those guys out just so they'd be tossed into another. She would *not* appreciate the irony.

"Is there a reason that you will need protecting?"

"Yes." *If I tell you before you agree, then you'll throw us in jail right now!*

Zaerin raised an eyebrow at her as he realized she wasn't going to offer up the information. "Are you going to tell me why?"

"I see no reason to trouble Your Majesty with such details if you won't grant this request. That way, you won't be taking part in the situation against your will."

There is no way in all the lands that he'll buy that! Iris could tell just from his expression that she was doomed. King Zaerin remained silent for what seemed like hours. Eventually he leaned slightly forward in his throne and narrowed his eyes at Iris.

"You're not really a Diviner's messenger, are you?" His words were an observation rather than a question.

The color drained from Iris's face. Her knees began to collapse, but miraculously, she remained standing.

"Why have you lied to me?" he asked with cruel calmness.

Iris swallowed hard. She didn't think she could speak even if she wanted to.

"Are those even Diviners with whom you travel? Or is that another lie?"

Terror gripped her heart. *Say something! Say anything! Don't just stand there!*

"Why would the lord of Saunskirt aid in supporting such a treacherous act toward your king? Speak, girl! Your life depends upon it!"

"Your Majesty, please forgive us." Iris bowed her head. "We meant no ill will toward you. Our reasoning for undergoing such an act was simply to meet with you with the speed and ease that a Diviner's party is apt to receive. We felt that the message we had to deliver was one that could not be delayed any longer."

"Then if your only reason was to see me more quickly, why continue with this façade while in my presence?"

"Because she was hoping to avoid the difficulty of having to explain everything to you! But apparently you'd rather complicate matters as usual," Darren called out in exasperation as he stepped forward.

"Who dares speak to me in such a way! Show your face, you insolent—"

"Now, now Uncle. Is that any way to greet your nephew after five years?" Darren smirked as he pulled down the hood from his Diviner's cloak, unbuttoned the area around his face, and stepped up next to Iris.

"Darren?" King Zaerin exclaimed in shock.

Uncle? Nephew! Iris screeched internally and swiveled her head between the pair. Her eyes grew three sizes. *Darren's related to the king? Talk about leaving out important details! So that's the reason for hiding his last name! Darren Turner! Nephew to King Zaerin Turner! Why didn't I figure that out? But why should I have? Nobles are not the only ones to carry that last name. Though it isn't very common. It was just too impossible to assume! So does that make Darren a prince? I can't believe he didn't tell me! Good grief, they even look alike! Was anything he told me before true?*

A crafty smile slowly spread itself across King Zaerin's face. "Darren, so you've returned. Then am I to assume that those other two back there are your old partners? Remove your disguises, boys; there's no use continuing with them now."

Kyle and Bryant took down their hoods and then bowed deeply to the king.

"Ah, yes, the infamous Kyle and that scourge of the night, Bryant. Where is the rest of your crew? Hiding within the city somewhere?"

"No, Your Majesty." Kyle responded with his head still bowed. "They did not travel with us."

"Hmmph, like I would take your word on anything." He snorted and then turned his attention back to Iris. "It seems that the only person I don't know here is the one who first spoke to me. Tell me, girl, what is your name, and how are you associated with such a vile bunch?"

Iris's head was still spinning from Darren's revelation. Had she really just spent nearly an entire week with royalty? Or was it a royal outcast? She was so confused! But she couldn't focus on that right now. She had to respond to the king even though all she wanted to do was just sit down for a minute.

"My name is Iris Straton, Your Majesty. These men are serving as my escorts to Alaster. We have come to tell you of an attack brought against your kingdom."

King Zaerin sat up straight at the last part of Iris's explanation. "An attack? Where? How long ago? By whom?"

"First, promise our protection, Uncle." Darren cut in coolly.

"Darren!" Iris whispered harshly to him. Was he insane to demand something from the king? Okay, so they were related, but still! That didn't give him free reign to speak however he pleased. *That's it. I'm done for. They'll take us away and chop off our heads!*

"You have three days of safety only. If any of you remain even a second longer than the allotted time, you forfeit your freedom, and my men will take you in. And to make sure you don't cause any problems within those three days, you will be accompanied by my best men every moment you remain within the walls of Alaster."

"Agreed." Darren nodded curtly.

Wait, what? He agreed; the king agreed? Did I just miss something here?

"Now, Miss Straton, deliver your message to me immediately."

"Yes, Your Majesty." *Holy Father, help me!* Iris took a shaky breath and began. "The enemy is unknown to me simply because I do not know how to distinguish such things. But I have witnessed their attack in Throansburrough where I lived. They came at the darkest point of the night. No one even heard their arrival until several explosions rang through the air. Our village was quickly engulfed in flames. As we focused on putting the fires out"—her throat constricted as the images bombarded her memory—"the soldiers were suddenly upon us. We didn't even see where or how. They quickly . . . s–slit the throats of those next to them and fired guns at those who tried to stop them. My family and I tried to run . . . everyone did. Our village guard assembled as quickly as possible to defeat them, but they were slaughtered in a m—matter of minutes . . ." Iris stopped speaking for a minute to collect herself again.

Her voice was quaking, and her vision was blurring. "Forgive me . . ." she apologized softly to the king. She bit her lower lip and forced herself to take another deep breath. After exhaling and wiping away her tears, she managed to continue with her speech.

"Once the guard was defeated and the head of our village murdered, these soldiers captured everyone in town." An involuntary shudder rippled through Iris. "People tried to hide but were quickly found. Those who escaped or who were left alive from the initial fight were taken to be . . . executed, separating men from women and the children from all . . ." Lori and Jacob's faces flashed before her, as a sob wrestled itself from her throat. Iris clamped her mouth shut. *Keep it together!* Clenching her hands into fists, she continued. "I escaped by running into the center of the fire, hiding in our house of worship. I hid all night. But when I came out the next day, they were all gone. Nothing was left standing . . ."

Iris's voice cracked with emotion as she trailed off yet again. She closed her eyes tightly, her face contorting with almost tangible pain. She opened her eyes again and forced herself to speak. "I am the only one who managed to escape alive, the sole survivor of Throansbur-rough. This enemy left no bodies in their wake, not even in Jaralynx, the next town to undergo the same horror as my own. We . . . didn't make it in time to warn them."

"We?" the king interjected with rapt attention.

"Darren and I. That was when we met each other."

"I see. And I'm assuming that from there, you went to Saunskirt and interacted with Lord Valomeer?"

"Yes, Your Majesty."

"Your desire for urgency was well-placed. I understand why Valomeer felt your ruse necessary. Sightings of my nephew and those other two creatures would have delayed you greatly."

"Y—yes, Your Majesty."

"And your tears speak the truth of your sorrow. Your report seems genuine."

Iris lifted a trembling hand and wiped away the streaks on her face.

"You really feel that this enemy is a threat, do you?" The king studied her intently.

"Well I did—do . . . at least for the smaller, less fortified towns along the east of the central road. That seems to be the path their destruction follows, but . . . now that I'm here in Alaster, I think . . . my fears have been misplaced. I beg your forgiveness if we have only wasted your time, Your Highness. But I knew that I at least needed to tell you of Throansburrough's and Jaralynx's fate."

"Your fears have not been misplaced, my lady. You are right in observing the greatness of Alaster, but there is still much you do not know."

Iris caught Darren nodding slightly out of the corner of her eye. How could that be? What was this flaw in Alaster's defense that made it vulnerable? King Zaerin was actually concerned about all this. And so was Darren. She was so confused! How could Alaster be threatened by *anyone*? Were they simply humoring her? No, they were truly worried. Something more was going on here, and she didn't like being left in the dark. Iris's gaze flitted between the king and Darren. Both seemed lost in thought. What was she supposed to do now? She had said her piece and had nothing left to discuss. She lifted her left hand to push back a strand of hair that had worked its way out of its tie. As her left arm dropped to her side, the king's eyes followed it.

"Our time is indeed limited." He spoke more to himself than to anyone else.

He then rose from his throne, walked to the side, and pulled a cord hanging from the ceiling that Iris hadn't even noticed until the king grabbed it. As soon as he let go, the main doors opened, and in stepped two guards.

"Take those two men"—Zaerin pointed to Kyle and Bryant—"to the guest quarters in the east hall. Give them a change of clothes and then guide them off palace grounds. They are to be watched at all times, two men for each one. They are to be protected from any harm for seventy-two hours from this hour. But after that, they *must* leave Alaster."

The guards saluted their king and then stepped beside Kyle and Bryant to lead them out. Iris watched as they left. Her attention was then drawn to the side of the room as a smaller servant's door was opened and one of the attendants from before came through. He stepped to the bottom of the throne's stage and bowed before the king, waiting attentively for his instructions.

"Gather the generals and captains in the Strategy Room and escort the lady there as well," Zaerin ordered and then addressed Iris directly. "When all those men are gathered, I want you to tell them exactly what you told me. Answer any and all questions they have for you. It is imperative that you do not withhold any details from them."

Iris nodded to the king while the servant stood once more, walked to her side, and led her from the throne room. As they were leaving, King Zaerin gave one more order to another servant.

"Make sure no one disturbs us. I and my nephew have much to discuss."

Chapter Nineteen

"So," Zaerin started, the first to break the silence. "It takes an act of war to get you to come back home."

"An act of war . . . then I was right?"

"As far as what your lady friend told me, it seems so, but only the generals will know for sure."

"Do you really have to put her through such severe questioning? I mean, we *just* got here."

"If it is who we think it is, then every second will count."

Darren sighed, dropping his head a little. "You're right."

Zaerin took a couple of steps off the throne's stage and walked over to Darren. "Tell me, boy. Are you still running along the dark path?"

"The dark path?" Darren chuckled bitterly. "Sounds like someone has been spending too much time with the Minister Teason."

Zaerin harshly grabbed Darren's shoulder, forcing Darren to look him directly in the eye. "This is no laughing matter! Tell me, are you or are you not still running with that scoundrel, Kyle?"

Darren jerked his shoulder out from under his uncle's grip. "And what if I was? Would you try to kill me again? No, I don't work with Kyle anymore! We split ways the day of the trial."

Zaerin stared Darren in the eyes for a few moments before responding. "You don't believe in the Holy Father anymore, do you?" Instead of compassion or concern, annoyance shone in Zaerin's eyes

"Do you?" Darren couldn't help but retort accusingly.

"How *dare* you question my faith!"

"Because you don't follow even the most basic of its teachings!"

"You have been absent for five years, boy. You know nothing of what I follow! I am the leader of all Alaster, of all Fitsengea! *I* am the religious guide of the people!"

"And yet you take council from Diviners? Isn't that forbidden in the Sacred Texts? 'Listen not to fortune tellers or psychics, for their ways lead to dissension and destruction!'"

"You have the gall to lecture me through Sacred Texts? You don't even believe! You have no right to utter those phrases with your unclean tongue!"

"Bet you still don't let the common people read the texts for themselves."

"Many of the common people, as you call them, are without an education. They don't know *how* to read! Minister Teason reads a passage out of the Sacred Texts every week!"

"Then why don't you educate the people!"

"Education is available to them *if* they want it! I can't *force* the people to learn. My stars, Darren! You're as frustrating as my brother! Did you really come all this way just to have it out with your uncle?"

Darren let out a sigh to calm his nerves. "You're right. We shouldn't be doing this now. So . . . how *is* my father?"

Zaerin shrugged. "We haven't really seen much of each other since you left."

"Have they been allowed to live within the borders again?"

Zaerin was quiet for a minute, crossing his arms behind his back as he was apt to do when discussing touchy matters. "When my father, Holy Father rest his soul, ordered that my little brother and his family be banished to live beyond the walls of Alaster, I never understood why. It took years for me to convince the officials to allow his children to even pass through." He paced as he continued. "Darren, you know that you were the first child they allowed to visit my palace. It was a privilege, a huge step toward letting you all back in."

"And now, since the trial, life has gone back to how it was before?" Darren filled in.

"Worse. They live within the walls now but are kept under constant surveillance and can only go place to place with a soldier's escort."

"But you're the king! Can't you force them to let my family be? What I did has to do with *me* not them!" Darren cried out passionately, taking a few steps toward Zaerin.

"I don't have as much power as you'd like to think, Darren. It took all I had to just make sure you and your friends wouldn't be sentenced to death!"

A new wave of guilt flooded Darren's heart. He really had destroyed the lives of everyone he cared about. He lifted his eyes to his uncle as a surge of anger rushed through him. All of this could have been prevented! Why had his uncle been so stubborn? Why wouldn't he believe his warning? He only cared about what Minister Teason—that cruel, wicked man who was a master at twisting words—had to say.

"You could have done more," Darren muttered under his breath.

"You may see them if you like," Zaerin continued, not hearing Darren's statement.

Darren nodded thoughtfully. "I would like to see them again. Do you think you could allow me a change of clothes before I go?"

"Certainly." Zaerin walked back over to his throne, stepped up on it, and pulled the cord that summoned the servants.

Within moments, a young girl entered through the servant's door. She quickly came before the king and bowed.

"Take my nephew to his old quarters and fetch him a change of clothes."

The girl rose from her position and walked over to Darren.

"Oh, and Darren," Zaerin called out as Darren was leaving. "Don't be too long; your presence will be needed once your lady friend has finished conversing with my people. And make sure to not mention any of this to your family."

Darren nodded stiffly and exited the throne room. The thought of facing Iris later unnerved him. The look on her face when he gave himself away verified his suspicion that she never grasped the weight of his full name. *That will not be a pleasant conversation.* That is, if she would even speak to him again. He followed the young woman down a different hall than they had first entered. She walked briskly and remained silent. Uncle Zaerin knew that Darren still knew the way to his old room. Darren knew the layout of the entire castle. He had spent so much time exploring the place that he didn't think he could forget it. Darren knew that this so-called guide to his room was more his watch dog than anything.

Might as well go along and hope that it will make things run more smoothly. As they continued walking, Darren wondered what Bryant and Kyle were up to. What exactly would they do for the next three days? He knew it wouldn't be difficult for them to lose their guards, but they couldn't hide forever. So it was either skip out and cause more trouble for themselves later or do as they were told and try to fix old problems with new, better actions. He doubted it would be the second one. At least he could try and repair his name. It wasn't up to him to look after the others. If they caused any trouble, they could get out of it on their own. It would probably be best for him to stay as far away from them as possible anyway. That way, *when* they got in trouble, he couldn't be blamed for or associated with it.

"If you could please wait here, your Grace, and I will go fetch a tailor for you." The woman spoke at last as she moved aside to allow Darren to enter the room where they had stopped.

"Thank you." Darren smiled at her before entering.

The girl gave a deep curtsey and then took her leave. *Heh, sure has been a while since someone called me "your Grace."* Darren laughed to himself. It felt odd hearing that again. It was weird being here. He never thought he would be back. Looking around the room he could see they never thought he would return, either. Dust encased everything, and cobwebs abounded. To the far side, sat his bed, which was still too big for him. As a child he had thought it would swallow him up. He made his way across the room to inspect it further. It had been stripped of all the covers, which were probably packed away. Darren turned to study the rest of the space.

Five years . . . it's been five years since anyone has lived here. Not even the staff has entered this place to clean. I wonder if the fireplace is still usable? I'll bet it didn't take long for them to remove all the valuables in here and give them to those they deemed more "trustworthy." Darren knelt down at the trunk at the foot of his old bed and checked. It opened up right away, though it was empty, save for a small old rusty chisel. *Why was a small chisel in his old trunk? Oh, that's right—now he remembered!* Darren reached inside and pulled it out, leaving its dust outline behind. Rising from his knees, he walked over to the fireplace.

Now where was it again? Was it the third stone to the left, the fourth? Or was it to the right? Darren looked at the square stone pieces that made up the floor in front of the fireplace. He stretched out his foot and tapped the stones with the toe of his shoe, feeling around for that one slightly loose stone. After a few moments, he found one that shifted slightly under pressure. Darren stooped down, took out the chisel, and pried up the stone slab.

He took a few minutes to set it free, but it eventually popped up under his persistence. Sticking his fingers in between the space he created, Darren lifted the stone from its place and set it aside. He smiled at the sight of the little box underneath, still in place in its hole. Darren put his hand inside and pulled it out. It was just slightly smaller than his hand. Slowly he lifted the lid off the wooden box. Inside all the letters were still intact. As Darren pulled them out, the glint of metal beneath them caught his eye. His heart skipped a beat as he pushed aside the papers and retrieved a small silver locket. As he held it up, the stone lights in the room reflected across the surface. How could he have forgotten about this?

Darren stood once again and pushed the stone slab back into place with his foot. He took the chisel with his right hand and placed it back into the trunk, fitting it to its dusty outline. After closing the trunk once again, he placed the letters and the locket back inside the small wooden box. Darren unbuttoned his Diviner's cloak a little and hid the box and all its contents in one of the secret pockets. Just in time, too, for as he turned around, the royal tailor entered through the open door. Maybe it was childish of him to still keep his little box, one of the few childhood memories he actually enjoyed, a secret. But he would continue to do so, nonetheless. He would hold onto it for as long as possible.

The tailor walked up to Darren and bowed deeply. He held some of Darren's old clothes from five years before. He had to admit he was more than a little surprised that they had kept any of his old things.

"If your Grace would not mind, I need to take some measurements to see if they need any alterations."

"Very well." Darren nodded.

He then unbuttoned the Diviner's cloak the rest of the way and took it off. Underneath the cloak, he wore the pants and shirt, which served as the undergarments for the uniform. Darren set the cloak atop his old dusty bed and then stood in front of the tailor, his legs spread slightly apart and his arms held straight out beside him. The tailor pulled out a string used for measuring and compared the length of Darren's arms and legs with the original lengths of those on the clothes. The tailor quickly finished his measurements and completed his alterations a few minutes later. *Physically I haven't changed much in the past five years.* Darren shrugged to himself.

Once the tailor's task was complete, he left the clothes with Darren and went on his way. At first, he had tried to dress Darren himself as part of his customary duties as the royal tailor. But with a little effort, Darren convinced him otherwise. He had never been one for letting others dress him, even during his younger days in the palace. It just felt strange to him. No, he'd rather pull his own shirt over his head and draw his own pants around his waist. Darren grabbed the vest that lay to the side and checked it for an inner pocket. When he found it, he took his box from the Diviner's robe and tucked it inside. He then put the vest over his tunic and pulled on his shoes. Once he left this room, his Diviner's clothing would be confiscated. After he dressed, Darren walked toward the door. When he opened it, he was slightly taken aback to see two soldiers standing at either side of the doorway.

"Can I help you?" Darren asked, already knowing the answer.

The soldier to the left turned to address him. "We are your escorts throughout Alaster."

Well, that was fast, didn't take them long to get here. "Alright, then. If you gentlemen could guide me to the household of the Duke Turner, we can be on our way."

"Certainly, your Grace."

Darren exited his old room and followed the soldier who first spoke to him while the other soldier took up the rear. They walked briskly down the halls and made their way back outside. In front, three horses were saddled up to take them back into town. Coming down the steps, Darren glimpsed Kyle and Bryant who were also leaving the grounds, each with two guards following closely behind them. He couldn't help but wonder where they were going and what they planned to do. He didn't waste much energy pondering it. Instead, he focused on keeping his horse in step with the soldier he followed. A ways down the road, he glanced back at the palace. He really *was* back here. It all kind of seemed surreal. He thought about Iris inside, talking with some of the most powerful people in all Alaster. Even he would have been nervous at that. Well, maybe not as much as she was, considering he had grown up with most of those men. But now that he was considered a criminal, he might have had just as much difficulty if he were in Iris's place.

Criminal . . . That's right, in the eyes of every single person here, I am a criminal. Uncle Zaerin never took away my family title, but to most, I'm no longer worthy of my nobility. Will my family even accept me? If they hated me, I couldn't blame them. After all, I did single-handedly destroy any chance of reintroducing them into full royal status. The idea that his father would refuse him entrance into his household made Darren sick to his stomach. His mother and father had always expressed their love for him, told him nothing could change that. Yet it was possible that he had finally found the one thing that would push them away forever. *Dad couldn't even look at me after the trial, even without hearing the details of Marriam's death.*

Darren glanced at the sun. From its position, it was just about eleven now. Interestingly, in his self-enforced exile, he had learned many useful little tricks. He used to be entirely dependent on his old pocket watch for the time. Now he could guess it by just the feel of the day; he could call it precisely by studying the sun's position.

They had ridden hard and were approaching the town now. Instead of heading back toward the buildings near the West Gate, Darren followed the soldier as he led him to the smaller homes by the North Gate. Right before they entered that section of the city, some daffodils were growing wildly a ways from the road.

"Hold up a minute!" Darren called out to his escort in front and warned the one behind.

Both soldiers reined in their horses and came to a stop along with Darren. Darren pulled his horse off the road a bit before dismounting. He handed the reigns to the guards and walked over to a patch of wild daffodils. He then proceeded to bend down and pick out the best ones. Using a piece of string from his tunic, he bound his little bouquet together. After retrieving the flowers, Darren returned to his horse and continued on his way.

Weaving down different streets, they went into progressively poorer areas of Alaster. Eventually, they came to a stop in front of a small two-story house of medium size. Though the buildings around it were in disarray, this home had owners who clearly did the best they could to take care of what they had. A small yard encircled it, affording some breathing room from the surrounding structures. *Well, at least it's better than what we lived in outside the city walls.* Darren dismounted from his horse once again and stopped to make a request.

"Please, gentlemen, if you could? I need to do this alone."

The men paused and looked at each other as if deciding whether to leave him unguarded.

"Look, I'm not going to try and make a run for it. If it makes you feel better, you can come in after me in thirty minutes if you don't hear from me."

They looked back and forth between Darren and each other before finalizing their decision. Eventually one spoke up. "If you do not show yourself every fifteen minutes, then we're coming in."

Darren nodded seriously. "Thank you."

Well, here goes . . . He took a deep breath then went forward through the knee-high fence that surrounded the home. He followed the circular stones that made up the short path up to the doorstep. Darren stopped directly in front of the door. Happy voices told of residents inside. He stood there for a moment, working up the nerve to actually knock. His hand hovered in the air for a few seconds before he rapped hard three times against the wood. Dropping his hand to his side, he strained his ears to figure out who would answer. The pattering of little feet grew louder as they came running up to the door, then stopped. The handle slowly turned.

Chapter Twenty

The wood creaked as the door pulled back, and two little blue eyes peeked out. The eyes grew two sizes at the sight of the bouquet in Darren's left hand. The child threw open the door the rest of the way to reveal a little blonde-headed girl who couldn't have been much more than four. She stood there for a second, eyes riveted on the daffodils, unmoving. With a friendly smile, Darren waved his right hand.

"Do you like these?" he asked, indicating the flowers. The girl nodded enthusiastically. "They're called daffodils. Here, you can smell them if you'd like."

She squealed in excitement, rushed forward, grabbed the flowers, and then ran back inside, leaving the door wide open behind her. Darren stood dumbfounded, not exactly sure what to do next. He just stared ahead and contemplated taking a step into the house and announcing his presence. He waited, though, as some of the voices floated toward him, discussing the little girl's find.

"What the—? Where did you get those?" The woman's voice paused for the hushed answer from the little girl. "You did what? Now what have we told you about that? You should know better! Go apologize at once, missy!" The girl's little feet ran away. "Oh, I don't think so! You are in so much trouble now! Get back here, this instant!"

"Is anyone going to talk to that guy at the door?" The frustrated cry came from somewhere else inside.

"I'm on it!" responded a young man who came loping up to the door to greet Darren. "Heh, sorry about that mister. My niece can be a little—"

Darren raised a hand to stop him and smiled, not wanting to get the girl in any more trouble. "No, no, it's quite alright. Um, just to be certain though, this *is* the Duke Turner's home right?"

The young man nodded. "Yes, sir, it is. What can we do for you?" As he spoke, he stepped farther outside, leaning slightly against the door.

"Well, I was—"

"Trevor, for Pete's sake, invite the poor man in already!" a familiar voice called from another room.

"Just give me a second, Liesel!" he called back to her and then added an exasperated "geez" under his breath. "Sorry again, sir. What were you saying, now?"

Darren's heart beat heavily in his chest. Could it be? Could this *really* be his little brother?! He looked so old! Well not old exactly, but older. But why wouldn't he? He *was* only fifteen when Darren had left. That would make him . . . *twenty* now. He really had filled out. And . . . *Liesel?* Liesel was here. Darren had to force himself to swallow hard a few times before he could start speaking again.

"T–Trevor? Are you really Trevor Turner?"

Trevor squinted into the setting sun behind Darren before responding, "Um, yeah? Do you know me or something?" He raised a hand to his eyes to block out the glare of the sun behind Darren's head so that he could get a better look at his face. "Wait . . . you look . . . familiar."

Darren couldn't suppress his grin. "Trevor! It's me! Your big brother! It's Darren!"

Trevor flinched, his jaw dropping involuntarily. "Darren . . ." A dark shadow quickly passed across his face turning him rigid as he frowned. "You're not welcome here." His voice dripped with bitterness as he went back inside, closing the door.

"No, Trevor! Wait—" Darren was cut off as the door slammed shut in his face.

Darren stood frozen for a few seconds, shocked at the anger and resentment in his little brother's voice. That couldn't *really* have been Trevor, could it? Darren's shoulders sagged from the weight that burdened his heart. If that had been Trevor's reaction to his return, there really was no point to going any further. Darren ran his hand through his hair and then let it drop to the side. *Not welcome . . .* He sighed and turned around. *Guess I'll just go back to Uncle's then. No point in hanging around here.* He made his way back through the front yard and was just passing through the gate when the door opened behind him.

"Darren!" He stopped in his tracks at the woman's desperate cry.

Darren turned halfway around to see a woman nearing sixty, her hair pulled back in a bun and standing a head shorter than him. His mother stood on the front step. Tears streamed down her face as her fists tightly clenched the skirt of her dress. Darren couldn't help but take a step toward her, unable to do anything but whisper. "Mom . . ."

"Darren!" She cried out as she sprinted to him. She threw her arms around him and hugged with all her might.

Darren hugged her back just as tightly, using all his restraint to keep from crying. His mother, on the other hand, made no effort to stop the follow of her tears.

"I knew it was you! When I saw Rachel pass by with those yellow daffodils, I just knew it had to be you!" She leaned her head back to look into Darren's eyes. Her arms shifted so that her hands could hold the sides of his face. "Yes, my baby always brings me my favorite flowers when he comes back home." She smiled through her tears, hands stroking his face and hair alternately. "Baby, my baby. You're home! You've come back to me! Oh Darren, I thought I'd never see you again." Her lips quivered with emotion.

Darren put his hands on top of hers, then pulled them to his mouth and kissed them. "Hi, Mom," he said with a smile.

A gasp behind them caught his attention. He looked up to see his sister Marguerite standing in the doorway with the young blonde girl at her side holding her hand.

"Darren?" she whispered.

Their mother turned at Marguerite's voice. "Oh, Marguerite, look! Darren's come home."

Darren lifted an arm to rub the back of his neck nervously, afraid of her reaction. He smiled tentatively. "Hey, Margie."

She raised a hand to her mouth, trying to collect herself as her eyes glistened. "You know I don't like being called that." She let out a short laugh intermixed with a sob.

"I know." Darren responded softly, his smile tentative.

Marguerite bit her bottom lip and held out her arms, beckoning to him, unable to speak. Darren walked past his mother, who let go of his hand reluctantly while stepping aside. He approached Marguerite, stopped a second, and then came into her hug. She rubbed her hands tenderly on his back and patted him a few times. Darren simply held onto her, his heart breaking from the stress and emotion of it all.

Eventually Marguerite pulled away from him. Still smiling, she rubbed her arms for a second and then turned to the child beside her. "Darren, there is someone I'd like you to meet." She jostled the girl forward a bit, who had suddenly turned incredibly shy. "Darren, this is your second niece, Rachel. Rachel, this man is your Uncle Darren. Say hi, sweetie."

Darren squatted down to eye level with Rachel. "Hi, Rachel. How are you?"

Rachel giggled up at him in turn and then rushed back behind her mommy's skirt, burying her face into it. Darren pushed against his legs to stand back up, realizing that he wouldn't be drawing Rachel out of her shell anytime soon. Marguerite smiled and rested her hand on Rachel's head.

"Don't worry, she'll come around."

"So how old is she?"

"She'll be four next week."

"Oh come on now," interjected their mother as she came up to Darren and linked her arm in his. "Let's all go inside to do our catching up. I have a fresh pitcher of lemonade just dying to be tasted."

Darren allowed himself to be led into the house, glancing behind him once at the guards sitting on their horses watching the scene attentively. *Fifteen minutes*, he reminded himself. Walking into the house, his mother directed him to a room off to the left, apparently their living room. The interior of the house wasn't lavish with only a few nice items, but it had been dutifully and proudly kept up. Darren sat down on the sofa with Marguerite sitting beside him. Rachel, anxious to go play, scampered off to another room in the house. His mother dashed off to the kitchen to bring back the drinks but not before asking Darren at least twenty times if he wanted something to eat. Darren did his best to assure her that he was fine. As they waited, he reached over and grabbed Marguerite's hand. It felt so wonderful to see his family again! Marguerite squeezed his hand in response, unable to keep herself from smiling.

"Oh!" Darren spoke up at last as a thought struck him. "Is Liesel here? I thought I heard Trevor talking to her earlier."

Marguerite's smile slowly faded away, but she still held his hand. "Darren . . . Liesel may not want to see you right away. She–she's still pretty upset."

Darren's happiness evaporated. "She's angry with me too?"

Marguerite gave him a questioning look. As understanding dawned, her eyes grew gentle. "Oh, you mean Trevor? He gave you a harsh greeting then? He's . . . angrier for Liesel's sake, more than anything."

"What do you mean?"

"You didn't hear?"

Darren gave her a look.

"Oh, right, dumb question. Sorry."

"So what happened?"

"Liesel's engagement was called off."

"What! Why?"

Marguerite sighed, hesitant to discuss the matter right then. "Steven did not want to be associated with a family name with such a dark mark on it as ours now has."

Fuming, Darren dropped Marguerite's hand and rested his chin on his clenched fists. "That little—"

"I think he was pressured to break it off from his own family. He seemed crushed when he delivered the news to Liesel."

Darren stood and walked to the other side of the room, much too upset to stay seated. "Could that coward not stand up to them!"

"That's easier said than done, Darren, especially in *that* family."

"That's a pathetic excuse!" Darren growled, spinning around. "Fine, then! If he doesn't have the nerve, then I'll talk to them myself! After all, I'm the one they have a problem with!"

"Darren," Marguerite called out calmly to stop him as he started to storm out. He turned. "You know she wouldn't want you to do that. Besides, if the guy really loved her, he wouldn't let something as dumb as this get in the way."

Darren walked back over to Marguerite and placed a hand on her shoulder. "Thanks, Margie."

She tilted her head to look up at him. "What for?"

"For trying to make me feel better, even when we both know . . . it's my fault that Liesel got her heart broken."

"Darren . . ."

"There we are!" came the triumphant call of their mother. "Lemonade for all, *and* I found the cookies that Jenny and I made yesterday evening. Well, what's left of them, anyhow. I hope they'll do." She beamed as she balanced the tray of drinks and food.

"Here, Mom, let me help with that," Darren offered, quickly stepping over to give her a hand.

She gladly passed off the tray to him and sat down in the middle of the sofa next to Marguerite. Darren placed it on the table, filled the glasses with lemonade, and passed them around. His mother then happily beckoned him to come and sit next to her. Darren obeyed after he had passed by the window to make sure that the guards saw that he was still present. His mother patted him on his leg a couple of times. She was so happy that she didn't know what to do with herself. All three of them sat silently, sipping their drinks. No one really knew where to begin, so an awkward silence settled around them. At last, Darren's mother decided to take charge and guide the conversation.

"Your father should be back from the market anytime now."

Darren played with the empty glass in his fingers. "That's great . . ."

"That's right," Marguerite added. "He went out with Kevin and Jenny so they'll be able to see you as well."

"How old is Jenny now?" Darren questioned.

"She turned ten just last month."

"Ten?" he spoke somewhat sadly. "I can't believe it." *Last time I saw Jenny, she was five. Now she's grown so much older, I doubt I'll even recognize her. She probably won't even remember me. Five years. I have to keep reminding myself that it's been five years.*

"Have you and Kevin had any other children aside from Jenny and Rachel?"

Marguerite shook her head. "No, just our two girls."

"Devon and his wife have a couple children of their own." His mother informed him.

"Really? That's great for him. He always loved kids. How many do they have now?"

"Eight."

Darren couldn't help himself but laugh. "Goodness, that's a big family."

"Only two more than us." Marguerite shrugged.

Darren kept chuckling. "I guess so, but I'm sure if anyone could handle them, it would be Devon."

His mother raised a finger. "And his wife, Lindsey. That woman is absolutely amazing."

Marguerite chuckled in agreement. "That she is."

"Oh, this is so wonderful, Darren!" His mother suddenly beamed. "Devon and his family will be coming for a visit at the end of next week. Mikkel too! Everyone will get to see you again!"

Darren shifted uncomfortably, placing his glass back on the table. "A–actually, Mom . . . I'm not going to be able to stay for long." The happiness crashed from her face. His stomach turned at her expression. "Believe me, I would be here longer if I could. But I was lucky to even get three days out of Uncle Zaerin—"

"Uncle Zaerin?" anger enveloped his mother's being. "You've met with *him* already?"

"Well, yeah. I had to. I wouldn't have even been allowed into Alaster unless I did."

"Why *did* he let you back in?" Marguerite asked curiously.

"I'm not really . . . allowed to tell you that."

"That sounds like Zaerin." His mother scowled.

She stiffly stood, picked up the empty glasses and put them on the tray with the now empty container of lemonade.

"Mom, why don't you just leave that for now?" Marguerite spoke gently.

"No, I'll get this now." She spoke harshly, though her anger wasn't directed toward Marguerite or at anyone in the room, for that matter.

She grabbed the tray and turned to leave for the kitchen. But before she could take a step, something behind them caught her attention. "Liesel, dear, I didn't even hear you come in. I thought you had decided to work in the garden out back."

Darren froze in place, staring straight ahead, afraid of what Liesel might do if he spoke to her. She was the one person in this whole family that he could not handle rejection from, his closest sibling. Though they were the same age, they were not twins and weren't even related by blood. Liesel had been adopted into their family when Darren was about two; her birth parents had died in a fire. She had been raised as if she were always meant to be a part of their family. Growing up, she had been his best friend. She understood him better than anyone else.

"Trevor told me that we had a visitor," Liesel explained dully. "I thought it would only be polite for me to at least make an appearance."

Darren forced himself to stand up and look at Liesel in the face. He had no idea what to say.

"Hello, Darren."

"Hey, Liesel."

Their words floated away in the air, leaving four people trapped in a sudden vacuum. Their mother cleared her throat at last to shatter the tension in the room.

"Well, I'm going to bring these back to the kitchen. Liesel, why don't you and Darren sit down and catch up for a bit? Marguerite, sweetie, could you give me a hand in the kitchen?"

"Mom I think—"

"Come along, now. I'm getting tired of holding this tray."

Marguerite reluctantly complied with an apologetic look toward Darren as she left. As she passed Liesel, she couldn't help but squeeze Liesel's shoulder tenderly, her way of conveying strength and kindness to her sister. When both Marguerite and his mother exited the room, Darren found himself just looking at his sister. What should he say? Should he offer her a seat? Should he try and approach her to convince her that all this wasn't his fault? But that would only work if he actually believed it himself. The only thing he could think of to do was to walk up to the window once again and show his escorts that he was still there.

"What are you doing?" Liesel spoke as if addressing a fool.

Darren dropped his hand from the wave and turned his attention back to his sister. "Just notifying my . . . escort that I haven't run off. I hear that soldiers follow you guys wherever you go as well."

Liesel shrugged and looked to the side.

"So . . . do you and Trevor live here with mom and dad, then? Or are you guys just visiting?"

"We have our own places."

"That's good." Darren looked up at his sister.

She hated him. Everything about her stance screamed how she wished he would disappear. Her arms were crossed tightly in front of her chest, her hands tucked into angry fists, her mouth in a firm down-turned line, and her eyes refused to meet his even once.

"Liesel. Do you really hate me?"

She didn't look at him, didn't even flinch.

Darren swallowed hard before continuing. "If so, then why did you want to see me? Why not just stay outside where you wouldn't be forced into this?"

Still nothing.

"If it's because you wanted to scream at me or something, then please go ahead. You know I've always preferred to get stuff between us out in the open." Darren paused and waited for an answer. When she still didn't respond, he sadly sighed and dropped his head a little while one hand tapped at his side. He crossed his arms and kept his gaze on the ground. "I only have about two more days until Uncle Zaerin kicks me out. I'll make sure to stay out of your way until then."

He reached into his vest pocket, pulled out the box from the castle, retrieved the silver locket, and then returned the box to his pocket. He moved to the table and set it down. "That's yours if you want it."

Liesel didn't even look up.

Darren ran his hand through his hair and walked past Liesel. "If mom comes looking, could you tell her I'm waiting for dad and the others out front?"

Darren took a few steps past Liesel but then stopped. Without turning around, he added one more thing. "I–I'm sorry I ruined your life, Liesel. The thought that I caused you such pain hurts me more than you'll ever know. I hope you'll find the happiness you deserve someday. I really do . . ." With that, he walked out of the house and sat down on the porch step.

Inside the house, Liesel stood still for a few seconds, then walked over to the table and picked up the locket. Opening it, she found the inscription inside. She couldn't help but read aloud the phrase they used to say as kids. The words Darren always told others so that she never felt like the odd one out in the family, words that showed their bond, words that made her feel accepted and loved.

"To my sister, Liesel, who's closer than blood."

Liesel grasped the locket as she sat down on the sofa and cried.

Chapter Twenty-One

"They're coming from the west! They must be attacking from Krine Island!" cried out General Kameron, a slender man of medium height in his mid-fifties. Sweat beaded on his wrinkled forehead, catching in his enormous bushy gray eyebrows.

"Impossible, the girl saw no tracks toward the east!" rebutted a taller thin man perhaps a few years the senior of the first. For a general, this man had a surprisingly scholarly build, as though he had spent a lot of time indoors.

"Well, they had to come from somewhere! They didn't just drop out of the sky!" General Kameron fired off in exasperation.

Iris sat at the long table, her chin resting on the surface. This heated discussion had been going on for hours. She had repeated different parts of her story at least twenty times. The arguing grew so intense at times that some of the men had to restrain the others from blows. The chaos unfolded before her. *This is ridiculous!* She sighed and folded her arms on the table around her head. If this was how Fitsengea's best generals normally went about preparing for war, it was a wonder they hadn't already been destroyed.

"Maybe they came from that continent above us, Sylphaen. That would explain the lack of tracks!" offered up a third general. Iris recalled his name was William. Of medium height and in his late fifties, he had neatly groomed white hair and a pointed beard. This man probably had more muscle mass than the first two generals combined.

"No, no! That makes no sense! Of all places, why would they target Throansburrough first? Why not one of our more important port cities?" Wiping the sweat from his gray eyebrows with one hand, General Kameron gestured to a map of Fitsengea spread out on the table with the other hand.

Throansburrough was important to me.

"Any word from Saunskirt? Have they seen the enemy coming?" questioned the youngest, shortest, and heaviest man of the group. General Franks was by no means a child, at least not in age. He was perhaps in his late forties though his tone and manner of presentation belied his importance as a general of Fitsengea.

"We need to study the warning we received three years ago!" the scholarly general offered.

"What about Saunskirt?" tried General Franks once more.

"That warning has nothing to do with this!" the robust General William challenged.

"Our duty should be to first set up a memorial for those lost in Throansburrough and Jaralynx!" The scholarly general spoke, shifting focus once more.

"Our first duty is to warn the people!" General Franks countered.

"No, we must first find the enemy and prepare for attack!" General Kameron protested.

Five generals and not a single shared opinion. I think they refuse to agree with each other solely on principle! Why am I still here? It's not as if they'd notice if I got up and walked out.

"Well, I say we wait for General Lance to return with the scrolls before we make any concrete decisions," The scholarly general finally said, seeming to give up on debating for the time being.

Oh great, they're adding another general to the batch. Geez, where are they all coming from?

"That boy is still wet behind the ears," complained General William.

"What does that have to do with anything, General William?"

Iris peeked up over her arms to see the same two generals at it again. They were the ones who almost had fist fight earlier. What was the other guy's name? He was one of the taller ones in the room. *General Allen, maybe? Yes, that's right, it was General Allen. And let's see, what are the other names? General Franks is the guy who keeps talking about Saunskirt. He seems oddly attached to the city, if you ask me. General Kameron is the one who doesn't think Throansburrough really mattered . . . jerk. And General Trent just kind of sits there and watches.*

"It has everything to do with everything! The boy is too green to take part in such a serious conference as this. He'll only slow us down with his inexperience!"

Ha! Like you're progressing so wonderfully right now!

"The boy will never gain experience unless he comes to one of these meetings, William," General Trent called out from the far side of the room.

"If you ask me, there's no reason for Alaster to have two generals anyway," General William growled.

"You're just sore that King Zaerin thought it necessary to divide up the control," General Trent responded dully.

"Well, how would *you* feel, Trent, if you suddenly had to split up *your* troops and now had to confer with another leader on every issue?"

"I'd be thrilled to have someone to share all the stress!" He laughed.

General William rolled his eyes. "I'm sure you would be."

You know, I think I liked it better when I had to put up with Kyle and Darren's squabbles. At least, then, there were only two of them, and they could still get stuff done despite their name calling. Everyone paused momentarily at a sudden rapping on the door to the strategy room. Curious as to who was calling, General Franks briskly walked over to the door and opened it. Four men entered, each with their arms full of books, charts, graphs, and scrolls. Three of the four quickly made their way over to the different generals. The fourth placed his materials on the table next to Iris. Intrigued, Iris sat up as her eyes roamed over all the papers.

"What took you so long, Lance?" William growled.

"*General* Lance," General Allen corrected.

And again, I say, too many generals! Iris half laughed, half sighed in her head.

"No, that's alright. I'm not one for formalities. Though I do believe introductions need to be made." Lance smiled and turned his eyes to Iris. Holding out his hand to her, he smiled broadly. "General Lance Richards, at your service. But please, call me Lance."

Charm and confidence exuded from his kind hazel eyes. Lance was a well formed man of thirty. He had a strong jaw and a thick head of slightly mussed chestnut brown hair. The beginning of a few wrinkles at the corners of his eyes strengthened his happy presence

Iris shook his hand and smiled back. "Iris Straton."

"It's a pleasure to meet you. Now I'm sure that these fine gentlemen have already introduced themselves, though I don't believe you've met the captains who came in with me." Lance turned to point each one out as he introduced them.

Lance had the odd ability of smoothing over the previous chaos just by simply being there. Something about his presence—maybe his warm smile—relaxed everyone.

"The man standing next to General Kameron is Captain Blake. Next, with General Allen, is Captain Peter. And then Captain Michael, who is under General Franks. General Trent's captain is currently on duty back up north in Tha'neos and couldn't make it to the yearly council."

"Nice to meet you all." Iris smiled and nodded at each one in turn.

So that's *why they were all able to get here so quickly. They were already in the midst of one of their yearly gatherings. I remember hearing about those before. But if all of the heads were supposed to come together then why . . .*

"Ummm, pardon me, but why isn't the general of Saunskirt here as well?"

Lance shrugged. "Apparently he had more pressing orders from Lord Valomeer to deal with first."

"In other words, he didn't want to come and begged off from the king on Valomeer's behalf," grumbled General Kameron.

"It's a wonder, though, that Valomeer didn't just send him along with you," General Trent commented to Iris.

"Yes, you would think that after hearing about the use of guns in the attack, he would send him posthaste. They are a newer technology, after all. Not many people have mastered gun powder yet, and since Saunskirt is in constant trade with warring countries, I'd imagine that General Roberts would have come as quickly as possible!" General Franks lamented.

Lance's eyes widened in surprise as he shifted his attention to Iris. "They used guns in the attack?"

"Very briefly," Iris explained.

"They also used some kind of explosives on the buildings when they first showed up," interjected General Allen.

"That's great!"

Iris shot a disgusted look at Lance. "What do you mean, that's *great?*"

"Oh no! I'm sorry; I didn't mean great in *that* way. I meant great as in it narrows down our options. Like General Franks said, not many have mastered the use of gun powder. We ourselves aren't exactly certain as to what all it's comprised of."

"Saunskirt is fairly close though," General Franks added.

In the corner, Iris caught the tail end of someone joking about General Franks' obsession with Saunskirt. Unfortunately she wasn't the only one who heard the remark.

"What was that, Kameron?" Franks growled.

General Kameron looked over in innocence. "I didn't say a word." His façade melted away as General William started snickering, causing General Kameron to break into laughter as well. *Jokes! They're making ruddy jokes!* Iris clenched her fists to restrain herself. She doubted if they were taking this seriously at all. If that was the case, she might as well head back to Saunskirt. After all, she still needed to have that device removed from her chest.

"Gentlemen, please," General Allen warned. "We need to focus. Captain Peter, could you please report your findings?"

Captain Peter nodded and stepped forward. He placed his materials on the table, first retrieving one of the larger scrolls and unrolling it he spread it out on the table. Drawn upon it was a rather large map showing all of Fitsengea in detail. Iris leaned over a bit for a better look. Captain Peter related how his information proved that such a quick attack could have only been completed by someone familiar with the terrain. The speed at which they were traveling was only more proof that it had to be some rebelling faction within their own land, for only natives would know how to move about as they did. This theory threw everyone into loud disagreements, some calling it wild conjecture, others fiercely defending the idea. Next another captain spoke. He used his own research to concoct another theory, which led to another uproar. The calm that Lance had created earlier quickly dissipated. It was as if every side thought the other a complete fool, and therefore anything that came out of their mouths was preposterous and wholly moronic.

Iris looked around at the room at those who refrained from joining the fray, but nearly everyone was in a heated discussion. *Actually it seems that as of right now, Lance is the only one keeping quiet. But I don't know how helpful that is since this situation really needs to be controlled, not ignored. Too bad they won't even hear anything I say.* Iris gave a small sigh and passed the time by pulling out some of the texts to read. The first couple of scrolls were nothing but battle strategies. She tried following along, but the shorthand notations on the side that were meant to act as a guide only confused her further.

Giving up on those scrolls she let her eyes skim over a few other items on the table before she settled on one of the bigger books. She opened it, flipped to the table of contents at the front, and found a section entitled "Throansburrough and Foreign Lands." Her curiosity piqued, she quickly turned to the beginning of that chapter. The first few pages provided an in-depth description of Throansburrough geography, topography, and all other sorts of -ographies. Iris thumbed past those pages. She had lived her whole life there; she knew the terrain, probably better than this book did. In the section on Throansburrough's history of interactions with foreigners, she spotted a hand-scrawled note along the sides of one of the paragraphs.

"See page 398," Iris mumbled aloud.

Next to it was an arrow that pointed to the word "danger," which was circled and underlined twice within that sentence. Iris followed those directions and turned to a subheading of "Threats to Throansburrough." Beside the title were more short messages. Apparently a recent researcher of this book found this section very important. Stuck between the two following pages rested an old piece of paper, the edges faded. Based on the notes, whoever had made the other comments had left it there. According to this person, Throansburrough was heading toward doom unless action was taken to protect it and fast.

An attack on Throansburrough signals the first of many attacks against all of Fitsengea. If the drought continues in the lands to the East, God, the one Holy Father, who the king of Alaster worships, will be blamed. To destroy this curse, they must first destroy Throansburrough (see prophecy). To succeed, they will kill them all. Must continue to seek solution to drought. In meantime, must increase guard around Throansburrough. If that city falls, Fitsengea is lost! Estimated time till attack: eight years. Holy Father, save us!

Iris flipped the page over to see if anything else was written. But the page had only the initials "A. H." that she assumed belonged to the author and a date from exactly eight years ago. Did this mean . . . did this mean they knew all along? That what had happened to Throansburrough, to Jaralynx, was preventable? Why had this been ignored? Why weren't they warned? Rage began to gurgle up in Iris's heart, she could feel her spirit burn. Jerking up her head, she threw an icy gaze at the men, who were *still* bickering. Iris shot up out of her chair and slapped her hand down hard on the table.

"Stop it!" she shouted, gaining their attention.

Everyone froze at her sudden outburst. Iris took a deep breath, forcing herself to calm down. "Someone, tell me"—she held up the note—"what . . . is . . . this?" She paused between each word for emphasis.

Please don't be what I think it is, please!

General Allen stepped forward and stretched out his hand. "May I?"

Iris handed it over, watching his reaction closely. General Allen's expression slowly transitioned from curiosity to fear. "It can't be," he mumbled.

"What is it? Hand it here, Allen!" William demanded impatiently.

Allen slowly came forward and laid the sheet on the table for all to see. Iris scanned the crowd, seeing similar responses from most. She tried to catch the eye of someone—anyone—but none could meet her gaze. They dropped their eyes to avoid her fierce stare.

"Tell me," Iris spoke with a soft fierceness. "What *is* it?"

"Ms. Straton, we really—"

"Did you know?" Iris cut off General Trent. "Had you really been warned?"

"Well yes, but . . . " General Kameron started but trailed off.

"And you did *nothing?*"

"You don't understand. We couldn't!" General Franks lamented.

"You had eight years! Eight *years* to do something, anything! Why? Tell me why!" Her voice rose in desperation.

Each of the men kept their mouths closed, glancing back and forth as if to say, "Should we tell her?" The captain's expression removed all doubt regarding their authority to even speak. A couple of them opened their mouths as if they were about to say something but thought the better of it and stopped themselves. Their failure to cooperate grated on Iris's already fragile nerves.

"Tell me *why*! I have a right to know!" she demanded once again, too impatient to wait any longer.

"Because we refused to believe him." General William sat down with a sigh, the first to ignore their typical protocol for information.

The rest of the men either nodded sadly or focused elsewhere.

"Believe who?"

"Andrew Hethers," Allen answered and pointed to the initials on the back of the page. "A. H. He was once the top historian in all of Alaster."

Iris waited for a further explanation; grating at their reluctance to talk. She crossed her arms and bored a stare right through them, finally connecting with Lance.

"Mr. Hethers wasn't just the top historian; he was *the* historian, covering all the main records for the king. But then one day, Mr. Hethers disagreed with a statement made by Minister Teason. Because of that, all his research was declared invalid. Minister Teason, with the king's blessing, decreed that all histories by Mr. Hethers were to be rewritten, burned, or locked away for all time," Lance explained.

Iris dropped her arms in exasperation and clenched her fists. "Did you even *look* at his warning, then?"

"Yes, and the research seemed impeccable but . . . General William groaned and dropped his head into his hands.

"But we ignored him. Called him a fool, even, laughed him out of the palace," General Kameron finished.

The conversation paused again as each person wondered what more to share or if they were even allowed to speak.

"He tried to go to Throansburrough and said that if we wouldn't listen, then he would warn them himself. King Zaerin ordered him not to go, but he tried anyhow, so he was put in prison," General Trent added softly.

"And none of you thought to even consider all of this earlier in your little meeting here *because* . . . ?"

General Franks shrugged. "No one has seen or talked about that man's work in years. How could you expect us to remember?"

"Well, you'll remember *now*, won't you. As far as I'm concerned, you're all just as guilty for the deaths of those thousands of innocent people as are the ones who actually killed them." Iris's glare and cold words tore through each of the men present.

Once again, no one could find the words to say. Minutes passed, and Iris stood still, throwing her convicting stare at each of them. They could have saved the cities, prevented the attacks. Or at least helped protect them. If only . . . if only it weren't for that one minister. If only these sniveling generals had stood up to the king and defended that historian. The king . . . yes, it was all his fault. He ignored it all; he abandoned Throansburrough. *That king who—*

"Judging from the silence in this room, it seems that Mr. Hethers' warning has been discussed?"

Iris spun around to the doorway as King Zaerin himself entered in all his glory. Her eyes narrowed. Everyone else bowed at his arrival; on the other hand, Iris stood rigidly before him.

"You knew." Iris confronted him.

"Ms. Straton, you stand before the king. Please, show the proper respect," Lance pleaded with her.

If Iris's demeanor didn't change, then she was asking for some serious trouble. But she didn't care.

"You knew what had happened when I first spoke to you. You knew even back then that your historian was right. You knew, and you did *nothing*. No, worse yet, you prevented others from doing anything! What kind of a king refuses to help his own people?"

"Girl, you will hold your tongue!" General William warned her.

King Zaerin motioned to General William that he could let Iris speak. "Such a speech is to be expected from the Woman of Prophecy. But really, my dear, those are words from the past. Though we might wish to, we cannot change them."

Iris balked. "What do you mean, *the Woman of Prophecy?*"

King Zaerin arched an eyebrow and smirked. He gazed over all the men before him and sighed. "So I see that they haven't told you *all* the details yet."

"Then stop wasting time and tell me now! What *else* is there to know?" Iris was in no mood for games.

King Zaerin nodded and motioned for Iris to take a seat. She complied hesitantly while the rest of the men found their own chairs. Zaerin sat at the head of the table and held out his left hand. An aide rushed to his side and handed him an ancient piece of parchment. Zaerin raised his right hand to retrieve a pair of reading glasses from another servant.

Lance leaned over to Iris to whisper a brief explanation of the old parchment. "This paper has been passed down through the generations as one of the ancient texts that only the eyes of the king are allowed to see."

King Zaerin cleared his throat once before he finally began to read. "Concerning the vision of the Prophet Grayten, recorded by the first scribe Leyos. In the third year of the second month of King Sephon's reign." He stopped reading to look at Iris. "King Sephon was my great grandfather, five generations removed."

Iris nodded, trying desperately not to roll her eyes. "Yes, Your Majesty, I'm aware."

He didn't reply but continued reading. "Let it be known that today a prophecy has been proclaimed within the Public Square by the Grand Prophet Grayten. His words were as follows: 'This very day, the Lord, our Holy Father, has set before me a vision. In this vision lay a blessing to our people, a warning to our rulers, and a promise to the kingdom. The Lord spoke to me, saying, "Son of man, tell my people my words. Oh, children of Fitsengea, you have been faithful in your ways to me. For this, I have blessed you so that you grow in number to reach far across the land. My people, your homes will be safe as long as you seek me first. Keep my commands and desire to know my heart, for this I will make you great above all nations. All you who are leaders in Fitsengea, seek me first, keep my commands, and desire to know my heart. Your forefathers knew me and prospered, yet they grew proud and forgot me in their greed. Their ways became detestable in my eyes, their arrogance brought their destruction . . . ”’” Zaerin trailed off, skimming ahead to a more important part.

Iris listened closely. She recognized this first part as one of the last sermons added to their Sacred Texts. She knew it well, which was why she could not understand why he was reading it now. This passage marked the new beginning of Fitsengea, reminding people how they needed to live and develop their own personal relationship with the Father. So how could *that* have anything to do with this prophecy mentioned before? And why did the beginning of the document call it a prophecy, anyway? Wasn't this section typically entitled, "A Sermon for the People"? Where was he going with all this? Iris started to voice her annoyance but before she could speak, the king began the reading again.

"That night, the Lord spoke to me once more. He said to me, 'Son of man, give this warning to the ruler of Fitsengea. Oh, king of Fitsengea, my eyes have seen deep into your heart. Though your kingdom prospers, though you have more than you need, still you desire more. Greed has threatened to ensnare you. Want has overtaken your heart. My people remain faithful to me, but your actions will lead them astray. Again I say, do not enter into treaties with foreign lands. Make no deals with the countries of witchcraft and devil worship. Take no part in soothsayers, in Diviners, in any forms of sorcery and wickedness. If you bring my people into contact with them, their hearts will be ruined.'"

The king looked up again. "Basically, my dear, the passage goes on to warn of the nasty repercussions if Fitsengea establishes a relationship with non-faithful countries. This is the first mention of a prophecy about the possible destruction of Fitsengea. The specific prophecy about you wasn't made until—"

"Ummm, excuse me Your Majesty," Iris interjected. "But if my memory serves me, I do not recall any of that message within the Sacred Texts. What text are you reading from, exactly?"

"You would know it as 'A Sermon for the People,' but it's no surprise that you don't recognize the other half. That section was deemed unnecessary for public knowledge."

"So you mean you've purposefully withheld Sacred Texts from the people?" Iris blurted out, horrified.

"My dear girl, initially this piece had nothing to do with the general populace. So why burden others with information that they cannot change? In fact, I had not even planned on reading this much to you, but when I came in, I felt . . . that when I looked at your face . . . something urged me to read on." He looked past her, his gaze unfocused as if entranced or in a dream. He shook his head slightly. "But we digress. You *do* want to know the prophecy, do you not?"

Iris couldn't believe her ears. Just because they couldn't control it was no reason for them to keep it from the people. What else had been exempted from their texts? What more had they hidden? Had she been taught incorrectly all these years? No, she knew what was right, what was true. At least she thought she did. She began to question everything. It scared her, so instead of facing it, she focused on the king, finally nodding to indicate that he could proceed with his explanation. At that, another servant stepped forward with a new scroll. Zaerin took it without looking at the attendant, undoing the scroll before he read from it.

"And the Lord said, for Throansburrough's faithfulness, out of her heart, I will raise up a hero, a child who knows me well. Through her, I will save the faithful of Fitsengea. She will be the rescuer of the nation, a woman unlike any other. Her presence beckons truth. Her voice will destroy the enemy. Her eyes will pierce the soul. I will give her the power of my name. She will be known as the Woman of Prophecy; she will heal the wounds of the land through my strength, and she will be mine."

Zaerin stopped speaking and looked up at Iris, waiting for her response. Iris almost laughed. That couldn't be about her! It just couldn't. Her eyes had never "pierced anyone's soul," and her words certainly hadn't kept her out of trouble so far. This had to be some kind of a joke—albeit a cruel one—considering the seriousness of their conversation, but a joke nonetheless.

"That's *not* me." Iris spoke at last.

"But my dear, who else *could* it be? You said so yourself, you're the *only one left.*"

Iris faltered. "But I–I–it couldn't—no, it can't . . . There's just no way!" *I'm barely even on speaking terms with the Holy Father right now!*

"Well, there is no one else, so it falls on you. A big responsibility is resting on your shoulders now."

"But how do you even know it's true? I mean, if you really thought it was from the Holy Father beforehand, wouldn't you have sent out a proclamation to Throansburrough letting us know about a prophecy spoken over us? And if my home really was so wonderful in the Father's eyes, then why was it the first place to be completely wiped out? What's your source? Who wrote the prophecy? Did you even check to see if the person was legitimate?"

"Mind who you're speaking to, girl!" General Kameron growled his warning.

Iris winced and looked at the king apologetically. "I–I'm sorry, Your Majesty, I don't mean to infer that you don't know what you're doing. It's just . . . it's all a little hard to believe!"

Zaerin nodded curtly. "It is, but it doesn't matter whether it is true or not. What matters is that the Yansairens think it is, and we can use that to our advantage."

"The Yansairens? Isn't Yansair the name of the land that resides to the far east of our borders?"

"Yes, it is a pagan land, one of our most bitter rivals. They consider anything that goes wrong in their land a curse from our own. That is the land to the east which Hethers, the historian, was referring to. About ten years ago, the king of Yansair, Thaylos, somehow got his hands on some of our copies of the texts. In them, he found the original manuscript of the prophecy which I just read to you, though this copy went into greater detail than what we have here. My resources learned that at the time, King Thaylos had received some sort of pagan prophecy about the danger of Throansburrough to their kingdom's power. Reading our own prophecy only solidified in his mind that the sole thing standing between him and all power was whoever this Woman of Prophecy was. So whether you truly *do* have the capabilities written here, it matters not, for your very existence will strike fear in their hearts like they've never known."

Once again, Iris could feel the anger and hurt swelling up in her heart. "You mean to tell me . . . that you *knew* almost *ten years* ago that some crazy king had it out for my village? That this enemy of our country, of our Holy Father, this power-hungry society, had somehow *gotten a hold of* our Sacred Texts? You *knew* that there was a threat, but . . . but you *ignored* it because Minister Teason told you to?"

"Minister Teason *never* tells me what to do, girl."

"I don't care! My family is dead, and you want me to play some role to help you win a war, a war that never should have started! Why? Why did you let it happen? How could you not care for your own people?" Iris's voice escalated as her own passion grew.

"It is not your place to ask such questions; you couldn't possibly understand all the matters a king must attend to on any given day. More important things were at stake at the time."

Tears of rage flooded her eyes at those words. "More important? *More important!*"

"Iris!" Lance grabbed her arm, restraining her as she moved toward the king. He didn't know what she planned, but this was heading south fast.

Jerking her arm away, Iris stared at him icily. She threw her chair back with a *screech* and stormed from the room. The men left behind looked nervously at their king to check his reaction. Did he want to force her to come back? Instead Zaerin merely lifted a hand and shook his head, signaling to leave her be for now. In the meantime, he proceeded to discuss the current threat on their land and what to do both diplomatically and militarily. Iris left them to their discussion, not wanting to hear any more of it. They could even lose the war, for all she cared. She wanted them to lose; she wanted them to taste the most bitter of defeats. Pain. She wanted them to know pain, the pain that their actions—or rather inaction—forced upon her.

Iris stormed down one of the hallways of the castle with no idea of where she was going, unable to see through her blurred vision. She blinked her eyes, hastily wiping away her tears as she went. She had to move; she couldn't stop, she just had to keep walking. As long as she put distance between herself and *those* men, that was all that mattered. They were supposed to come to her aid. They were supposed to be the ones who fixed all this for her. She was going to come here and report her findings, handing over all her worries for them to take care of. They were to rescue her from this mess. They weren't supposed to be the ones who caused it!

Hiding texts. Hiding prophecies. Refusing to warn people or to take other's warnings seriously! What kind of a kingdom does that? What kind of a king *allows that? Is there* anything *trustworthy about him? About his generals? Preventable, it was all preventable! They could have stopped it! Or at least, they could have lessened the devastation. My family even—* Iris gasped and stopped in her tracks as her hand flew up to her mouth involuntarily. *My family . . . my family could have* lived! This thought poured bitterness upon her heart's wound. The very idea that even one of her family members could have been by her side during the last few days, guiding her, helping her understand.

In their place was only hollow pain, utter awareness of her loneliness. She had nothing because of King Zaerin! No, that wasn't right. She now had this device on her chest and the possibility of life imprisonment because of Zaerin. Yes, she blamed that on him too. Everything that had happened since the beginning could have been stopped. She was hurt by her loss. But even more so, she was angry. Iris clenched her fists tightly, fingernails digging into her palms. It was all because of the king. It was all because of *him.*

"All because of that—that . . ." Iris bit her lip, wanting to let loose a thousand curse words, but she restrained herself through force of habit.

Instead, she released a cry of anguish and punched her fist against the stone wall, which proved to be a foolish idea. Iris yelped in pain and pulled back her hand and shook it, wincing. She sucked in some air through her teeth and jumped around a little bit. Glancing at her hand, the knuckles were red with a few scrapes on them. She glared back at the wall. *Stupid wall!* This time, she kicked it in frustration, keeping herself from further self-injury. Iris sighed heavily. *This is dumb. Why am I berating an inanimate wall? It has nothing to do with this.*

"My, my, causing trouble again now, are we?"

Iris spun around as an elderly man approached her. He wore the long brown robe indicative of the men from Alaster's church council. She had never really seen one before, but she had viewed so many paintings of that exact outfit that she would bet her life that this man held one of those esteemed positions. Iris couldn't help but grimace a little as the man continued toward her. She was *not* in the mood to be rebuked by some random old guy for doing something she didn't even know she had done!

"Now are we going to have to have that talk again? Hmmm? How many times do I have to tell you not to pick fights with guests? Why, it's inhospitable. Not to mention, it's just plain rude!"

Iris's jaw dropped at his words. Was this guy crazy? *He's talking to the wall!*

"What if the other walls hear about this? They would be so disappointed in you. Shame on you." The man stood beside Iris but looked only at the wall, shaking his finger at it as he continued his scolding "Now I want you to apologize to this fine lady at once."

"Uhh . . . sir?"

The man turned to her with a gentle smile and winked playfully. "Walls these days, always causing trouble."

The man chuckled a little, forcing Iris to smile slightly. He wasn't crazy. It was just his sense of humor. It sounded like something her father would have said. Iris rubbed her hand absentmindedly. Her cheeks flushed as he had seen her earlier outburst. The man reached out his hand and placed it gently on her shoulder.

"Now, my dear, would you mind telling me what was so horrible that it did to you to make you act out so?"

Iris looked up into his eyes. He reminded her of her grandfather, except this man had a grey beard and more hair on the top of his head. But the eyes were the same: kind and twinkling from inner merriment, the type meant to comfort others.

"It's just that I . . ." Iris's voice cut off as a sob caught in her throat. The tears she had fought so hard to keep in check rolled down her cheeks. Something inside broke. Iris couldn't hold back her feelings any longer. She abruptly flung herself into the man's arms, letting loose her bitter sobs as her hands clung to him tightly.

"Oh, dear me. You poor child!" The man wrapped his arms around her and softly stroked the back of her head. He cooed, "There, there, girl. It's alright. Tell Uncle Peter all about it."

Chapter Twenty-Two

Lori rested her face against the steel bars, their cool numbness nearly unnoticed against her cheek. She had been sitting there, unmoving, with her face pressed against them for hours. The other girls in the cage had tried repeatedly to convince her to lie down and rest with them. If they huddled together, they would be warmer; at least that's what they kept trying to tell her. They had been served their lunch rations a few minutes ago and had nothing else to do. So they decided to try and sleep. The girls begged Lori to rest with them because they'd all be more comfortable, but she ignored them and refused to budge. She wasn't being stubborn, rather defeat overwhelmed and saddened her.

The numbness extended beyond her face to the very core of her being. They had taken her Jacob away from her. The bad men had forced all the boys to go on the first big machine, the "trans" something. She didn't understand why they had to be separated. After all, weren't they on one now anyhow? She wanted Jacob so badly. He needed her; she had to protect him, but she couldn't do that if he wasn't with her. Why did they take him away? She wanted him back. Was he going to be okay? She couldn't help but whimper. What if she never saw him again?

Lori wrapped her arms more tightly around the bars as another whimper slipped out. Her eyes stayed trained on her feet. They limply hung below her between the bars, swinging back and forth with the slow motion of their cage. They had been hung up in the air inside this big "trans" machine. The bad men had wanted to make sure that the girls couldn't cause them any more trouble. That didn't bother Lori much, though. She was farther away from the bad men who slept underneath, the few who were left, at least. Most of them had gone on the first machine with the boys. This machine carried the girls and all the wagons and other supplies.

Off to Lori's left a gentle shuffling noise was made as Sara knelt down beside her. Lori didn't respond to the girl's presence. Sara tenderly worked her fingers through Lori's soft hair, saying nothing. Simply stroking Lori's head in her motherly fashion. Slowly the warmth of Sara's actions began to break through to Lori. She was reminded of how her mommy did the same thing whenever they cuddled. She had always loved the tickling sensation it sent down the back of her neck. The reminders made Lori long desperately for home.

She moved her face back from the bars and turned her eyes up at Sara. Sara didn't seem to notice the change in Lori's position but continued her gentle strokes of Lori's hair and kept her eyes trained out the giant window in front of them. Lori pulled up her legs from outside of the cage. She shifted to lean against Sara now instead of the bars. Sara looked down at Lori and drew her in closer, cradling her in her arms as one hand dutifully pet her hair.

They sat together like this for a while before Lori finally whispered, "Sing to me, Sara . . . please?"

Sara kept playing with Lori's hair as she thought for a second and then sighed. "Lori, I'm sorry, I can't . . . If they heard me, we'd both get in trouble."

Lori burrowed in closer. "Please, Sara . . . you can whisper it into my ear. I want to hear a song from home. Please. I want to hear something my mommy would sing."

Sara took a deep breath and slowly exhaled. She angled her head so that she could see the soldiers resting on the bunks below. They had been drinking heavily again and probably wouldn't be easily woken. She finally nodded.

"Okay, Lori, did your mommy ever sing the 'Everywhere' song from the night meetings?"

Lori nodded. "Mmhmm."

"Okay, I'll sing that one then." Sara leaned in closer to Lori, putting her lips next to her ear and began to whisper the words.

When you feel broken,
And your heart is sad,
Look up to heaven,
The Father is there.
If you feel empty and alone,
Look to your side,
The Father is there.
If you feel scared,
Or if you feel mad,
Look around,
For the Father is there.
His arms open wide as He smiles,
Look in your heart,
The Father is there.
He'll never leave you,
You're never alone,
For His love is with you,
Wherever you go.
Close your eyes and drift off to sleep,
Look in your dreams,
The Father is there.

When things get hard,
And you have no more strength,
Don't worry, for the Father is there,
Yes, the Father is everywhere.

When Sara finished, Lori looked into her face. "Again?" she pleaded.

Sara nodded with tears in her eyes. As she started to sing, Lori picked up some of the words with her. Each time they stopped, Lori begged her to sing it once more. Sara complied because she wanted to keep singing too. Eventually some of the other girls came over to them. Before long, the entire group had huddled around Sara and Lori, each singing the song as softly as possible. Even the girls from Jaralynx had joined in. No one complained about repeating the same song, and no one grew tired of it or wanted to stop. The song became their way of mourning what they had lost, but even more than that, it unified them.

Lori looked at all the precious faces around her. Something was different about them now. Tears fell from the eyes of many, but they weren't the same tears of fear and brokenness from before. A change permeated the atmosphere around them. With each renewed verse, Lori felt it grow inside her. How could she describe this? Whatever it was, she wanted it to continue.

Sara looked at Lori who wore an expression that she hadn't seen in a while. Sara held the child tightly and kept on singing. She knew what this feeling was, and she didn't want to let it go. They were finally feeling hope.

Chapter Twenty-Three

An out-of-place wooden cottage sat on the castle grounds. While it wasn't exactly small, compared to the rest of the stone structures around it, it looked miniscule. The more prominent figures on the church council were required to live on the palace grounds. Most resided in the actual castle, but the few who didn't had their own homes built nearby. This was the only cottage, though, and it was as far off the palace grounds as physically possible, right next to the wall.

The inside of the home lacked many of the typical luxuries afforded to those close to the king. Not because Zaerin hadn't offered them but mainly because the resident of the home felt no desire to accept them. Peter was a simple man when it came to material needs. In other words, he simply felt no need for them. If it had been up to him, his current residence would not have even been as big as it was. Allowing the king to build the cottage was an act of appeasement.

Peter brought the weeping Iris to this modest abode. He thought that it would probably be the most neutral of grounds. There was nothing like sitting in the parlor and drinking some tea to help soothe a person's heart. It seemed to do the trick as Iris dried her eyes and talked to Peter more calmly.

"My, my." Peter couldn't think of anything else to say.

Iris sat across from him, holding the teacup with both hands. She had just told the man everything, and by everything, she meant *everything*. Not only did she describe her experience in Throansburrough and what she saw in Jaralynx, but she also thoroughly discussed her interactions with Darren, Kyle, and Bryant. She told him about Valomeer and the device he put over her heart. She told him about trying to trick the king and about the anger she now held against him.

In any other circumstance, Iris would have never poured out her heart to a complete stranger. But something inside her urged her on and told her to speak to this man, holding nothing back. Iris looked down at the tea in her hands. After baring so much of her soul, she felt better, if not a little embarrassed. She couldn't bring herself to look at him just yet.

"Thank you, Iris, for sharing all of that with me. Now I know that it has been you all along."

Iris peeked up at him quizzically "All along?"

"From the time you described the horrible beginning of these events, to our very meeting, the Father has been pressing hard upon my spirit to pray for a young woman. I did not know for whom, why, or what to say, but pray I did." He chuckled softly. "Not that I had much choice about that. He hasn't allowed me a decent night's sleep since."

Iris looked at him, flabbergasted. "You–you've been praying for me?"

Peter nodded kindly as he took another sip from his cup.

"But . . . are you sure it's *me* the Holy Father meant?"

"He told me that I would meet the girl I was praying for today. I had been bugging Him for quite some time about needing more specifics in my prayers."

"But I–I was sure that . . . I was certain the Holy Father had rejected me."

Peter cocked his head slightly to the side. "Rejected you? My dear girl, you should know that the Father never rejects His own. You're free to reject Him, but He would not do that to you."

"Then why hasn't He helped me? Why has He let all these terrible things happen? Even with your prayers, He's done nothing!"

"Oh, I wouldn't say He's done *nothing*," Peter responded calmly. "It seems to me that there were plenty of times that things could have been worse, but He saved you."

Iris couldn't help but throw him an unbelieving glare. "Like what?"

"Like when you had your first encounter with Bryant. That hole you fell into might have seemed like more bad luck, but did it not rescue you from your attacker?"

"I suppose you could look at it that way. It did bring me to Darren in the end."

"Precisely, and then there was the way those birds just *happened* to come at the exact time you were sneaking across Valomeer's yard. If not for them, you would not have been able to tell where to step."

"I guess . . ."

"And where do you think your courage to speak to such powerful figures has come from? Or even the fact that you *did* speak to them without being immediately locked up?"

"But why hasn't He done more?! Why did He let me be sentenced to prison? Why would He let Yansair, if it really *is* them, attack us? Why didn't He make the king do something? Why did He let my family die?"

"Why, indeed. May I share something with you that I've learned from my years on the church council?"

Iris nodded.

"No one will ever understand the Father. If we could define Him, put all His reasonings in a little box, and then come up with the obvious outcomes, He would no longer be the Father. He is too great to be defined."

"I know that, but . . ."

Peter sighed. "Sometimes bad things happen in the world, Iris. That does not mean it's a curse from the Father. Sometimes they happen simply because our evil hearts have caused them. Most often, they happen because honestly, Iris, my dear, we are continually under attack from the Great Deceiver. But the Father always has plans to work through difficulties and through us. If we're lucky, He'll tell us how, but we usually only see it after the fact. I am not saying the Father planned this. I am not saying what has happened is in any way your fault. All I am saying is that when we ask why in times like this, we are only trapping ourselves. We become stuck asking why when we will probably never know. Instead, we should just move forward and ask the more pertinent question of 'what now?'."

Iris let her gaze fall back down to the cup. He was right, and she knew it. But that didn't mean she wanted to admit to it just yet.

"I can only say these things to you, Iris, because I have felt as you do. I know that I will never understand the extent of your pain, but I have asked why and how the Father could let certain things happen and why and how He could not change these situations for the better. I know those feelings all too well. Yet I hold on to the truth, knowing that the Holy Father *is* good, and so turns *all* things to good for those who love Him, eventually. The point is, though, even if the Father told you all the whys and explained the final outcome, would it really make accepting the deaths of your family any easier?"

"I suppose I would still be angry and hurt and would have asked Him to use someone else."

"Exactly."

"Even so, what you said doesn't make me feel any better! It still feels as if He's turned His back on me, which doesn't seem right, because I've always tried to be faithful to Him! I read and studied the Sacred Texts; I went to worship, and I did my best to keep His commands. I prayed to Him every day, practically all day long! I know I'm not perfect, and I've messed up plenty of times before. But I always thought that He still loved me, no matter what. That even though life isn't fair, even though I'm no better than the next person, that as long as I gave myself to Him, I could trust Him to take care of me. So why hasn't He? Where was the Holy Father in all of this? He promised to never leave me! He promised to love me! I don't get it. I don't understand, and I don't know if I even *want* to understand!"

Peter set his cup down on the little table between them. Iris watched him carefully. He'd probably lecture or scold her now and show her the supposed error of her ways. Or maybe he would just give a rote answer like she'd heard in the past. "The Holy Father uses adversity to help you grow." "It was all for a purpose." "The Holy Father gives His toughest battles to His strongest soldiers" or something along those lines. But really, she couldn't care less about some so-called greater purpose right now. She didn't want to be used. She didn't want to be a catalyst for anything. She just wanted to be home, to have a home, to have her family. If the Holy Father really loved her as she much as she had been told—as much as she believed for all these years —then wouldn't He have kept something as awful as all this from happening? The Holy Father had abandoned her, plain and simple.

Peter's chair creaked slightly, bringing Iris back the present. He had risen from his chair and was walking over to her. The kindly old man put his arms around her and hugged her. Iris didn't move; she didn't know what to do. Of all things, she hadn't expected this. Should she hug him back? She couldn't bring herself to stand or even to raise her arms and return the gesture. Instead, they both remained in that position with Peter embracing her like a father and Iris sitting in the chair, looking at the man like he was crazy.

"I *am* still here." Another voice that Iris had never heard before spoke. Yet, she knew it.

The words hadn't come from Peter because they went straight to her heart. All her rigidity evaporated at this voice. Warmth blanketed her body as a peace she had never known before entered her mind. Iris finally raised her arms and hugged Peter back. As she did, a vision appeared before her eyes. She was standing now, but she wasn't holding onto Peter. In his place stood a man, a light, a spirit, a mist. She couldn't comprehend the form; she had no words. All she saw was the brightness—a blinding brightness that somehow did not hurt her eyes.

Iris felt her soul vibrating. She let out a gasp and almost let go from shock. Yet she held on because something in the deepest part of her said she never wanted to let go. She dropped her head in awe at the greatness of the presence holding onto her. Her heart beat so hard that she was certain it would burst. She knew this man. She had known Him all her life. She wanted to speak to Him, but no words came. The power of this man arrested her tongue's ability to make a sound. Happiness and joy poured through her like never before. She felt safe. Her arms gripped Him more tightly. She felt it was ok to not speak, that He already knew everything she wanted to say. Every fear, every worry, melted away as His arms held her. Finally, Iris could feel something loosen the grip on her tongue. Even so, only two words came to mind, only two words she wanted to speak.

"Holy Father."

Iris felt a soft chuckle vibrate in the man's chest. She wanted to weep with joy at His laughter.

"Yes, Iris. It is I."

She couldn't see His face, but she knew He was smiling as He spoke. It was the first time Iris had ever *felt* a smile. She felt more alive than she thought was possible.

"Oh, Iris, I've missed you."

Confused, Iris asked, "Missed me? But I never left You."

The Holy Father chuckled again. "You forgot me."

Iris looked up at him. "How could I forget You? I never forgot You. You left *me*, remember?"

"I never leave. I have always pursued you. You were trying to outrun me, but you know that, don't you."

Iris paused for a second before answering reluctantly. "Yes."

"I've missed our talks, Iris. I always love to hear from you."

The sadness of His longing for her spread into her heart, making her want to weep. She *had* stopped praying to the Holy Father. She hadn't *really* prayed since before the night of the attack. Sure she had, solely out of habit, breathed His name in her thoughts now and again, but she had purposefully cut off any real communication with Him. She used to share her heart about everything with Him. Since that night, she had done her best to avoid Him.

"I–I was just so mad . . ."

"That's okay; I don't mind. You're allowed to be angry with me. But was it really because you were *just* mad at me?"

"Ummm . . . no . . . I was afraid."

"Afraid of what?"

The Holy Father wasn't asking because He didn't already know the answer. He was doing what her dad used to do. He would ask her questions just to get her to admit things to herself that she hadn't wanted to think about before.

"I was afraid that . . ." What *was* she afraid of? She had already admitted her fear that the Holy Father had abandoned her. But deep down, she knew that wasn't true. She had known the Holy Father for too long to ever *truly* believe that. "I was afraid of what You would tell me to do. I knew that if I did talk to You, I'd then have to face whatever it was You wanted me to do, and I'd have to do it alone."

"But you haven't been alone, have you?"

"I guess not . . . not really, but it still *feels* like I am. But I guess . . . if I had talked to You . . . I would have at least felt like You were with me."

Iris rested her head upon the Holy Father and whispered, "I'm sorry."

"It's okay. All I want is for you to keep talking to me."

"I will, or at least, I'll try to . . . ummm . . . Holy Father? What *is* it that I'm supposed to do? I mean, there's got to be something that You want, right? I've been upset before in life, and You've never come down personally to give me a hug and make me feel better back then."

The Holy Father chuckled again, but this time it grew into a full-fledged laugh so beautiful that Iris couldn't help but join in. They laughed hard together for quite some time. As their laughter died down, Iris found herself wishing it wouldn't.

"Oh, Iris, I didn't do this because I wanted to ask you to do anything. I came to calm your heart. I wanted to remind you of how much I love you. Yes, there is something you need to do, but now isn't the time to talk about it. Now is the time for you to reconnect yourself to me so that you *can* do it."

"Oh . . ." Iris peeked up as she prepared herself for the response to her next question. "Whatever it is that You want me to do . . . do You . . . do You *really* think I'm capable of it?"

"I wouldn't ask you if the answer was otherwise."

"Right . . . I knew that . . . I think."

Iris relaxed as a hand brushed her hair away from her face.

"Trust me, Iris."

Iris nodded. "I'll try."

The Holy Father smiled and pulled her in closer for a goodbye hug. "I chose well when I chose you, Iris Straton."

Iris closed her eyes and hugged Him back tightly. When she opened them again, her arms were around Peter once more. They both released their hold simultaneously. Peter stepped backward into his chair in a daze. Completely drained yet totally revitalized, Iris wondered, *Did that really just happen?*

"Woah . . ." Peter breathed out.

Iris looked up at him, his face mirroring her own.

"In all my years . . . I've *never* had something like that happen."

"Did–did you see Him too, then?"

Peter scrunched his eyebrows together. "See Him? No, I *felt* Him, though. I heard Him speak to me."

"What did He say?"

"He told me to hold you. That's why I got up in the first place. He kept telling me to hold you . . ."

"Wow . . ." Iris couldn't think of anything else to say.

I was just hugged by the Holy Father! A chill ran up and down her spine at the thought.

"This . . . this really is bigger than the both of us, isn't it?" Iris said.

"I believe so, my dear."

"Did the Holy Father tell you anything else?"

Peter nodded slowly. "He wants you to go back to King Zaerin. The king has something to talk to you about."

"Now?"

Peter nodded again.

Iris couldn't help but frown. She didn't want to leave just yet. The presence of the Holy Father still lingered around her. She didn't want to lose that feeling. She wanted to sit and stay with Peter, a man who knew the Holy Father, who heard the Holy Father speak and listened to Him. He really trusted the Holy Father. Iris sighed. Peter trusted Him. *Just like I said I would. Okay, Holy Father, have it Your way. I'll go see that man again.* Iris stood from her chair and smiled at Peter.

"Thank you *so* much for all you've done."

Peter stood and clasped her hands. "My pleasure. You'll be in my prayers."

Iris nodded and bit her lower lip. Tears of gratefulness welled up in her eyes. She took a deep breath, smiled at the old man once more, and then showed herself out. As she closed the door behind her, guards approached from a distance. Iris left the cottage and smiled at them politely. She had to walk toward them because they were in the path that Peter had taken her to go from the palace to his home. She would have gone another way if she'd known one but this was her first time here and due to her natural ability of getting lost, she thought it best to take the route she had used at least once before.

As she approached them, she didn't know how to act. Should she avert her gaze or just keep looking at them and smile until they passed each other? She didn't want to seem rude or stare, but she didn't want to obviously ignore them either. Perhaps it wouldn't have been such a dilemma if the men hadn't been paying such close attention to her as they approached. Iris wanted to blurt out, "What?" just so they'd realize the awkwardness they created. *Calm down. You'll pass them soon enough. Really, it's not like it's that big of a deal!*

"Ms. Iris Straton?" the one on the left called out sharply just as they came face to face.

Iris halted in surprise. "Ummm, yes?"

"We have been ordered to find you and retrieve you," the man on the right explained.

"Retrieve me? Let me guess. The king wishes to speak with me, right?"

"Ummm, yes. How did you . . . ?"

Iris waved the question aside. "Don't ask. Shouldn't keep his High-ness waiting. Lead the way, gentlemen."

The men paused for a second but then turned around. "This way."

Iris walked in between the two soldiers back to the palace. Upon entrance, they went down a couple of halls and finally back into the throne room. The pair took their leave and left Iris standing before the king on his throne. Iris had to fight the sarcasm building up within her, making her want to spout off with, "What do you want now?" But that would be highly inappropriate, no matter how much she wanted to do it. *Okay, Holy Father, You want me to talk to You, so here I am, talking. Please, Holy Father, help me put up with this guy.*

Even though she didn't think that this man deserved her respect, Iris decided to be civil and offer him a lady-like bow. "You summoned me, Your Highness?"

"Yes. I have finished my discussion with the military council for now. I have decided that our first order of business is to bring you back to Saunskirt."

"Sir?"

"I will be ordering Lord Valomeer to remove the device from your chest and then send you back here. Oh, don't look so surprised, girl. Did you honestly think that your king would not have noticed that bracelet on your wrist or know what it symbolizes? You are of a greater use to me here than decaying in a Saunskirt dungeon."

"So I am to act as this Woman of Prophecy, then?"

"Yes, your very existence will strike fear into the hearts of every man, woman, and child in Yansair. It is an advantage we cannot afford to lose."

Iris could not think of a response other than to nod. Anything she wanted to say would be highly improper. She inhaled deeply in an effort to calm herself.

"I will be assigning a section of my royal guard to accompany you to Saunskirt and back for your protection."

"If you don't mind my asking, Your Highness, how long will I need to stay in Alaster?"

"For as long as it takes—a couple of months or even a year. We're dealing with war, girl. No one can predict how long it will last. But do not worry. During that time, I will give you a place to stay here in the castle."

Iris grew quiet as she pondered the idea of going from being a prisoner of Saunskirt to one of Alaster. At least the accommodations would be better, and it wasn't as if she had anywhere else to go. An idea then blossomed in her mind.

"Your Majesty, I was wondering if I could make one request in regards to my protection."

Zaerin paused for a second, curious as to what she might be plotting. "Continue."

"Well, I was wondering if I could be allowed to choose the head of my personal guard? After all, they will be protecting *my* life."

Zaerin stroked the beard on his chin as he considered this new proposal. The king did not appear to be a great fan of this idea. *Lord, please let him say yes! Please, Holy Father, let this work!*

"Very well. You may choose whomever you think best suited for the position. I can arrange for one of my men to introduce you to the very best we have, and once you have decided, you will leave immediately on the next transport."

"So you promise that I can have whomever I choose? Even if you don't like my decision, you give your word that I can keep him?"

Zaerin scrunched his eyebrows together. "I give you the word of your king, and nothing can take that back."

"Very well, then, I have already made my decision."

The king sat up a little straighter "But you haven't even looked anyone over yet."

Iris couldn't help but let a small smile escape. "I choose Darren—uh—I mean the Marquis Darren Turner to be by my side."

Zaerin's face flushed with anger as he realized that Iris had just tricked him. "Are you *certain* that's who you want?"

"Yes, my king. I can think of no other who would do a better job."

And this way he can live in Alaster as long as I have to. Now he can spend time with his family.

The King unhappily stared at Iris for a second. The color in his face returned to normal as a new idea crossed his mind. "You are an interesting woman indeed, Ms. Iris."

"What do you mean?"

"Well, you are surprisingly willing to trust your life to someone who, as far as I can tell, has done nothing but lie to you about who he really is. He never did tell you that I was his uncle, did he?"

Iris faltered at his words. "W–well, no." It was true, she didn't trust him. But she wasn't doing this for herself. "Even so, he has shown himself quite useful in the time I've spent with him."

Zaerin leaned to one side with a smug look on his face. "Tell me, girl, why are you trying so hard to help my nephew?"

"I—umm . . . Iris let her eyes fall on her hands as she fidgeted uncomfortably. *Why* am *I so concerned about his welfare?*

The king didn't bother to wait for her answer. "Very well. If it is Darren you want, it is Darren you'll have. A king does not go back on his word. I will send my men to bring him to the transport station. My servants have taken the liberty of preparing some supplies, and I have had my tailor create clothing more befitting of a woman of your importance. My attendants will take you to change, and from there, you will be taken to the transport station so that you can be quickly on your way."

As he spoke, two women stepped into the room from the servant's entrance. They walked over to Iris and waited patiently behind her.

"That is all for now. You will be expected at another meeting when you return. The Holy Father's speed to you, Iris Straton."

Iris gave the king another bow and then turned to follow the women to be fitted for her more appropriate attire. Once in the changing room, they pulled out a regal white gown. Iris looked at herself in the mirror. The dress had long romantic sleeves and silver trim about an inch thick lining the edges of the whole ensemble. The cut of the collar showed off her shoulders. They had tied her hair up in a bun, crisscrossing a long silver ribbon through it. The ribbon hung between her shoulders.

The dress clung attractively to her bust and waist, flaring out softly as it fell to the floor. Iris rolled her eyes at the sight of it all. Yes, it was a beautiful dress but was clearly not suited for travel. So this was how she had to present herself from here on out. *So much for not drawing too much attention to myself.* She looked at the other dresses packed for the trip. All of them were practically identical. *Well, at least my new uniform is pretty. I suppose that's something to be grateful for.*

The servants had packed everything so that the dresses wouldn't wrinkle. Once Iris had changed, a couple of soldiers entered to escort Iris to the carriage. This carriage was different than the one she had ridden in before, which was for Diviners only. Her new ride was an enclosed black carriage with white curtains over the inside windows. In addition, the horses themselves were the purest white she had ever seen. Curious as to if this motif symbolized anything special, Iris asked one of the guards walking her to her ride about the meaning of the colors.

"This carriage is for only you, my lady. It is a symbol of the Woman of Prophecy, similar to the garment you now wear."

Iris thanked him for the answer but couldn't help but think how ridiculous the whole affair was becoming. As they pulled away in the carriage, the men at the gate announced that the Woman of Prophecy was coming through. *News sure travels fast here, doesn't it? I didn't realize how much King Zaerin had intended to play this up within his own kingdom. Why do I have the feeling that this won't end well?*

Iris moved her hand to pull back the curtains and watch the scenery fly by. While she could free herself from Valomeer's control, could she really do what King Zaerin asked? She knew he didn't honestly believe that she was this Woman of Prophecy. Iris agreed with him about that, but she was still expected to act as if she was. Exactly how *was* a Woman of Prophecy supposed to act, anyhow? She was the first one, so maybe she had to make up the rules as she went. That would probably be too good to be true, though. And yet it was exactly what she was doing.

I don't know if this is what You want from me, Holy Father, but I pray that through it, You make things right again. Iris easily flowed back into the habit of prayer. True, she was still uncertain about nearly everything, and the gaping hole in her heart still hurt, but she was much more willing to at least attempt to seek the Holy Father. That might have only been because she had such an extraordinary encounter with him. She was still stunned at how unbelievable it was, like a dream. It was only a couple of hours ago but seemed like a memory from years past. And yet it was so real that it was as if she had just stepped out of it. These conflicting emotions, in of themselves, were enough to keep her head spinning.

Iris lifted her gaze at a slight cough across from her to the soldier riding inside the carriage. The men had been ordered to take certain positions before leaving. Two were to sit up front, one to be stationed at the back, and a fourth to be placed inside. For the life of her, Iris couldn't figure out why they needed to orchestrate these strategic positions. Would she be attacked on her way to the transport? Talk about unlikely. That didn't really bother her as much as the unnerving silence of the ride. She hated the uncomfortable silence, but she didn't know what to say. Not only that, but she didn't know if she was allowed to say anything. Could she converse with her guard? Would he even respond if she tried?

The man stifled another cough. *Well, that's as good of an excuse as any to strike up a conversation,* Iris thought as she quickly planned out her starting speech.

"Ummm, excuse me? Are—are you alright?" Iris began tentatively.

The man gave her a questioning look.

"I couldn't help but notice your cough. You're not sick, are you?"

"If I am causing the lady distress, we can pull over so that I can switch places with one of the other men."

"No, no! It's not that at all. I was just concerned about you. You're perfectly fine where you are." Iris gave him a friendly smile.

The soldier smiled weakly in return and then turned his gaze else-where. *Okay . . . That could have gone better. Maybe I should try the direct approach.*

Iris smiled cheerfully. "My name's Iris."

"I know that, miss," he responded.

Oh, good grief! Work with me here, mister! Iris leaned forward a little to get his attention. "So . . . what's your name?"

He looked at her with a sidelong glance. "Grayson."

"Pleased to meet you, Grayson." Iris offered him her hand to prove her sincerity.

Grayson looked at it and then back up at her face, finally accepting it with his own stiff shake. His standoffish manner left Iris frustrated. She sighed in exasperation.

"Tell me, Grayson, have I done something wrong? Did I offend you or something?"

Grayson's eyes widened in surprise at the suggestion. "No! Not at all."

"Hmmm, okay. Then I take it you're just not the talkative type?"

"It's not that. I just . . . don't know how to talk to a woman like you," he admitted softly.

Iris smiled at him, bemused. "A woman like me? And what type of woman would that be, exactly?"

Grayson looked at her as if she was crazy for not knowing what he meant. "Well, according to my general, you're the most important woman in all Fitsengea, and there is more honor in protecting your life than in winning a hundred battles! To speak to someone so great as yourself is a bit nerve-racking, miss."

Iris's eyes widened with shock at such an outlandish statement. She pressed her lips firmly together as laughter bubbled up inside her, trying to suppress an outburst. But the more she thought of the absur-dity of it all, the more difficult it became to keep from laughing. Iris finally gave in until she laughed so hard that her sides began to hurt. She kept laughing for a couple of minutes as Grayson stared at her in confusion. Iris forced herself to calm down, taking a few deep breaths between the last prevailing chuckles.

"S–sorry about that. But it seems that your general has taken a bit of poetic license in describing me."

Grayson gave her a soft smile. "Maybe, but you sure do look the part."

Iris giggled gently. "Really? How so?"

Grayson scratched his head uncomfortably. "I–I don't know. You kind of look like . . . well you're really . . ." He sighed in frustration as he tried to find the right words. "Please don't take offense to this. I know it's improper for me to say such a thing, but there's just no other way to put it."

Iris arched an eyebrow in curiosity. "Go on. I promise not to get mad."

"Well, you *look* like a savior." He cleared his throat and braced himself for Iris's reaction. "You look very, ummm, celestial."

"Oh . . ." The warmth of a blush ran up Iris's cheeks. "Well, that's just because of the clothes. King Zaerin had his tailor create these for me." She spoke quickly and laughed nervously. She never did know how to handle compliments.

Grayson shook his head. "No, that's not it. I mean, it does help, but there's just something special about you, something about your eyes."

Iris dropped her gaze to the floor in embarrassment. "Th–thank you."

Iris twiddled her thumbs as the conversation stopped. *Me? Celestial? That's very sweet of him to say, but really, now. And what's so special about my eyes? Surely, he just messed up and chose the wrong words. I've done that a thousand times before myself. Okay, so the Holy Father chose me to do something. That still doesn't make me more important or special than anybody else. The Holy Father chooses tons of people to do many different things every day. He didn't pick me because I was so great. He picked me because He wanted to work through me. I'm certain that if He asked someone else, they'd be just as good, if not better than me. The Holy Father wanted me for this. I don't know why, but He did.* Suddenly a new question popped into Iris's mind.

"Grayson?"

"Yes, my lady?"

"Who is your general? The one who told you about me, I mean."

"Oh, that was General Lance."

"Did he say anything else about me?"

"Not in particular." Grayson paused as a playful smile spread across his face. "He would kill me for telling you this, miss, but from the way he talked about you, I gather you left quite an impression on him."

Shoot! My face is turning red again. I can feel it. Iris cleared her throat and tried to respond casually. "Really, now? That's surprising to hear, considering we barely just met today."

"If you ask me, you don't seem like the type who's easily forgotten."

Iris floundered at his words. "I–uh . . ."

Grayson grimaced. "Sorry, my lady, I believe I overstepped my boundaries again, didn't I?"

"It's okay, Grayson, really. I'm not one for formalities, anyway."

"Hmm, sounds like what General Lance always says."

"I guess that means we have something in common, then." Iris smiled pleasantly.

Grayson smiled back at her. Even though she was terribly embarrassed, Iris smiled as he had relaxed a little bit by now. This time, the silence between them was a little more comfortable. Iris was still reeling from the idea that Lance thought so much of her when they had exchanged so few words. She wasn't as angry at him as she had been with the other generals. Surely, since he was such new blood, he wouldn't have taken part in causing Throansburrough's destruction. Iris stifled a gasp as a new horrible thought hit her.

Had Darren known too? Was that why he was so scared from the beginning? He had lied about practically everything else, so why not this? The idea sickened her. How could he not tell her all this *before* she met with the king? Why didn't he try to do something about it? It might not have changed anything, but he could have at least tried! He was a Marquis, after all! *Someone* would have listened to him. The feelings that had died down from the meeting slowly came to the forefront of her mind. This time they held a stronger sense of betrayal than before. *Wait a minute now, Iris,* she thought, trying to calm herself. *You don't know if that is really the case here. Maybe he was so worried for another reason.* Iris looked down at her hands sadly. She wished that were true, but she knew that her first assumption was more likely.

Chapter Twenty-Four

Iris turned her eyes to the window, pulling back the curtain with one hand to enjoy the magnificent sight. They were approaching the buildings around the West Gate. The tall stone structures gleamed in the sunlight. The whole place was surprisingly clean with no evidence of poverty anywhere. *It must be wonderful to live in Alaster.* She smiled a little at the thought but frowned in the next moment.

Why am I getting so worked up about Darren? By all rights, I shouldn't give him another thought, not with all his dishonesty. I should just push him out of my mind, be civil in person, but make no effort at reconciliation. So why do I desperately long to be able to trust him? Maybe it's because he's the first person I met who tried to help me after all this started, and now I've created an unrealistic relationship in my head. That would certainly make sense, but I'm not so sure. Iris softly sighed. *Holy Father, please explain this to me! I don't understand!*

Iris leaned her head against the window. All the different emotions she had been experiencing lately were exhausting. *And this is just the beginning, isn't it?* She smiled grimly. *Holy Father, I need Your strength. Please, please keep reminding me that You haven't left. I need You . . .*

"We're here, my lady," Grayson announced as the carriage pulled to a stop.

Iris sat up and smiled at him. "Thank you, Grayson. And please, call me Iris if you want."

Grayson only smiled and nodded. He turned to the door and opened it. He quickly glanced around. One of the guards already stood to one side of the door, giving the all-clear motion. Grayson stepped down and then offered Iris his hand. She accepted it and exited the carriage gracefully, one hand holding Grayson's and the other holding up the hem of her dress so that she wouldn't trip on the step. Grayson and another soldier walked beside her as they went through the gate and approached the transport platform.

Iris had to admit that she wasn't too thrilled with the idea of getting back on another transport so soon. After all, she had only gotten off one this morning. Now she would spend yet another four days cooped up with a bunch of strange men by herself. Hopefully these men would be more trustworthy than the last crew she was stuck with.

In the distance, a man paced up and down the platform unhappily. As they drew near him, she discovered that it was none other than Darren looking so disheveled. *What in the lands could be bothering him?* Iris didn't want to confront him just yet and steered her escort off to the side. But her plan didn't last long as Darren caught sight of her.

"Iris!" he called out and jogged over to her side.

As he drew closer, he slowed down considerably, noticing the change in her appearance. His jaw dropped slightly, and eyes widened. In a daze, he took a few more sluggish steps toward her. The hold of his eyes quickly made her feel self-conscious, forcing her to look away. Iris just barely caught him whispering "wow" under his breath. She wished he would stop staring at her.

"What?" she cried at last.

Darren snapped back to attention. His countenance instantly changed, and he snarled, "Iris, how could you not tell me what Valomeer made you do?"

Iris gazed back, her eyes narrowing slightly. Did he honestly have the nerve to attack her for not sharing something with him?

"Forgive me," she said icily, "I had other things on my mind, *Your Grace.*"

He backed up a step. "Iris, I . . ."

She crossed her arms and waited for him to continue. After a few moments of silence, Iris rolled her eyes. "Well now, that clears everything up, doesn't it? I'll just excuse myself to go wait for the transport." She gave him an exaggerated curtsey and then walked briskly past him.

Grayson and the other soldier allowed her to go alone. She wasn't that far away, and as long as she was in view, they were satisfied. They instead reported in to Darren. After all, Iris *had* made him the head of her protection. Iris now wondered what had possessed her to do so. Releasing an irritated sigh, she focused instead on watching the workers prepare their transport. The other two soldiers from the carriage helped the men load the food supplies. *Good grief, I know a few more of us are coming than last time, but they're putting enough on there to last us a month!* As she watched, she noticed that two of the soldiers looked familiar to her. *That's just silly. I don't know a soul in Alaster! Even so, they remind me of someone.*

Iris was so busy trying to figure out who they were that she didn't hear Darren come up behind her.

"Look, I'm sorry for yelling at you and . . . I'm sorry for not telling you about, well everything, but you have to understand. It wasn't something I was ready to share."

Iris gave him a dirty look. "So you decided to just drop it on top of me in front of the king?"

"I hadn't planned on doing that, but at the moment, it seemed like the best idea."

"No, the best idea would have been for you to be forthright with me from the start!"

"Well, what about you? You haven't necessarily been open with me, either." He gestured at the bracelet on her wrist.

"*That* I hid because I didn't want you to feel responsible or guilty about it. What *you* hid was because *you* felt guilty and wanted to save face." They both knew she was right.

Since Darren was at a loss for words, Iris chose this moment to ask him the question that had been weighing on her. "Darren, for *once*, be completely honest with me. Did you know about the prophecy?"

"Well, I . . ."

"No games, Darren, I want a straight answer. Did you know?"

"I was running around with Kyle back then and only cared about myself. I know that's a stupid excuse, and I wish I could change it—"

"So, it's yes then. You knew all along, which is why you panicked the first time I spoke to you." Iris was surprised to find that, more than anything, she felt disappointed. "Why didn't you tell me?"

"I didn't think it was necessary."

"What is it with you people? Your uncle didn't think it was very important either and look at how well *that* ended!" she spit back at him bitterly.

"Look, telling you the reason for the attack before wouldn't change what happened and sure wouldn't help you feel better!"

"No! But I could have been more prepared. For crying out loud, I would have appreciated an advance warning about being this Woman of Prophecy!"

Darren blinked a couple of times. "Wait, what?"

"Apparently I'm it! All the little soldier men know. How could you have not heard? How could you have not connected the dots for your-self, for that matter?" Iris shook her head in unbelief.

"Look, I never actually read the prophecy. I only heard it second-hand from Professor Hethers, and I wasn't paying very close attention back then."

"Wait, did you say Hethers? As in, Andrew Hethers?"

"Yes? He was my history tutor for a time, but why—"

"Do you know where he is now?"

"No? No one does. He was supposed to go to prison for spreading treasonous ideas, but one day, he just disappeared from his cell. No one has seen him since."

Iris sighed unhappily.

"So what is the Woman of Prophecy supposed to do?" Darren asked nervously.

"Be the savior of all of Fitsengea."

"How are you going to do that?"

"How would *I* know?! I just found all this out, remember?" she snapped.

Darren sighed. "Iris, I really am sorry—"

"Alright, looks like you're all set."

Darren and Iris looked up as the Master of the Transports, Flyn, walked toward them.

"She's all packed and ready to go. Oh, and my boys told me that you were on a tight schedule, so I took the liberty of coating the stone lights in my special formula."

"And what formula would that be, exactly?" Darren asked skeptically.

"Don't worry, it's been thoroughly tested, so it's perfectly safe."

"I'm sure it is, sir." Iris smiled kindly. "But what does it do?"

"Oh, it makes the transport go twice as fast!" Flyn nodded proudly. "It should only take you two days to get to Saunskirt instead of the usual four days."

"Does the king know you've created this formula?"

Flyn looked at Darren and puffed out his chest a little bit. "Of course, the king knows. It was his idea to start this project in the first place."

"Then I'm certain it will be fine." Iris spoke up, noticing that the man was becoming irritated. "Thank you very much, sir, for doing this for us. I'm sure it will be very helpful."

Flyn blushed at Iris's attention and rubbed at his nose out of habit. "Aw, it's nothing, miss, I just do what I can." He addressed Darren, his tone harshening. "You're good to board. Just make sure you're all securely fastened in before it takes off." He nodded to Iris. "Safe journey, miss."

Iris thanked him again as he walked back to his post. When Flyn was out of earshot, Darren tried to pick up their conversation from where he had left off. But Iris wasn't in the mood to hear any more of his excuses. She held up her hand stopping him.

"We'll finish this later, okay? For now, let's just get out of here." She strode away from Darren and onto the transport.

To her surprise, the interior was much different than the transport from Saunskirt. Instead of a big open space in the middle, this transport had tons of chairs bolted in place, each equipped with their own securing straps. The two soldiers who helped load up the transport were already seated along the front row and ready to go. Iris went to introduce herself to them and sat down by the one closest to her. Just as she was about to speak, Darren came through the doors and made an announcement.

"Alright, everyone, strap in. We're pulling out."

With that, he walked over to the nearest seat to buckle in. Grayson and the other soldier came jogging in to ready themselves. Iris quickly followed suit and snapped the buckle securely. The doors released, hissing as they slowly closed. The chemicals sprayed loudly underneath. In the next second, the entire transport shot forward. The force of the momentum was much greater than Iris expected and seemed double the strength of that of the other transport. *Wow, that new chemical sure does have a kick to it!* Iris thought as her whole body melted into the chair. Iris gripped onto the armrest instinctively. Fighting the force, the soldier beside her reassuringly placed his hand on top of hers.

"Just hang in there, princess, it's almost over."

Princess? Iris moved her head to the side. "Kyle?"

Kyle sat pressed against his seat as well but gave her a cocky smile and wink. *How in all the lands did* he *get here?* The next instant, the transport jolted and slowed to a constant, though faster-than-normal, speed. The change in speed slammed everyone against their restraint devices for a second. Now that the speed had stabilized, everyone breathed a collective sigh of relief and released themselves from their chairs. Nearly everyone rose immediately, doing their best to stand on wobbly legs, a side effect of adjusting to the intense speed that they now traveled. Iris, however, remained seated, staring in surprise at Kyle beside her.

"How did–when did–where did you—" She stopped and pressed her lips together, forcing her mouth to say what was on her mind. She inhaled deeply and started again, more slowly this time. "Kyle, why are you on this transport?"

Kyle shrugged. "Sounded like fun," he teased.

"Kyle," Iris warned.

"Ha ha, okay, okay. Bryant and I needed a ride back to Saunskirt to meet up with Malachi and Aaron."

Iris suppressed a frown. "Bryant's here too?"

"Yep." Kyle craned his neck around until he caught sight of him. "Ah! There he is, being cornered by Darren."

Iris followed his gaze to see that, sure enough, a not-too-pleased Darren was busy talking with Bryant. No wonder the other soldier had looked so familiar! Iris sighed and shook her head.

"But why *this* transport? You could have chosen any other one without disguising yourself."

Kyle shrugged again, crossed his arms behind his head, closed his eyes, and leaned back in the chair. "Maybe I just like the challenge."

"But you still had three days left in Alaster. Didn't you want to spend time with your family?"

Kyle's body went rigid at the suggestion. He took a moment to respond quietly. "They wouldn't want to see me anyway."

"*You!*"

Iris whipped her head around as Darren stomped toward them. Iris could see the veins throbbing beside Darren's temple. Kyle peeked out one eye but didn't even flinch.

"What in the lands do you think you're doing?" Darren exclaimed as he positioned himself directly in front of Kyle.

"Relaxing in a chair. What are you doing?"

Darren lunged forward and grabbed the collar of Kyle's uniform. "Don't get smart with me!"

"I'm sorry, does it hurt you that much to think?"

Iris jumped out of her seat and forced herself between the two. "Darren! Kyle! Knock it off!"

Darren stepped backwards reluctantly, keeping his eyes trained on Kyle, the hate evident. Kyle simply readjusted his stolen uniform.

"I am *not* in the mood to put up with either of you right now!" Iris stated as her gaze flickered between them. "Yes, Darren, you're right to be angry. They shouldn't have done this. We don't even know how they confiscated those uniforms, and I, for one, don't care to find out! It's been a *really* long day, and I have absolutely no desire to add fighting to the long list of crap I've had to put up with. So save it for when I'm not around. Got it?" She put her hands on her hips and stared at each of them in turn, driving home the message.

Both Kyle and Darren nodded reluctantly at her and then avoided each other's eyes. Iris sighed in exasperation and walked away. Maybe the best thing for her to do right now was just to lie down for a bit. She really didn't want to talk to anyone or even be around anyone right now. She wished that all this was over, but she had a feeling that it would be quite some time before she experienced any semblance of true peace. In the meantime, she would just have to suck it up and take a break wherever she could.

Iris flopped down on one of the bunks at the back of the transport. She rolled to her side, away from everyone else. Her mind ran a mile a minute, keeping her awake. Her body, on the other hand, betrayed its true exhaustion as soon as it hit the mattress. *Well, if I can't sleep, at least I can rest here for a bit. That'll be better than nothing, I suppose.* Iris tried to calm her racing thoughts to give her mind a break. She tried just staring numbly at the wall, but she just had too many questions piled up from today for that tactic to work. She finally resorted to telling herself the stories she had heard as a child. She relaxed at their comforting familiarity.

She imagined each scene, playing them out thoroughly in her mind. This distracted her so well that she didn't notice that night was falling. She would have continued in this exercise through the night if it hadn't been for the gentle tapping she felt on her shoulder. Iris moved her head slightly to see who it was.

"Excuse me, my lady, I'm sorry if I woke you. But I wanted to let you know that dinner is ready if you want any."

Iris rolled over to face him. "It's alright. I wasn't asleep. Thank you for letting me know." She propped herself up on her left arm. "So far, I know everyone's name here but yours. Would you mind sharing it with me?" Iris smiled.

The soldier smiled in return. "You may call me Jason, my lady."

Iris sat up and put her legs over the side of the bed. "Thank you, Jason, and you may call me Iris."

Jason offered her his hand to help her stand. Iris accepted it politely. She walked with him to a section of chairs where the others were seated. Everyone else had already started eating their meals. Darren sat apart from Kyle and Bryant. Grayson was seated in between the group. Iris went and sat by Grayson; Jason followed her and handed her a portion of the meal. Maybe she would relax more around these two new men. They were likely to be more loyal and trustworthy than her other male escorts. After all, these two had trained to be honorable soldiers under King Zaerin, and right now, their sworn duty was to protect her.

The mere physical presence of the pair gave Iris a better sense of security. *At least I won't have to babysit them like I do Darren and Kyle.* Satisfied with that thought, Iris ate her meal of dried meat, Askgan cheese, and sweet Brenberry fruit, washing it all down with a cool glass of water. Just as she was finishing up, she noticed Kyle out of the corner of her eye. He had shifted himself in his chair so that he was now sitting backwards and faced Iris directly.

"So tell me, boys, are you secretly Diviners in training, or did Bryant's face scare you so badly that you *still* can't find your tongue?"

"Hey!" Bryant spouted beside him in between mouthfuls of food.

"Honest is honest, Bryant. You've gotta face the facts someday, old friend."

Bryant muttered under his breath as he continued eating. Kyle gave up trying to decipher his words and refocused on the soldiers.

"You boys didn't answer my question. In fact, neither of you have made an effort to speak to me at all since we've been here. I'm beginning to worry if you know *how* to speak."

Grayson calmly took a sip from his cup before responding. "We simply prefer not to waste our breath on scum like you. But ignoring a direct question is childish, which is why I have answered."

Kyle feigned a look of pain. "Why, dear me! Whatever could I have done to upset you boys so? I mean, it couldn't be the fact that my compatriot and I were so easily able to do away with your fellow soldiers and then take their place without notice. No, it couldn't be *that.*"

Don't tell me they . . . "Kyle, what do you mean by 'do away with?' You didn't . . ."

Kyle's face turned serious. "Don't worry, Iris. That would have been far too easy. Not that apprehending them wasn't easy enough."

Iris breathed to slow her racing heart. She prayed that Kyle was telling the truth. She wouldn't know how to handle the situation if she had to deal with murderers on the transport. Thankfully, Kyle's response was as sincere as they came, well, at least for Kyle, that is.

Kyle turned his attention on Jason. "And you have nothing to add? No other attacks on my character? Or are you just going to sit there and continue this child's game of the silent treatment?"

Jason didn't even look at Kyle. He took the last bite of his food, stood up, and went to the bathroom to rinse his plate. Kyle rolled his eyes and turned around in his chair.

"I fear this will be an extremely boring trip, my friend," Kyle stated to Bryant. Bryant chuckled in reply.

"You brought it on yourself," Iris pointed out.

"And how, exactly, did I do that?"

"Kyle, you're anything but innocent, so don't even start with me! You know *exactly* why they're treating you this way. And something tells me that you *want* them to! Is it so that you can reaffirm your preconceived notions of an Alastrian soldier?"

Kyle stood from his seat. "I'm going to bed."

As Kyle walked away, Bryant stood as well. "Right, since we're announcing our actions now, I'm gonna go take a shower. If anyone else needs the bathroom, tough. I plan on taking my time."

Iris rolled her eyes. At least she could look forward to finally being rid of that brute when they reached Saunskirt.

"You're a very sharp individual."

"Pardon me?" Confused, Iris turned to Grayson.

"What you said back there to that Kyle fellow; you struck a nerve, miss."

"Well . . . it wasn't really my intention."

"I don't mean to make you feel uncomfortable. I just wanted to point it out. Very well said, Miss Iris."

"I–I suppose . . . Thank you for the compliment, Grayson."

Grayson nodded and rose from his place.

"Though I was wondering," Iris called out to him before he left, "if maybe you and Jason could *try* to be civil with them. I know I have no right to ask this of you, but it *would* make our situation easier for the time being . . . a–and you would be proving him wrong if you want of think of it that way."

Grayson paused thoughtfully before smiling. "Very well said indeed. Alright, Miss Iris, I will do my best to be civil with them and will notify Jason of your wishes. Goodnight, my lady." He bowed slightly before turning and heading toward the bunks.

Iris sat silently for a minute, looking out the large window in front of her. The sky was growing dark. Soon the lights on the outside of the transport would come on, which meant that the ones indoors would shut off. *I can't wait to sleep in a normal bed again instead of in these transport bunks. And getting more than just a couple of hours of sleep at a time will be nice.*

"Ahem."

Startled, Iris looked up at Darren standing next to her, waiting until he had her attention. "This seat taken?" he indicated to the one on Iris's left.

Iris pursed her lips together. "Yes."

Darren remained standing, not exactly sure how to respond. Iris quit tormenting him and sighed heavily. "But this one's not." She patted the seat on her right.

Darren smiled slightly at her joke, then sat in the chair she pointed to. Both of them remained silent beside each other for a while. Iris contemplated starting a conversation, but she just couldn't bring herself to do it. After all, why should *she* be the one making all of the effort? Any bad blood between the two of them was his fault anyway—well, mostly. Iris's stubbornness finally won out.

"I believe . . . it's my turn again." Darren spoke at last.

Iris looked over at him, waiting patiently for him to continue. Darren dropped his gaze and nervously played with his hands. "I want to tell you I'm sorry, Iris, but right now, those words sound so empty. Cheap, almost. I can put as much feeling behind them as I can muster, but . . . it wouldn't be enough, would it? To say that things have been tough for you is an understatement, and I sure as heck haven't done anything to help you through that. I've made things worse, harder for you and . . . you were right. I should have told you about my uncle *before* you met him and maybe even mentioned the prophecy. And I—"

"I'm sorry I didn't tell you about my arrangement with Valomeer."

Darren raised his head, surprised.

"To admonish you for not being completely honest with me while I wasn't truthful with you is hypocritical. For that, I'm sorry."

Darren dropped his head again. "I guess, in the end, we both messed up." He gave a half smile, which quickly faded "I wish . . . I wish you felt like you could have trusted me enough to tell me sooner."

Iris cocked an eyebrow.

"I know, I know. And I should have trusted you enough to tell *you* everything. I'm sorry that I didn't."

Iris sighed "We barely know each other, Darren. That's all this proves. Maybe . . . our expectations were too high?"

Darren's voice dropped lower "You needed someone to believe in. I *should* have been that for you . . ."

Iris's heart ached at his sincerity. The poor guy looked miserable. Iris wanted to stay angry with him, but she was rapidly losing this fight. Now she wanted to tell him that everything was okay and to not worry, but that would have been a lie. And yet . . . maybe it all would be okay in time. But how much time? And would she be able to trust him again? Really, it depended on whether or not he proved himself trustworthy. She hoped he would.

"So . . . why did you choose me?"

Iris focused her attention back on their conversation. "As the head of my protection, you mean?"

Darren nodded.

"Because I knew that King Zaerin would demand that you go wherever I went, and if I had to return to Alaster, you could spend more time with your family."

Darren raised his head slowly. "You did that . . . for me? Even after everything you know?"

Iris shrugged. "I just don't think it's right to keep a family apart." Her voice faded to almost a whisper. "If you're lucky enough to have one, you should cherish them as long as you can."

Darren lowered his head sadly, whispering another, "I'm sorry."

Iris clasped and unclasped her hands together a few times as she thought carefully about what to say next. She finally worked up the nerve to continue and broached the subject that had been weighing on her mind.

"There's . . . a lot more to your story, isn't there? The whole thing that happened between you and Kyle, the trouble in Alaster. You haven't shared all of it with me yet, have you?"

Darren sighed. "No."

Iris waited for him to continue, but he said nothing. "Are you going to tell me?"

"I . . . I will, but I just can't right now. Please try to understand."

Impatient, Iris bit her bottom lip. Even so, she really had no choice but to agree. "Okay, Darren, I'll wait until you're ready to talk. Just promise me that you won't forget to get yourself ready."

He chuckled softly. "Right. I promise."

Iris let go of a sigh and then pushed herself out of her chair. "Well, now that *that's* all been taken care of. I suppose it's time we say good-night. I want to be well rested for when we reach X32 tomorrow. Maybe this time, I can actually see some of the town!"

Darren smiled thoughtfully and rose as well. They walked together over to their packs and pulled out their night attire. Iris waited outside the bathroom as Darren went in and kicked Bryant out so that she could change in private. Once she finished, she made her way toward an empty set of bunks. Everyone was already in bed, and she didn't want to wake anyone. In addition, she was uncomfortable with the close proximity to so many men at night. As she prepared herself for bed, she looked over her shoulder at Darren on the other side of the room. He was looking back at her. He raised a hand and mouthed, "Good night." Iris smiled and waved back. She laid down and pulled up the covers over her shoulders. *Click.* All the lights in the transport turned off. Iris relaxed and closed her eyes, thankful to rest. Today had been a *really* long day.

Chapter Twenty-Five

A ray of sunlight danced upon Iris's heavy eyelids. She didn't want to open them. Her body begged her for more sleep. She thought about rolling over and pulling the covers over her head to keep out the persistent rising sun. But any true hope of going back to sleep was soon thwarted by the click of the inner lights turning on. The others moved around, rustling as they got ready. *If everyone else is getting up, I guess that means I really should too. Who knows what they'll think of me if I'm the only one who stayed asleep for a few more hours? Oh, the extra rest sure would be lovely! Oh well, another time, maybe.*

Relinquishing to the light, Iris pried open her eyes. Sitting up, she looked around groggily. She spotted a trunk positioned near the head of her bed on the floor. *That's strange. I don't remember seeing that there before I went to sleep nor did I hear anyone move it here this morning. Wonder why someone decided to place it there of all places? Maybe it really was there last night, and I just didn't notice. I can't believe how oblivious I can be sometimes!*

Iris gave a small yawn and then stretched. Oh well, it wasn't that big of a deal anyway. She decided to put it out of her mind as she dropped her feet to the cold metal floor. She hopped around in search of her shoes at the drastic change in temperature after snuggling under her warm, cozy blanket. Finding the shoes beneath her bed, she immediately scooped them up and pulled them on. Now the floor was more bearable. She looked for an outfit for the day and snuck to the bathroom before anyone else claimed it.

She made it in just in time to beat Bryant. For someone who was often ill-groomed and disgusting on all levels, he sure enjoyed taking his time in front of the mirror. She couldn't understand how unattractive men had such distorted mental images of themselves. True, he probably wasn't as hideous as her mind made him out to be, but what she knew of his character tainted her perception of his physical appearance.

Iris didn't take long to shower and dress. Her only problem was deciding what to do with her damp hair. Since it was so thick and long, it would take forever to dry if she put it up or braided it, but if she just left it down, it would constantly fall in her face. After some thought, she made two small braids from the hair that framed her face and tied them back with the ribbon she had worn the previous day.

Iris double-checked herself in the mirror. Yes, this style would do the trick and keep her hair out of her eyes. It didn't look half bad either. She smirked slightly at her reflection. She was overdressed in the silver-and-white gown she wore, but she really had no other choice. Still, a part of her couldn't help but enjoy the frills a bit. As a child, she and her sister often pretended to dress as she was now. She wondered what Julie would say if she saw her like this. She wished she could show her. Tears welled up in her eyes at the thought of Julie. A few raps at the bathroom door brought her back to reality.

"Are you done in there yet?" Bryant called out impatiently from the other side. Iris frantically brushed the tears from her eyes and responded through a forced smile.

"Coming."

She quickly gathered up her night gown and her towel. With a glance in the mirror, she wiped away the last remaining tears and all traces of sadness from her face and then exited the room.

"Finally." Bryant grumbled under his breath as he rushed past her. Iris rolled her eyes at his attitude, that of a self-absorbed teenage boy although he was one of the oldest guys here. Iris shook her head to rid her mind of her annoyance and headed to see what the other guys were up to after putting away her things.

Grayson, Kyle, and Jason all sat around each other in the chairs at the center of the transport. Grayson and Kyle were still clothed in their night wear, waiting for their turn in the bathroom. On the other hand, Jason looked refreshed and ready for anything. As Iris approached, Kyle smiled and waved in greeting.

"Morning, Iris."

Iris smiled back. "Good morning, Kyle. Sleep well?"

"Just fine, thanks."

He sure seems like he's in a good mood. Iris moved her eyes to Grayson and Jason. *They don't look agitated. Maybe they actually* are *trying to get along. Now* that *would be a great change of pace. Though if it's true, it sure is suspicious how easily things smoothed over between them.* As Iris came up to them, Grayson stood and stepped aside so that Iris could sit among them all. He bowed slightly as she passed by.

"Good morning, my lady."

Jason echoed the gesture as Iris sat next to him. Iris smiled at both of them and wished them a good morning as well. Grayson sat down beside her, and Kyle remained in his turned around position so that he could visit with everyone more easily. Grayson, Bryant, and Kyle had not been up much longer than she had, but Jason, as she had assumed, had been awake since dawn. Kyle and Jason remarked that they shared of the commonality of both tending to rise early. Preferring to sleep in, Iris agreed with Grayson about not understanding morning people. As they continued to joke and talk, Iris felt the need to ask them about why they were all getting along so much better now.

Jason looked at her seriously. "Because you asked us to."

Iris blinked a couple of times at the straightforward response. "Well, yes, I did. And I'm glad that you're all trying. But I'm surprised at how quickly you reconciled yourselves."

"Well, I was raised to try my best to do as a lady's request. And I don't think my mother would be pleased if she heard that I mistreated my cousin." Jason shrugged, looking at Kyle.

"Wait! You two are *related?*"

They both nodded.

"Well, why didn't you say something earlier?"

"Because neither of us figured it out till this morning," Kyle answered. "We're actually second cousins, and we haven't seen the other since we were kids."

"We didn't connect the dots of our family names until today."

Iris simply shook her head and turned to Grayson. "And what about you? You don't happen to have some hidden connection with anyone on this transport, do you?"

Grayson laughed. "Not that I'm aware of, my lady."

Iris chuckled in turn. Just then, the door to the bathroom opened, and Bryant stepped out with a loud, pleased sigh. He stretched and looked around causally until he spotted the group sitting in the chairs. He sauntered over and plopped down next to Kyle. Kyle looked at Bryant and then back at the others before rising.

"Right, then, my turn to get all prettied up."

"I don't think we have enough time to wait for *that* to happen."

Kyle looked down at Bryant and smiled. "Now we're even for my comment about your face from before, huh?" Laughing, he grabbed his toiletries and clothing and then went to change.

As Iris watched him, she looked around again. "Is Darren still not up?"

"The Marquis Turner? No, I believe he's still sleeping. Do you want me to go wake him?" Grayson responded dutifully.

"N–no that's okay, let him be. I guess he didn't sleep too well last night then."

"Well, since everyone else is up, I suppose we should prepare the portions for breakfast. Would you mind giving me a hand, Lady Iris?" Jason asked with a polite smile.

Iris nodded happily. Maybe this meant that he would stop treating her so formally if he was actually asking for help. "I'd be more than glad to."

Iris followed Jason over to the far side of the transport where all the food supplies were kept. None of the food needed to be cooked as there was nowhere to do so. Food preparations included finding the right container, dividing up the food, locating the dishes, and carrying everything to the others so they could all eat. It wasn't hard, but Iris was happy to help. The idea of standing on ceremony annoyed her. She would do whatever she could to prove that she really was just a normal person.

About halfway through the preparations, Jason stopped and glanced up at Iris. "I know I have no right to ask this, but . . . Lady Iris, what is your relationship to the Marquis Turner?"

Iris tilted her head to the side. "You mean Darren? Well, I . . . hmmm . . . I'm not sure, really, why do you ask?"

"I–I was just wondering. I'm sorry I brought it up."

Iris scrunched her brow; he wanted to say more but was afraid he was stepping out of line. She moved over and placed a reassuring hand on his shoulder. "No, go ahead. What is it?"

He looked over at her, his inner struggle obvious from the expression on his face. Iris smiled encouragingly.

"It would seem . . . that possibly the Marquis thinks more highly of you than you realize."

Iris couldn't help but step back, fighting the urge to laugh nervously. "W–what do you mean?"

Jason sighed and rubbed his left arm. "Look, I would never do this normally, but something about you makes me want to reveal everything to you."

"Okay . . . ?"

"Last night, I got up to get some water after everyone else was sleeping. You were tossing and turning a lot. It seems as if I wasn't the only one to notice. Marquis Turner got up and went over to you. He put that trunk by the head of your bed and sat next to you. I don't think he noticed me walk by. When I got up this morning, he was still there. But he saw me and went back to bed. I think he had been there all night."

Dumbfounded, Iris's mouth gaped wide. Speechless, she wondered, *Why would Darren do that?* "Did you see what he was doing?" she asked tentatively.

Jason shook his head. "No, not exactly. It was very dark, and he was angled away from me. But I could tell that he had no ill intent."

Iris's mind reeled at this new information. "Th–thank you, Jason . . . for letting me know." Her eyes moved in a dazed manner to Darren's bunk across the transport. *What in all the lands could* that *have been all about?*

"Could you do me a favor, Jason? Don't mention this to anyone else, okay?"

Jason nodded solemnly. "As you wish, my lady."

They both turned silently back to the supplies. Iris was thankful that Jason didn't feel like talking anymore. She didn't think she could have focused if he had. She was too preoccupied, her mind doing back flips and jumbling up all sorts of thoughts. What bothered her most right now was that she really wanted to ask Darren what he was doing, but she had no idea how to approach him or if she even should. She did not want to think about this anymore, but her thoughts her were stuck. What would she do when he woke up? How could she face him without giving away that she knew? Things were going to get very awkward.

Jason and Iris brought the plates of food over to where the rest were seated. By this time, Kyle had already returned, and Grayson was dressing. Everyone ate their food quietly, but it wasn't long before Kyle started cracking jokes. Eventually even Jason joined in, sharing stories about their relatives that Kyle didn't know. Grateful, Iris enjoyed the easy-going atmosphere and light banter. She couldn't worry about talking to Darren until he was actually up, and he probably wouldn't awaken for quite a while since he had been up all night. Instead, she focused on spending her time with the others. She enjoyed just sitting and listening to their different stories. When they couldn't think of a tale that connected to the previous person's story, they told some sort of riddle they had learned from home to test the other's wits. Kyle was often the first one to solve them.

The day continued in similar fashion: talking, joking, and getting to know each other better. Grayson and Bryant showed off some of their favorite escape techniques, taking the time to explain them to Iris just in case she found herself in a position to use them. Iris didn't think that she would ever be in a place where she needed this knowledge, but she still had fun learning. A few simple moves could bring down a grown man, and the others seemed to get a kick out of watching her too.

When she finished, Jason led her up the ladder in the wall of the transport to the upper railing. Passengers weren't supposed to go there; only technicians were allowed to keep tabs on the transport's condition. But since Jason's father had helped build some of the transports, he knew just the spots to check out the transport more thoroughly. On her way to Alaster, Iris had just been shown some of the basic features. This time, she actually crawled into some of the spaces used by the technicians.

At first, Jason tried to dissuade her for fear of ruining her clothes. But Iris didn't care and convinced him to let her go, not that it took much persuading. Once they finished exploring those cramped spaces, they joined the others. Lunch time was nearing, and Iris was ready for a bite.

"So are you planning on becoming a transport worker after all this?"

Iris looked over her shoulder as she stepped down the ladder. Darren stood there smiling at her. He had finally woken up while she and Jason were busy. Iris's heart hammered in her chest. *Act naturally, just calm down, and pretend like you don't know anything!* After the last step, she turned to him and smiled.

"I'll need *some* way to earn my keep in the future, won't I?"

Darren laughed at her joke. "Guess so."

"Lunchtime!" Grayson called out from the side, bringing out the next batch of food.

Iris gave a mental sigh of relief at the interruption. Everyone soon took their places and began eating with less talking than before. As far as Iris could tell, Darren's presence shut Kyle down, which, in turn, affected the whole group. Iris just wished that they would somehow get over it and start fresh. Maybe she was asking too much. She still didn't know the full story between them. She wanted to take Kyle aside and ask him to tell her everything, but if she did that, she would betray Darren's trust. She knew how badly that felt, so she refused to do it to him. With no other choice, she instead focused on the food and ate in silence.

They relaxed a little after lunch finished, mainly because the group had splintered once again. Kyle and Darren moved as far away from each other as possible. Iris ignored them both and stood in front of the large window. It wouldn't be much longer before they reached X32. They were really flying along the road now, thanks to that special chemical the Master of the Transports had concocted. As Iris looked into the distance, she wondered what lay ahead. She concentrated on the enemy she now faced.

How far had they traveled now? Had they already tried to attack Saunskirt? They left nearly a week ago. She hoped and prayed that Valomeer hadn't ignored her warning after all. Maybe he had taken action to protect their city. Or better yet, maybe the enemy had bypassed them altogether. *I wonder if our enemy is truly the Yansairens?*

Iris absentmindedly shook her head. She couldn't help but hope that the king was right in his claim. Yes, they were very dangerous, but at least she could put a face, a name, to this mysterious enemy. And if it *was* them, then the Father already had some kind of plan to make things right again. Although that did little to comfort her because it brought forth the question of exactly what she was expected to do. In addition, *all* of this could have been avoided. *I know . . . I know. I have to trust that You know what You're doing, but . . . I can't help it if it still hurts to know that you didn't save* my *home. And now you're asking me to save everyone else . . . when You didn't save them. Forgive me, Holy Father, I am too weak to even try to understand.*

Iris wrapped her arms around herself and stared beyond the window without focusing on the landscape. She was distracted by her racing thoughts, so lost within herself that she didn't even realize that Darren had come up beside her until after a few moments. She finally looked at him sideways, thankful that he didn't ask what was bothering her. As her emotions swirled, she didn't think she could keep it together. She wanted to hide her tears from the others. Iris breathed slowly to calm herself down before turning to Darren. Before she could say a word, he interrupted her.

"I was trying to help you sleep." Darren spoke without moving his head to look at her.

Iris closed her mouth and stared at him in confusion. "What?"

"You were having nightmares again. I've done the same thing every night since we first left Saunskirt. I noticed that . . . as long as my fingers moved through your hair, you could sleep peacefully."

"I . . ."

"That first night when we fell asleep under the window, that's how I found out. That's why I always take naps during the day."

"But how did you . . ."

"How did I know that you knew about last night? I asked Jason if he had told you. Don't be mad at him. I kind of . . . *ordered* him to be honest with me." Darren clenched his fist and turned to face Iris. "I'm telling you all of this because I want to be honest with you. I know it might take a long time for you to get over what I failed to tell you before, but I–I want to try and make it right."

Iris froze at his revelation and the inconceivable embarrassment of his words. She was grateful for his desire to be honest, but she was floored by how he went about it. Besides, it wasn't as if she wasn't just as embarrassed as he was. Laughing off his confession, she made a joke in an attempt to diffuse the tension.

"Oh, come on, Darren, you were just worried that I'd think you were some creepy man who liked to watch girls in their sleep. That's why you're telling me this now. Admit it!" Iris gave him a teasing smile and laughed nervously.

Darren didn't take the bait. Instead he waited for her to answer seriously. What did he want her to say? Did he want her to flip out and demand he stop, or was she supposed to ply him with praise for being so considerate? Did he expect her to tell him that his actions secretly melted her heart while adding to her internal confusion and awkwardness. Or that there was still a side of her that thought this whole thing really *was* weird? She had no clue what to say, but she *did* know that she wished he would stop waiting for her to speak! And yet, she knew she would have to say something eventually. Why was no one around to interrupt a conversation when you wanted them to?

"I . . ." She sighed and pushed a strand of hair behind her ear. Her eyes dropped to the floor. She couldn't bring herself to look back into his. "I really don't know what to say. I'm . . . I'm not mad at you, if you were worried about that, and I *do* like your forthrightness and honesty with me. But I have too much on my mind right now to think about this too. So . . ."

"That's okay, I understand."

Iris peeked up at him, catching the gentle look on his face. Good, at least she hadn't upset him.

"Fifteen minutes to checkpoint! Prepare yourself for arrival!" Kyle bellowed off in the distance.

Iris raised her head at the announcement. She turned to the window to see if she could see X32 yet.

"Hey! There's something wrong with the road up ahead!" Darren called out to no one in particular as he strained his eyes to see.

Iris followed suit but couldn't see anything amiss.

"Grayson!" Jason called up to him from below the platform along the side. "Pull out the magnification scope!"

Grayson dashed to one end of the walkway, pulled a series of levers, and readjusted some stone lights before a device popped out of the wall. He hunched over and put his face up to it, moving a dial on the wall with his right hand to focus the device on the correct spot. Once he had the scope on the area Darren had indicated, he cried in horror and spun around to yell down at the rest.

"The road is out! A wide trench is in its place!"

Darren spun on his heel, "*What*! Activate the emergency shut off! We've got to stop this thing before it crashes!"

Grayson ran to the other end of the walkway and slipped into one of the small spaces that Jason had shown Iris before. On the main floor of the transport, Jason had run to one of the walls beneath the walkway and was removing a panel that hid one of the emergency switches.

"Iris! Get strapped in now! This is going to be a rough stop!" Darren shouted at her as he ran over to give Jason a hand.

Iris rushed to one of the seats on the front row and followed his orders. "But what about you and the others? How will you keep yourselves from being thrown around?" she shouted to him over her shoulder.

"We'll be fine! Kyle, look after Iris!"

Kyle ran up to where Iris was seated and positioned himself next to her. Bryant also ran to a nearby chair and strapped himself in.

"Everybody, hang on!" Jason cried out. "Now, Grayson!" And with that, Jason and Darren pulled down the switch in the wall as Grayson maneuvered some wires upstairs.

An ear-splitting whine echoed throughout the entire structure. In the next moment a body-wrenching jolt flung Iris harshly against her straps as the transport decelerated. Sitting back up, she looked at Darren and Jason, who had survived the slow down by hanging onto the handles next to the lever. *That was close!*

"It's not enough!" Grayson shouted in a panic from above. He shoved himself from the room and threw himself against the railing. "It's not enough! The transport is going too fast! We can't slow it down anymore!"

Darren backed up from under the walkway to look into Grayson's face. "What do you *mean*, it's not enough?!"

"We're going too fast! We won't stop in time!"

"The ravine is coming into sight!" Kyle shouted his warning.

"That blasted transport master has doomed us all!" Bryant moaned bitterly.

"Grayson, get down here!" Darren ordered as he and Jason rushed to their seats.

Grayson ran to the ladder, putting his hands and feet on the railing and sliding down it to the bottom. Once he hit the floor, he rushed over to the chairs. Just as he sat down to strap himself in, Iris looked out the window. Her eyes doubled in size as a gaping hole appeared where the road should have been. They really *were* going to crash!

"Brace yourselves!" Darren warned from behind her.

Holy Father, please! Don't let us die! Iris closed her eyes tightly and threw her arms over her head to protect herself. She didn't even have time to scream as her stomach dropped to the ground in the next instant. The transport careened over the edge of where the road had once been. The hole wasn't as deep as she had first thought because instead of falling to their deaths, the transport smashed into the bottom. The front crashed with such great force that the entire vehicle flung forward, flipping the back end completely over them. As they flew upside down in the air, the giant glass window in front of them shattered, flinging glass toward them.

At the same time, Kyle partially undid some of his straps and draped himself over Iris to the best of his ability. Iris tensed in fear as she tried to curl up into a ball. Kyle flinched as the glass showered over him. A second later, the transport bounced to the other side beyond the hole but was then thrust to its side from the strength of the impact. They were now doing barrel rolls across the landscape. With all the crashing and rolling, the chairs bolted to the floor were jarring and shaking. The bolts jolted so harshly they stripped from their holds. Jason and Bryant cried out as some of the metal pieces propelled through the air, hitting them. Kyle broke through his remaining straps and took off. Iris reached for him but was too disoriented to know where to grab. The metal sides of the transport crunched from the pressure. Iris widened her eyes for a second before another jolt launched her head backwards into her chair. Her head slammed into it, and her vision went black as the horrible sounds faded away.

Chapter Twenty-Six

———————————————

"O www. . ." Iris moaned.

What . . . what happened? Why . . . do I hurt all over? Another groan escaped. Her mind felt like it was trying to shake itself from a dream. *Open your eyes . . . everything will make sense if I can just open my eyes . . .* With great effort, Iris slowly peered them open, taking a moment to register the devastation before her. Chaos was the first word that came to her mind. *Crash . . . the transport . . . and the road. I need to move . . . please, Holy Father, make me move. I have to know if everyone's okay. Help me move!* Iris's arms were stretched out before her. She gingerly pulled them beneath her, pushing herself up onto her knees. *I guess this means I was somehow flung out of my chair.* She was no longer strapped into her chair and could move freely.

A cry caught in her throat as she attempted to stand. Her head was throbbing; her chest, ribs, and stomach ached. Her legs felt too weak to hold her up. Her dress was torn, and her hair fell in a tumbled mess around her shoulders. Iris steadied herself against a nearby wall. She surveyed the scene around her. How could *anyone* survive this? *Well, I'm alive, so maybe . . . they* have *to be!* She opened her mouth to speak, but nothing would come out. She swallowed and tried once again.

"H–hello? Can–can anyone hear me? Darren? . . . Grayson? K–Kyle? Jason . . . Bryant? Please, answer me!" Her stomach churned. "Please, somebody, say something! Where are you? Hello?"

A groan from above caught her attention, and Iris immediately searched for the source. The transport had landed upside down. The last few rows of chairs that had not been torn off were now where the roof should have been. As Iris peered at the chairs more closely, two forms were still strapped in. She forced herself from the wall and climbed over some of the wreckage to take a better look. She crawled slowly as her ribs burned at every motion. She gasped at the sight of Darren and Grayson trapped above.

"Darren, Grayson! Can you hear me? Darren! Please, open your eyes! Darren!" Her eyes searched for any sign of movement as her ears willed them to make a sound.

Every second she waited seemed like a year. *Please, Holy Father! Please!* Her heart skipped a beat at a faint cough, followed by a groan. Who made the noise? She couldn't tell which man it was. She stood stone still trying to see if the swaying arms were due to conscious effort.

"I . . . ris."

She nearly missed the soft whisper of her name. "I'm here!"

"Iris . . ."

Her heart pounded as Darren called out to her. "Darren! Darren, can you hear me?"

Slowly Darren pulled his arms toward him. Dazed, he moved his head, trying to find the source of Iris's voice. Her face danced between happy relief and angst. He was alive! But was he okay? How would she get him down? She needed help, but she didn't know where anyone else was. Just then, crunching glass behind her caught her attention. She turned carefully at the sound. The transport's interior was engulfed in darkness, but the sun poured in through where the window used to be, making it difficult for Iris to see. Squinting her eyes, she made out the forms of men scrambling over debris from outside. They were making their way into the transport. *Oh, thank you, Holy Father!*

"Hey! Over here! Help!" Iris shouted to them as she limped across the interior wreckage toward them.

She moved slowly because she kept tripping over the chairs and other scraps of metal in her way. Just as she was about to reach them, her footing gave way. She threw out her arms to catch herself but still fell to her hands and knees. Upon landing, pain ricocheted through her ribcage, winding her and forcing her to stay still. Before her were the feet of one of the men. He didn't say a word as he looked down at her. Panic surged through her instinctively as she looked at the distinctive designs on his footwear. Fearfully Iris lifted her eyes to the man's face. She recognized that uniform. All color from her skin vanished. She thought she might throw up. He was one of *them*, one of the murderers who destroyed Throansburrough.

"No . . ."

The man smirked down at her, bent over, and grabbed her by the arm, yanking her to her feet. At the sudden movement, starbursts of pain shot through her vision. Iris couldn't even move. The man took his other hand to pull down the neckline of her dress. At that, Iris snapped back to reality. She tried to push him away, but he gripped her too tightly.

"No!" Finding her voice, Iris screamed.

The man pulled the neckline down farther, stopping when he reached the metal badge over Iris's heart. Upon seeing the device, he pulled back his hand from her dress and quickly grasped her other arm.

"It's her! I've found her!" he shouted over his shoulder.

Adrenaline pumped through Iris's veins. She wrenched herself away from him. He fought to hold on. Iris remembered the moves she had been taught earlier. She twisted her body, pulling against his thumbs, to break free from his grasp. It worked. She quickly turned to run but wasn't fast enough. Just then, one of the man's comrades tackled her to the ground. Iris screamed out in pain and fear. She kicked, scratched, punched, and bit her attacker, doing whatever she could to escape.

"Help!" she screeched at the top of her lungs. "Somebody help me!"

Two more men were soon upon her. She fought with all her might. A couple times, she wriggled free from their clutches, but in her weakened condition, they soon grabbed her again.

"Let me go! Nooooo! Stop it! Let. Me. Gooooo!"

The men didn't say anything. They just concentrated on dragging her from the transport. She couldn't let them take her outside. She knew that once she was outside, all hope would be lost.

"Help me! Please! Darren! Darren, help me! Darren!"

Two of the men grabbed her arms; the third took her legs.

"No! Holy Father, please! Holy Father, help me!"

Tears streamed from her eyes. They were closer to the opening.

"*Darren!*" She screamed with all her might.

In the next moment, they had pulled her through the opening. Iris and her captors disappeared into the sunlight.

"*Aaralee*."

The powerful voice called out once again, running through the deepest parts of her heart and mind.

"*Aaralee*."

The ground beneath her feet rumbled as the wind tore her black hair all around her. Aaralee's body trembled at the ferocity of her surroundings, but more so at the power in that voice. A sense of dread swept over her as she took in the bareness of the landscape. Where was she? What was going on? Slowly shadows in the forms of buildings began to take shape. She knew those buildings; she knew this land. It was her home, but it was covered in *such* darkness.

"*Aaralee, hear my voice*."

Aaralee sensed the voice behind her and turned around fearfully. Light struck her so forcefully that her knees buckled, and she fell to the ground in terror. She felt so unclean, so imperfect next to that light. She had no right to face it and could barely speak.

"Wh–what do you want with me?"

"Aaralee, your home, your people are in great danger. Soon they will be destroyed. Not one will be spared."

Somehow, Aaralee knew this voice spoke only the truth. Terror coursed through her at hearing of their nearing end.

"H–how c–can we stop it?" she trembled.

"Protect my prophet, heed her words. You will save the people."

Aaralee's eyes shot open as she awoke. Her hair was plastered to her sweat-soaked skin; her heart beat rapidly in her chest. The dream still weighed heavily on her mind, and she shot out of bed and ran to the window. She threw back the heavy red velvet curtains as her panic-filled eyes scanned the horizon. A calm starry sky greeted her, the only stirring the warm night breeze. Aaralee exhaled deeply in an attempt to calm herself. *It was only a dream.* She smiled to herself. *Albeit a very real and very terrifying dream.* Still it disturbed her. This was the fourth time she had had this dream in the past two weeks. What could it mean?

Suddenly an excited rapping came at the door to the bed chamber. Aaralee turned to see her husband rise from their bed. Instinctively he grabbed and unsheathed his sword, threw on an over cloak and went to the door. As he did so, Aaralee, too, reached for her own cloak and protective dagger within it. Upon opening the door, a servant immediately knelt down, his face to the floor.

"King Thaylos, I bring great news!"

The dress of the servant showed that he was one of the court's special runners, tasked with delivering messages directly to the king. She relaxed her grip on her dagger. But her husband maintained his stern stance as he waited for the runner to continue.

"Your Highness, they did it! They have captured the woman! They're bringing her to the dungeons as we speak!"

King Thaylos stood a little taller and smiled. "Thank you, runner.

Now go summon the Great Mother and bring her to my chambers immediately!" He watched the runner leave for a moment before closing the door and turning to his wife with a broad smile. "We've done it, my Queen." He crossed the distance between them, set down his sword, and wrapped his arms around her. "We have won. We've saved Yansair."

Though his embrace should have filled her with joy, dread washed over Aaralee instead. Her dream of a land and people destroyed flashed through her mind. Would this really save them? *Protect my prophet . . . save the people . . .* The words echoed in her heart. Could she trust the dream? She should have been at peace, but deep inside, she knew this was far from over.

Acknowledgments

I can remember back when I was eight years old sitting in my bedroom, when I made the conscious decision that someday I would become a published author. Reading hadn't come easy to me thanks to Dyslexia, but the passion for reading was able to fight past those hinderances, thanks to parents who read to me and fought alongside me to conquer my initial limitations. I grew up in a world that told me Dyslexia disqualified me, but my parents showed me the beauty of its ability to reveal the world to me in ways no one else could see. Mom and dad, thank you for showing me a label isn't an identity and how to find the amazing blessings within them.

To my sister and best friend Morgan, you unwittingly trained my story telling abilities through our vast worlds of make-believe and Barbie sagas that had full family histories and *all* the drama. As adults you continuously strive to connect with a sister who lives a very different, and highly nerdier, life than yours. Thank you for allowing me to geek out over all my passions and never diminishing what I love. You not only give me room to be myself but also champion it. And to my brother-in-law Matt, thank you for letting your weirdo sister-in-law feel free to bust out in song and dance with your wife and kiddos at any given moment! You've given me space for breakdowns and just a place to chill, thank you.

To my nieces and nephews, I am deeply thrilled by your passion for reading and more so just love who you're growing into. Maddie and Max, your intense enthusiasm for my stories and all the things I create have thrilled my heart and have helped keep me inspired. I am so honored to be known as your Sippy. I hope to continue to create stories that all of you can continue to love for years to come.

To Jennifer J., Jennifer M., Jasmine, Dulce, Brianna, and Laura S. - the friends who have stood with me for the years it took to bring Iris's story to print, thank you. You have patiently, and sometimes not so patiently, waited a *long* time for its release and the subsequent sequel (which I promise will come out *much* faster than this book did!). You guys were my sounding boards, my confidence boosters, my beta readers. You helped me catch errors. You yelled at me for torturing your favorite characters. And most of all, you refused to let me believe I couldn't do this. Your prayers and consistent words of encouragement brought this story to life.

Glory to my Savior who kept me on this earth and wouldn't allow darkness to destroy me. I would not exist without You. You showed me the power of a story, and constantly remind me that mine are worth being told.

Finally, to my readers. Thank you for giving Iris's world a chance. Some of you have been waiting for a while for its release, others are just now discovering it. This story is for any of you who also fight through pain and places of hopelessness. No matter your world view, your history, or your current circumstances I hope this book can help you feel seen and even the slightest bit less alone. You are worth the fight, please don't give up.

About the Author

Canadian born but Texas raised, Tiffany Grant completed a master's degree with a split major in history and English from Texas A&M University Texarkana. She is no stranger to living in "different worlds," from her upbringing to her time living in Asia teaching English in Thailand and India. Though Dyslexic she has held a deep passion for reading and writing since she was eight years old. When not writing she balances her time between her developing YouTube career and being a beloved aunt to five amazing nieces and nephews.

Sign up for her newsletter to stay up to date on new releases!
https://mailchi.mp/choosethepen.com/home-page

She loves getting to connect with readers! You can visit her website here: www.tiffanygrant-choosethepen.com

And find her on these sites:

facebook.com/choosethepen

instagram.com/choosethepen

youtube.com/@choosethemouse

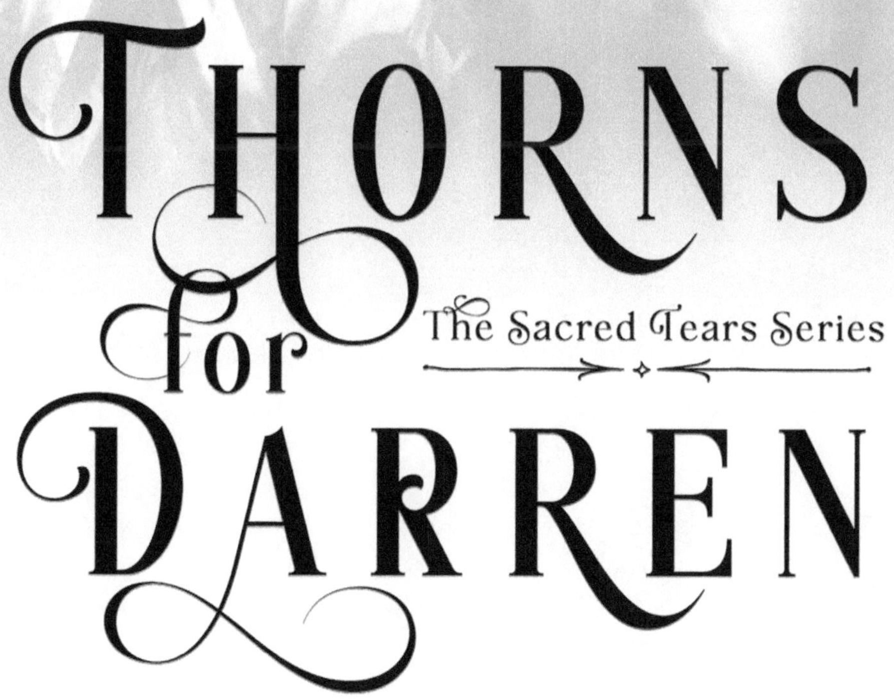

TIFFANY GRANT